For Hal Martin

THE
PROSECUTION

LYING ALWAYS CAME EASIER TO ME THAN TELLING THE truth. When I was a small boy, I climbed onto the kitchen counter to get to the cookie jar and knocked my mother's favorite crystal bowl over the edge. Watching it shatter into pieces on the floor, I knew in my heart that if anyone ever found out I was as good as dead. Carefully, I gathered up the shards of glass and tried to hide them behind some pots and pans in the cupboard. Holding one of the largest pieces in his hand, my father asked me that evening if I knew anything about it. I did what anyone would have done: I denied it.

He did not seem to believe me. Sitting in his chair, he put his hand on my shoulder and started telling me about George Washington and the cherry tree. I knew then I was finished. That story was everywhere. You couldn't run away from it. Every father told it to his son, and every schoolteacher told it to her class. You might go all the way through grade school without knowing anything about American history, but you knew young George had ruined it for the rest of us when he made his famous confession, "Father, I cannot tell a lie."

I stood there and stared down at the laces on my shoes. There was no way out of it, but I still could not bring myself to lift my eyes and say those words. The best I could do was nod my head and hope that this excruciating silent admission would be the only punishment I had to endure. It was not clear to me even then whether the lesson was never lie or never get caught.

I have not always told the truth in my life, but I never lied in a court of law, and I spent years defending murderers and rapists and thieves. I did not need to lie; the law itself allowed me to make certain that people who should have been punished were set free. I had wanted to be a lawyer who never lost a case because every client was innocent; instead I became a lawyer whose only concern was preventing anyone from ever proving that my client was guilty.

I had no qualms of conscience, no late-night regrets, about what I did or how I did it. I was a criminal defense attorney, sworn to put on the best defense I could for my client. When one trial ended, another began, and I never thought twice about what might happen because someone guilty had been acquitted; not until, as part of an exquisite scheme of revenge, the only truly innocent man I ever knew was charged with murder, and I was betrayed by the only woman I ever loved.

Leopold Rifkin was the most honorable and decent man I have ever known. The senior circuit judge, he had done everything he could to help when I was just starting out, a graduate of the Harvard Law School who did not know the first thing about trying a case in court. From the very beginning, I was drawn to the power of his mind. Learned in ways I could only imagine, he studied the classics in the original languages and owned the largest private library I had ever seen. After I had become known as a lawyer who seldom lost, he worried

Praise for
D. W. Buffa's *The Defense*

"An accomplished first novel . . . It ends with a couple of twists that are really shocking. And it leaves you wanting to go back to the beginning and read it over again."
—*The New York Times*

"*The Defense* has more thought behind it than any three Grisham stories. . . . A legal thriller that manages to both thrill and show the inherent weaknesses in the legal system."
—*Rocky Mountain News*

"Stunning legal reversals . . . Fine, flowing prose . . . Its points of ethics land with the most devastating impact."
—*The New York Times Book Review*

"[*The Defense*] boasts a startling conclusion that transforms it into a more thought-provoking book. . . . It might not be a bad idea to make this book required law-school reading."
—*Mademoiselle*

"An ingenious, riveting legal thriller . . . A fast-moving, thoroughly gripping entertainment that has the moral and emotional authority of a literary novel. . . . The surprise ending packs a powerful punch."
—*Publishers Weekly* (starred review)

Also by D. W. Buffa
Published by The Balantine Publishing Group:

THE DEFENSE

Books published by The Ballantine Publishing Group are
available at quantity discounts on bulk purchases for pre-
mium, educational, fund-raising, and special sales use. For
details, please call 1-800-733-3000.

THE
PROSECUTION
A Legal Thriller

D. W. Buffa

BALLANTINE BOOKS • NEW YORK

A Ballantine Book
Published by The Ballantine Publishing Group
Copyright © 1999 by D. W. Buffa

www.ballantinebooks.com

ISBN 0-449-00690-5

This edition published by arrangement with Henry Holt and Company, LLC.

Manufactured in the United States of America

First Ballantine Books Edition: November 2001

10 9 8 7 6 5 4 3 2 1

that I won too often and wondered if I understood the price I might one day have to pay.

The day he warned me about finally came, and the price was higher than even Leopold Rifkin could have foreseen. I suppose there is a certain irony in the fact that the first time I cared more about the defendant than I did about myself was the first time I thought I might lose. Unwilling to take that chance, I defended him for a crime he did not commit by committing one of my own. I told a witness to lie, and, as a result, Leopold Rifkin walked out of court a free man. A few days later, he took his own life, and the day of the funeral, Alexandra, the woman I wanted to marry, walked out of mine.

It had been more than a year since a jury found Leopold Rifkin not guilty of a murder he had not committed and for which he should never have been prosecuted, more than a year since I abandoned the practice of law. In that time I never returned to the courthouse. There were too many memories, too many things I did not want to think about. If Horace Woolner had not asked me, I might never have come at all.

THE COURT REPORTER GAZED AHEAD AS HIS FINGERS pressed the silent keys of his machine. At the counsel table an assistant district attorney looked glumly at the floor, his hands shoved into the pockets of his dark blue suit. The only spectator, I sat on a wooden bench in the back, remembering the last time I had been here, waiting to hear the verdict of the jury in a case in which I had convinced a witness to lie.

Now Horace Woolner was on the bench, presiding over a simple sentencing. Determined to let everyone know what he thought, the prisoner raised his shackled wrists and extended the middle finger of each hand in a gesture of double defiance. A few feet away, a deputy sheriff moved forward. Woolner raised his hand and shook his head. The deputy stopped and backed away.

Resting his arm on the bench, his huge shoulders hunched forward, Woolner narrowed his eyes, measuring the young man on whom he had just passed sentence.

"That will be six months for contempt of court," he said finally. "To run consecutive to the twenty-four-month sentence you were just given on the burglary charge."

His lawyer tried in vain to stop him. Screaming an obscenity, the prisoner thrust his two raised fingers into the air again, his blue eyes fierce with rage. The deputy grabbed him by the shoulder and threw him down into the empty chair as the lawyer looked on in open-eyed astonishment.

"You knew what the sentence would be before you were brought in. You filled out a plea petition," Horace said, waving an eight-page document stapled at the corner. "This is your second felony conviction. You knew exactly where you stood, exactly what the sentencing guidelines call for. We went through this petition." He indicated the document. "You said you understood it. You said you had reviewed it with your lawyer. There were no surprises, Mr. Merriweather. Despite that, you have to put on this little show of yours to demonstrate how tough you are. Is that the game we're playing here?"

Straining under the hand that held him down in the chair, the prisoner retreated into a scowling silence.

"I can give you another six months for contempt, if you'd like," Horace said. His deep voice seemed to come from everywhere at once. "And then you can give me the finger again, and we can keep doing this, over and over."

The deputy was holding the prisoner down as hard as he could. Merriweather had the lean, well-muscled look that prisoners his age often have. Tension rippled down the tendons of his neck.

"Let him go," Woolner ordered, as he got to his feet.

You could see the surprise register on Merriweather's face as Woolner moved around the bench and came toward the table. It was one thing to challenge a heavy-set black man with graying hair and a judicial robe flowing over his rounded shoulders. It was something else to watch the distance close between yourself and a thick-necked man you just realized had to be at least six foot two and well over two hundred fifty pounds, a black man coming right at you with cold-eyed confidence.

"What . . . ?" he asked, his eyes darting from the judge to the deputy and back again to the judge.

Standing directly in front of him, Woolner laid a huge hand on the prisoner's shoulder and gazed into his eyes.

"I wish I didn't have to do this," he said, in a quiet, unhurried voice, "but I have to. So why don't we both handle it like men?"

The tension seemed to drain out of the prisoner. With Woolner's hand still on him, his shoulders slumped forward and, lowering his eyes, he slowly nodded his head.

"Let's go back to the beginning," Woolner said, resuming his place on the bench.

Standing next to his lawyer, Merriweather looked smaller and younger than he had before.

"In accordance with the guidelines, I sentenced you

to twenty-four months in the care and custody of the state department of corrections," Woolner went on, in a calm, firm voice. "Is there any comment you would like to make about that sentence?"

Merriweather stood there, blinking.

"Is there any comment you wish to make, Mr. Merriweather?" the judge repeated.

This time Merriweather understood. "No, sir," he said politely, shaking his head for emphasis.

"Very good. In that case, the six-month sentence formerly imposed for contempt of court is withdrawn." As the deputy started to lead the prisoner away, Woolner added, "One more thing, Mr. Merriweather. This is your second felony conviction. Don't let there be a third. You understand my meaning?"

The prisoner was taken out of the courtroom, and the lawyers began to gather up their papers.

"Welcome back to the criminal courts, Mr. Antonelli," Woolner called out in a clear, jovial voice, from his place on the bench.

Both attorneys stopped what they were doing and looked up.

"That's right, gentlemen, Joseph Antonelli really does exist."

He led me into chambers, where I sat down in front of his desk and watched him remove the black robe and hang it on a rack next to the door.

"Alma is going to kill me," he said, examining a hole in his pants. "I just got this suit last week," he explained, as he slid into the chair behind the desk. "She's just going to kill me. I got to stop doing this," he mumbled to himself.

The words had barely left his mouth when he began to laugh, a deep, rumbling noise.

"When that kid gave me the finger, I got so mad I started to grind my fountain pen into my leg. Damn good thing it isn't real!"

"You didn't look mad. You looked like you were in complete control the whole time."

It was almost instinctive, the way he deflected praise. " 'Judge beats twenty-two-year-old defendant to death with bare hands' isn't the best headline to get when you have to run for reelection, is it?"

"You saved him from himself, and no one is ever going to read about that," I replied.

He dismissed it. "He's just an angry kid. Can't really blame him, either. Both his parents were drug dealers. Start out like that, not much chance you're going to do all that well, is there?"

His voice had become so quiet I could hear his breath underneath the words he spoke. He leaned back in the chair and let his gaze drift across the book-lined walls of the room. The venetian blinds on the room's only window were open, and gray light cast a dreary pallor over the desk and our thoughts.

"I didn't know you had taken Leopold's courtroom, not until I walked in here this morning."

Horace was staring out the window. "I didn't want to," he said finally, turning back to me. "It didn't seem quite right. Besides, I liked the one I had. It was bigger, and I was used to it. But then, after Leopold died"—he hesitated, tactfully avoiding any reference to suicide—"I didn't like the idea of some other judge having it, either." He shook his head with disdain. "They were all so willing to believe he must have been guilty, even though he was acquitted."

His head jerked back. "Strange, isn't it? We're the only two people who know what really happened, and you inherited his house and I ended up with his court-room. . . .

"You look different, Joe," he said presently. "More relaxed." He changed his mind. "No, that's not it. More concentrated." Beaming, he exclaimed, "That's it, isn't it? It's that damn library. You're starting to get like Leopold. It's that same look, something behind the eyes."

"The only change, Horace, is that I'm not carrying a couple dozen cases around in my head, trying to remember what I'm supposed to be doing an hour from now."

Leaning forward, a shrewd glint in his eye, he got right to the point. "Leopold never did what you're doing. He didn't lock himself up behind those iron gates and spend all his time in his library. He came down here every day, five days a week, year in, year out, and did his work. He came down here every morning because he knew he had certain obligations to the rest of us. You have obligations too. You're a hell of a lawyer," he said firmly, "and it's time you got back to doing it."

"We've been through this before, Horace. I'm not coming back. I can't."

Folding his arms across his chest, he moved his hand along the side of his face, down to the chin. In the silence, he looked at me. "There's something else I want to talk to you about," he said finally. "Do you remember the murder of Marshall Goodwin's wife?"

Marshall Goodwin was the chief deputy district attorney. His wife had been viciously murdered, and the case had never been solved. I had forgotten most of the details, but what I remembered was bad enough.

"She was killed in a hotel room somewhere. Her throat was slashed."

"That's right. Do you know Goodwin?" Horace asked. He closed his long thick fingers into a fist and then opened them, over and over again, like some ritual exercise.

"I tried a couple of cases against him. He was good."

"I hired him," Horace remarked, as he watched his hands at work. "Probably the best deputy I had. Always prepared. He usually won, too," he added, as he looked up. "Except when he had to go against you."

I missed the courtroom, but it was so far removed from the way I now lived that it was like being told how good you had been at something in high school. It no longer mattered. It was not even viable as a form of nostalgia.

Picking up a ballpoint pen, Horace began to tap it on the desk in a slow rhythm. "His wife's name was Nancy," he said, with a solemn expression. "As nice a person as you'd ever want to meet. She worked for an electronics firm. She was in Corvallis for a conference when she died, one of the few times she ever spent the night away from home."

Horace dropped the pen and reached inside a drawer. He pulled out a large file folder held together with a thick rubber band.

"Three months ago, a guy was arrested for a double homicide down in Los Angeles. Travis Quentin. Murdered a man and a woman in their bed. The kind of record you'd expect, major felonies, armed robbery, assault. They have him cold, so he offers to tell them about another murder if they'll agree to life instead of going for the death penalty. After what he tells them, they get hold of the Oregon state police, who interview Quentin, and then conduct their own investigation. This is what they've got," he said, resting his hand on top of the file. "I'm not sure it's enough." He looked down at the floor, a pensive expression on his face. "Or maybe I just don't want to think it is," he said, raising his eyes.

I had been following everything Horace said, and I understood why he did not want to believe it.

"They think Goodwin killed his wife?"

"Hired someone to do it. Goodwin was right here," he said, nodding toward the door that led to the outer office and, beyond that, to the hallway. "While his wife was being slashed to death, Marshall Goodwin was in a conference room in the DA's office, getting ready for his next day in trial, prosecuting someone for murder. Can you imagine a better alibi?"

I remembered something. "He got married again, didn't he?"

Horace nodded. "Yeah, about a year after his wife's death. Another prosecutor, Kristin Maxfield. That's how they met. Everyone thought it was the best thing that could happen to him."

With one hand on the desk and the other on the arm of the chair, Horace pushed himself up. Squaring his shoulders, he adjusted his weight over the two artificial limbs that had given him mobility for more than half his life. Out of the corner of his eye he saw me watching.

"They may not be too good for running"—he shrugged, grinning—"but you ought to see what I can do to a door if I get really pissed off!" He stood next to the window and gazed out at the sky. "This makes me angry," he said, his voice suddenly subdued. He pointed back toward the bulging file on his desk. "That one of our prosecutors might actually have had his wife murdered for money."

"Does the district attorney know yet?"

Leaning against the casement, Horace lowered his

eyes. "The state police came to me because they needed a warrant for a wiretap, and because I used to be the DA. They figured they could trust me to keep my mouth shut until they made an arrest." His eyes still fastened on the floor, he brushed the side of his face with the back of three fingers held tight together. "I haven't told Gwendolyn yet and I'm not going to tell her."

He raised his eyes and looked at me.

"What do you think she would do with this? Do you think she'd prosecute her own chief deputy?" His eyes stayed fixed on mine. "It doesn't get much worse—her own chief deputy accused of murder."

"She can't just ignore it," I said, as Horace moved across the room to his chair behind the desk.

"Can't she?" he replied, with an indulgent glance. "The case isn't that good," he observed, tapping the file folder with his index finger. "It's the word of a confessed murderer against the word of one of the major law enforcement officials in the state. She could bury this case, and believe me, that's exactly what she'll do."

Intelligent, ambitious, and rich, Gwendolyn Gilliland-O'Rourke had wanted to be governor from the day she was born; becoming district attorney was just a stop on the way. So far as she was concerned, the power of her office had no more legitimate use than the advancement of her own career.

"There isn't much you can do about it, Horace. She's still the DA."

"Yes, there is," he insisted. He put his hands on the arms of the chair and rocked back. "There's a statute that allows the appointment of a special prosecutor, someone from the district attorney's office in another county, or even a lawyer in private practice."

I was familiar with the statute. It was used when a

case required particular expertise that was not generally available. Small rural counties sometimes invoked it to obtain the help of an outsider in a case that was too specialized. Usually, the request came from the district attorney's office itself. Obviously, that was not going to happen here.

"I have the authority," Horace asserted.

"Who are you going to choose?" I asked, assuming he already had in mind a district attorney from one of the surrounding counties.

"I want you to do it," he replied.

"I'm a defense lawyer," I protested, astonished.

He corrected me. "You used to be a defense lawyer."

"You're right," I agreed. "I'm not a lawyer anymore. And I'm not going to be, either." I said it firmly. "You know what I did," I reminded him, with a baleful look.

"You got an acquittal for an innocent man," he replied. "Gilliland-O'Rourke would have sent him to prison for the rest of his life." He paused for a moment, glancing away. When his eyes came back, he was as serious as I had ever seen him. "I'm asking you for a favor. I need someone I can trust to decide whether Goodwin should be prosecuted or not, and if you decide he should be, I want you to do it. This case is too big to give to some prosecutor from another county or some lawyer in private practice. And everybody remembers how good you are. No one can accuse you of trying to make your reputation on this."

Reading the hesitation in my eyes, he pretended to be sympathetic.

"I know it's a big decision," he said, as he stood up. "You don't have to decide right away. Take the file, read it over. You can let me know this weekend." He came around the desk. "We can talk about it at the dinner on

Sunday. I already have your ticket," he added, before I could begin to phrase a graceful regret. "Alma insists you come," he went on, certain this would put an end to any thought of refusal. "And then you can tell her how bad you feel that you accidentally tore this hole in my pants."

"And just how did I manage to do that?" I asked, as I rose from the chair.

"Oh, hell, I don't know," he said, with good-humored impatience. "One thing at a time. I'll think of something."

He gathered up the file and handed it to me. Placing his hand on my shoulder, he looked me right in the eye, and I felt the same thing the prisoner must have felt, the sense that somehow he understood more about you than you did yourself.

"I want you to do this. It's important." Then, without a moment's pause, he reverted to his normal light-hearted banter. "And as a bribe," he said, slapping me on the back, "I'll buy you lunch."

"What about your pants?" I asked, glancing at his trousers.

Reaching across the desk, he tore off a piece of Scotch tape and, drawing together the two sides of the tear, placed it on top.

"That'll do for now," he announced. "Maybe after lunch I'll find a needle and thread." He considered it as we headed down the hallway together. "I used to be pretty good at mending. Learned during the war. About the only thing I learned worth remembering."

LATE IN THE AFTERNOON, I LEFT PORTLAND AND FOL-
lowed the river road to Lake Oswego and the house
where I had lived in almost perfect seclusion for more
than a year. The gray April drizzle had stopped and the
sun broke through the clouds, coating the towering
green fir trees with a silvery mist. At the bottom of the
long spiral drive, I got out of the car and shut the damp
iron gate behind me.

At the top, I parked the car and climbed the steps to
the porch that curved around the front of the rambling
two-story structure. A hardwood floorboard creaked as
I walked down the hall to the library and dropped the
case file on the desk.

The artifacts of Leopold Rifkin's existence, the photographs of his wife, a few pictures of friends taken at
different points in his long life, awards he had received
for years of honorable and largely anonymous public
service—everything that had made this room his own
had been placed in storage because I could not bring
myself to throw them away.

Everything else was the way he had left it. The bookshelves lining the walls and climbing to the ceiling were
still filled with the greatest works ever written: the
dialogues of Plato and the treatises of Aristotle; the

14

speeches of Cicero and the histories of Tacitus; the scientific works of Bacon, Descartes, and Newton; the political writings of Machiavelli, Hobbes, and Locke; the astonishing creations of Nietzsche and Rousseau—all of it was here, organized in an order that was seldom apparent and not always chronological. Even after all this time whenever I opened one of his well-worn books there was always a moment when I felt like a stranger.

I went upstairs to the bedroom and changed into a pair of khaki pants and a short-sleeved shirt. Barefoot, I went down to the kitchen and made a cup of coffee and then slid onto the high-backed chair at the desk in the library.

Directly in front of me, left open at the page I had spent part of the morning trying to understand, was an English translation of Aristotle. For months I had labored over the six works of the *Organon*: the *Categories, De Interpretatione*, the *Prior Analytics*, the *Posterior Analytics*, the *Topics*, and *Sophistical Refutations*, in which Aristotle had fixed the rules of right reason and established the foundation of logical thought. I had struggled on, until finally I had managed to get through most of Aristotle, including even the *Physics*. Then, opening the first page of the *Metaphysics*, my eye fell on the first sentence, perhaps the seven most hopeful words ever written, a simple declaration of what had once been an article of faith: "All men by nature desire to know."

It was hard to imagine that many of them wanted to know much if anything about the *Metaphysics*. I put down the coffee cup and glanced across at the file folder straining against the rubber band. Horace had known I would not be content to just stay here forever like a cloistered medieval monk. Placing a scrap of paper inside the volume to mark the place, I closed the copy of Aristotle and moved it to the side.

For the next few hours I worked my way through the written record of the police investigation into the murder of Nancy Goodwin. I had spent my life reading reports like this—the tedious chronicle of an act of violence, written in a monotonous prose, the perfect expression of the utter banality of evil. It always left me with an oppressive sense of dull indifference, a feeling that how the victim died was somehow more important than how she had lived. It was the ultimate obscenity of the criminal law: not that a woman had been killed, but that what had been done to her at the end had become the only thing about her that mattered. The victim of a homicide was put on public display. Whatever else it was, murder was always an act of lewdness.

A motel maid found the naked body of Nancy Goodwin, her head hanging over the corner of the bed, her hair caked with the blood that had drained out of her knife-slashed throat. Her mouth had been taped shut and her wrists tied behind her back. According to the coroner she had been raped, probably more than once.

A woman with whom she worked had driven down with her from Portland and had the room next door. They had sat together at the conference dinner and shared a drink afterward in the motel bar. Around eleven they had walked back to their rooms and said good night. The next morning the woman assumed that Nancy Goodwin was sitting somewhere in the darkened conference hall watching the same presentation. Two hundred people had attended the conference that brought Nancy Goodwin to Corvallis, and none of them had noticed anything unusual. The police found dozens of fingerprints in her room and fibers all over the floor, but it was a motel room used by hundreds of different strangers every year. No arrest was ever made.

Leaning back against the corner of the chair, one leg draped over the wooden arm, I gazed out the window. The skies had cleared and the late afternoon sunlight drenched the budding trees at the far edge of the lawn. Scattered between them, azaleas and rhododendrons were already in bloom, a visible reminder that winter was giving way to spring.

Police reports had not changed, but I found I was reading them differently from the way I had before. Determined to find any oversight, no matter how small, any gap, no matter how narrow, in the chain of evidence, I had never read them just to learn what had happened. Long before I ever began the study of Aristotle, I had known something about the use and abuse of analytical thought.

A hundred miles away from where she had been murdered, Marshall Goodwin was finishing the cross-examination of a witness when he was told of his wife's death. The judge, who had been given the task, had called him into chambers and then listened in horrified silence as Goodwin, overcome with grief, cried out that his wife had been four months pregnant with their first child.

I could see him in my mind, arguing a case in front of a jury. Marshall Goodwin was good at what he did, better than most lawyers who made their careers prosecuting criminal cases. Thorough and precise, he had a quick smile and an easy, relaxed manner. There was none of the raw-eyed irritability that betrayed the desperation of someone who could not keep up and paid the price for it with sleepless nights and eighteen-hour work days. On the contrary, Goodwin gave the appearance of a self-assurance so complete it would have been dismissed as arrogance had it not been accompanied by a certain friendly civility. He was the kind of lawyer who was the first to offer his congratulations on those rare occasions when he lost. Whenever Gwendolyn Gilliland-O'Rourke decided the time had come to run for governor, nearly everyone assumed Goodwin would become the next district attorney.

Though they never admitted they were giving up, the police eventually closed their investigation, and the death of Nancy Goodwin became another unsolved homicide, a file folder gathering dust, until, two years later and a thousand miles away, the killer was caught in an unrelated murder. Faced with the prospect of the gas chamber, Travis Quentin tried to save his life by confessing to another murder. The transcript of the interview in which he accused a deputy district attorney of conspiracy to murder contained no discernible trace of remorse. He had been given a photograph of the victim and told where she would be staying the night. He was to kill her and then be paid ten thousand dollars for the job. Rape had been his idea.

The lengthy criminal history of Travis Quentin reflected the even-tempered barbarity of a sociopath and the utter inadequacy of the systems in place to do something about it. He committed his first murder when he was fifteen years old by throwing a twelve-year-old boy off the roof of a ten-story building. More disturbing than the absence of any attempt at justification, or even a simple explanation, was his apparent inability to understand why one was needed. Instead of a death sentence, or even life in prison, he was confined in a juvenile facility until he became an adult. If he learned anything from his brief incarceration it was how to become more careful in the crimes he committed. Thirty years of frequent arrests and occasional convictions had done nothing to reform his character or protect his victims. Counting Nancy Goodwin, he had killed at least six people and, as reparation, had thus far served a total of seven years on two convictions for manslaughter.

On the front page of the criminal history of Travis Quentin was his photograph, a grainy black-and-white mug shot. He had a pock-marked face, with a narrow forehead, thick eyebrows, and a broad, bulbous nose. The back edge of his left ear bent forward as if he had slept on it, and the lid on his right eye drooped down at the corner. He had the look of someone who sweats profusely the moment he begins to exert himself.

There was no serious question about whether Quentin had really killed Nancy Goodwin. He knew everything about it, including details that had never been released to the public. The real question was whether it had really been a murder for hire. He said it was, but he had a great deal to gain and nothing to lose by implicating someone else. It was the only way he could save his own life. He agreed to take a polygraph and he passed it, but there were still doubts that he was telling the truth.

I got up from the desk and took my empty cup to the kitchen. Outside, the shadows lengthened over the lawn as the last glimmer of twilight stretched across the western sky. Through the open window, the soft sigh of an evening breeze started up and then died away.

With a full cup in my hand, I wandered back and gazed at the shelves lined with thousands of cloth- and burnished leather-bound books collected over the course of Leopold Rifkin's long life. The library was more than the repository of what Rifkin had read, more than a visible reminder of what he had spent much of his life thinking about; it was a sanctuary from the changeable inconsequence of the world. It was the place that had given him a perspective about the things he did down in the city, inside the courtroom, where he decided the fate and fortune of everyone who came before him. Scattered across the desk, the fragmentary reports of the unfinished investigation into the murder of Nancy Goodwin and the possible complicity of her husband almost seemed to belong here. Settling into the chair, I picked up the page where I had left off.

According to the account of Travis Quentin, he had first met the chief deputy district attorney while he was in the Multnomah County jail. The police had found him parked late at night on the side of a road less than two blocks from a fashionable neighborhood. They claimed that when they approached the vehicle—an old junker that no one who lived there would have been caught dead in—he reached under the front seat. Fearing for their safety, the two officers drew their weapons, ordered him out of the car, and proceeded to search it. All they found under the front seat was a small bag of marijuana, but stuffed behind the back seat they discovered a large quantity of heroin and, inside the trunk, three handguns, a sawed-off shotgun, and an assault weapon that could cut a man in half with a single one-second burst.

It was a questionable search. Any decent defense attorney would have attacked it with a vengeance. The law of search and seizure was a shambles, in which appellate courts attempted to give guidance to the discretion of the police by producing as many opinions about what they should have done as there were judges to write them. It was standard procedure to file a motion to suppress, argue it before the trial court judge, and see what happened. If the judge ruled that the search was valid and the evidence admissible, you went to trial, and if your client was found guilty you had the chance to convince an appellate court that the police had failed to follow a rule on which they themselves had never been able to agree.

Nothing like that happened here. Two days after his arrest, Travis Quentin was brought to the district attorney's office where he was interviewed alone by Marshall Goodwin. The deputy sheriffs who took him, bound and shackled, from the county jail thought Quentin was a potential witness in a major narcotics case that supposedly involved some of the most prominent people in town. After Quentin met behind closed doors with Goodwin for more than an hour, all the charges, except for a single misdemeanor count for possession of marijuana, were dropped.

No one thought anything about it. Plea bargains were made all the time, and if there was anything different about this one, it was only that it had been made so quickly. And far from raising any suspicion, the absence of a defense lawyer only increased the respect in which the chief deputy district attorney was held. The police knew which prosecutors they could count on and which ones always insisted on the letter of the law. Goodwin was smart and tough and, most important of all, he never blamed a cop for a case that went bad.

Shortly after his private conversation with Quentin, Goodwin stood beside Gilliland-O'Rourke while the district attorney announced indictments returned by the grand jury against a dozen upper-middle-class citizens, not one of whom had ever before been in trouble with the law, on charges of conspiring to sell narcotics. All of them proclaimed their innocence, demanded their day in court, and then took the best deal they could get. There were no trials. There was no need for anyone to testify about anything. Travis Quentin was released from county jail at the end of his thirty-day sentence and no one gave him a second thought.

Travis Quentin gave a more interesting account. He claimed that when he was brought to Goodwin's office, the two officers who were holding him by his arms were told they could wait outside. Their reluctance to leave Goodwin alone and unprotected was dismissed with a smile. Frowning, they pushed Quentin down onto a wooden chair in front of the desk and turned to go.

"You can take the handcuffs off," Goodwin announced. He was sitting on the front corner of the desk, one foot on the floor, the other leg swinging idly back and forth. "Mr. Quentin and I are going to have a friendly conversation," he explained. "I'll be fine," he added as the two officers exchanged worried glances.

As soon as the door shut behind them, Goodwin reached inside his suit coat pocket. "Cigarette?" he asked, pulling out an unopened pack.

Rubbing his wrists, Quentin nodded and waited for Goodwin to open it and give him one. Instead, Goodwin tossed him the pack.

"Keep the rest. I don't smoke," he said, as he got to his feet and moved to his chair behind the desk.

Quentin had next to nothing in the way of formal education, but he knew something about lawyers and the way they worked. Most prosecutors dressed like funeral directors and talked in flat voices with a sort of grim-faced impatience. Goodwin was wearing a double-breasted blue blazer. Quentin remembered the shiny gold buttons. Lounging in his chair, an ankle crossed over his knee, he acted as if he had nothing but time and no better way to spend it than in a long, desultory conversation about how best to solve someone else's problem.

"You have an interesting record, Mr. Quentin," Goodwin remarked, without a trace of indignation.

Quentin had opened the pack and taken out a cigarette. Reaching inside a drawer, Goodwin found a matchbook and flipped it to him.

"Manslaughter, burglary, armed robbery," Goodwin observed, as he glanced at the thick compilations of arrests and convictions that constituted the only biography Travis Quentin would ever have. "I'm afraid it's the kind of record that doesn't leave much room for leniency. No, I should think that with these new charges you're looking at eight to ten years, minimum."

Pausing, he leaned his elbow on the desk. "Unless you'd just like to save everybody the time and trouble of a trial."

Quentin was on his guard. They did not bring you to the district attorney's office to negotiate a plea bargain. Your lawyer did that, and he did not have one yet. After a long drag on the cigarette, Quentin asked the only question he cared about. "What do I get?"

Instead of casual amusement, Goodwin's eyes now reflected a serious interest.

"You plead guilty to misdemeanor possession of marijuana. You'll do thirty days in the county jail, with credit for the time you have to wait before you're sentenced."

Quentin had just begun to inhale. He choked on the smoke. "Who do I have to kill?" he said, laughing.

Standing up, Goodwin shook his head. "No one right now," he remarked. "Do we have a deal?"

It never occurred to Quentin to say no.

The day he was released, he was met outside the county jail by a woman who handed him a large manila envelope containing a black-and-white photograph of Nancy Goodwin, the name and location of the Corvallis motel, and the date she would be spending the night. There was also $5,000 in hundred-dollar bills and a key to a bus station locker where, according to the written instructions, he would find an additional $5,000 waiting for him when he finished the job.

The money had long ago been spent, and the photograph and typed directions to the location of his victim destroyed. Quentin agreed to call Goodwin and threaten him with exposure unless he paid more money. With the police listening on another line and a tape recorder preserving everything that was said, Goodwin answered the phone and, as soon as he heard who was calling, said he did not know anyone by that name and hung up.

The case against Marshall Goodwin consisted of the testimony of Travis Quentin and very little else. Quentin had been arrested, and he had spent nearly an hour alone with the chief deputy district attorney. The charges that could have been brought against him were dropped, and instead of years in prison he had served thirty days in the county jail. That was it, all of it, and it was not nearly enough.

Drifting over to the French doors that led out to the patio, I watched the lights glittering in the distance and found myself wondering what Marshall Goodwin was doing at that moment. Most murders had something of the commonplace about them, ordinary acts of brutality by dull, dimwitted people for whom violence was the principal form of expression. But this was not an act of violence committed in a moment of rage, not if Travis Quentin was telling the truth. This was murder for hire, carried out with a clear mind and a cold heart. What possible reason could Goodwin have had? And if he had done it—hired Travis Quentin to murder his wife—had he managed somehow to put it all out of mind, the way every prosecutor and every defense attorney forgets about each case they try as soon as the verdict comes in and they start thinking about the next one? Was it really that easy?

Turning away, I glanced at the clock on the desk. It was a few minutes after nine, not too late to call.

Horace answered on the first ring. "You been expecting my call?" I said with a laugh.

"No, I thought it was Alma. I've barely seen her this week. Every night she's got a meeting, getting ready for their fund-raiser Sunday."

I had forgotten the fund-raiser. "Listen, Horace," I began, trying to think of the best way to get out of it.

"*Listen, Horace* yourself," he growled. "You're not getting out of it. I have to go; you have to go."

The absence of logic in this was irresistible. "No, Horace, you have to go because you're married to the woman who's in charge. And because you're a judge who might want to get reelected. I don't have to go anywhere."

"I understand all that," he said placidly. "I have to go; you have to go. I have to go because I'm married to Alma, and you have to go because she wants you there. Now tell me, you get through all that stuff I gave you? What do you think?"

"You mean, do I think he did it?" I paused, trying to draw some conclusion that made sense. "If I didn't know him, if I'd never met him, if the only thing I knew was what this guy Quentin says, I suppose I'd think there was a chance."

For a moment, Horace was silent. Finally, he said, "You don't think there's enough there for a conviction, do you."

I hesitated. "I'm not even convinced the case should be prosecuted. Are you?"

"It's like I told you. I hope he didn't do it."

"But you think he did. Why?"

"Couple of things. The polygraph, for one. Quentin passed it. The meeting with Goodwin and the way all the charges were dropped. The way Quentin knew where Nancy Goodwin was going to be. But maybe more than any of it, there's something about Goodwin. I can't put my finger on it. I don't want to believe he did it, but when the state police told me I didn't have the kind of reaction you have when you just know something couldn't have happened that way."

I knew what he meant: the certainty that someone was innocent and the awful doubt that you might not be able to prove it. If there was anything worse than defending someone who was convicted of a crime they did not commit, it had to be prosecuting the case that sent that innocent person to prison. It was the fear that every decent attorney felt, and the sense of danger that gave an edge to everything that happened in the criminal courts.

Horace had a gift for listening to the things left unspoken.

"Joe, you have all the right instincts. If Goodwin didn't do it, you'll know it."

"What makes you think I'm going to do this?" I asked.

"What makes you think you won't?"

FROM A SMALL CITY OF GRAY STONE BUILDINGS YOU
could walk across in ten minutes, Portland had grown
into a maze of misshapen skyscrapers and interlocking
freeways. The federal building and the county courthouse, once two of the most prominent structures in
town, were now buried in the shadows of the surrounding office towers. For nearly a hundred years
Portland had been a center of the timber trade. Lumber
was one of the things the world could not live without,
and the men who knew how to make money from it had
left behind mansions that were monuments to their own
bad taste and children educated in a way that made certain they would have neither the vices nor the virtues of
their fathers. The sons of pirates became gentlemen, and
the daughters of whores became ladies, and if there was
a certain loss of raw energy in all this, it seemed a cheap
enough price to pay.

The first generation had been driven by the desire for
wealth, and the second by a sense of honor; the third
generation was not driven by anything at all. Other
names were now better known, more familiar: the
names of new founders, men, even women, who had
come from nowhere, without money or connections but
with that same narrow-minded determination to make

27

their mark. Whether they had old money or new, everyone wanted to be invited to the Convention Center, to attend what Alma Woolner had managed to turn into one of the social events of the year.

Built on the east side of the river, where there had once been nothing but warehouses and railroad yards and corner taverns for the men who worked there, the Convention Center was a fairly recent addition to the city, a green glass tribute to postmodernism with a flat three-sided spire that shot straight up toward the heavens. The Cathedral of Notre Dame had taken a hundred and forty years to build as a tribute to an eternal God; this had taken less than two years to complete as a center of commerce. It was all a question of what you prayed to.

The lobby was jammed with men in black tie and women dressed in everything from slinky black dresses to bright floor-length gowns. Taking a glass of champagne from the first waiter I passed, I made my way through the undulating crowd, searching for Horace. With my glass above my head, I gradually reached the other side and found him against the wall, proudly watching his wife.

Barely touching the hands that reached out to her, Alma spoke to one person and then to another. Turning away from a wizened old lady wearing a beaded jacket over her stooped shoulders, she spotted me. She smiled at a stout, square-faced woman and moved past her. "I knew you'd come," she cried, placing her hands on my shoulders. She rose up on tiptoe to bestow a kiss on the side of my face.

"Thank you," she whispered, as if I had done her some great favor. She let go and took my hand. "Look who I found," she announced, as she led me to her husband.

Horace was waiting, his eyes exuberant with malice. "Have you met the chief justice?" he asked innocently.

The balding middle-aged man next to him extended his hand. His tuxedo and the ruffled white shirt that went with it were both a size too large.

"Jason Cornelius," Horace continued with cursory formality, "Joseph Antonelli."

For an instant, his grip weakened and then, as if to compensate, grew even more firm than before.

"Yes, yes, of course. Mr. Antonelli. I remember," he said, with a faint smile.

Eager to avoid embarrassment, he had once recommended to me that Leopold Rifkin resign from the court when he was accused of murder. I had suggested in turn that a judicial system strong enough to survive Cornelius's own incompetence could certainly endure a false accusation brought against an innocent man. Like most politicians, Cornelius might never remember a promise, but it was not likely he had forgotten that exchange. Before he could say anything more, I turned to his wife and introduced myself.

"Your husband and I both had the good fortune of counting among our friends the late Leopold Rifkin," I explained.

She had no idea who I was talking about. "Rifkin?" she asked, glancing at her husband.

"Yes, dear, Judge Rifkin. He died a year or so ago," he said. "It was all very sad, very sad indeed." And he patted her on the arm as he led her away.

Leaning against the wall, his arms across his chest, Horace chuckled under his breath. "Well, you handled that with your usual charm."

"What did you want me to do, tell the truth?"

He laid his hand on my shoulder and looked past me,

surveying the glistening faces of the crowd. "You never want to do that with someone like Cornelius," he said, so no one else could hear, "unless you really want him to think you're lying."

The crowd around Alma Woolner shifted first one way and then the other, gradually moving her away from where we stood, until all we could see of her was the jet-black hair that swept up from the slope of her neck. Horace never lost sight of her.

"Alma looks wonderful," I remarked admiringly.

"Alma always looks wonderful."

"You're a lucky man, Horace."

He turned to me. "You have no idea."

And in an instant he started in on me. "Why don't you wander around? Maybe you'll find a really attractive woman just dying to spend her nights with a guy who likes to spend all of his in a library."

He began to move away, working through the crowd, one eye on Alma, the other darting back to me. "Lot of possibilities here," he taunted, nodding his head and raising his eyebrows every time he passed anyone in a dress.

"They're all taken!" I yelled over the din.

He stopped and grinned broadly. "Not all of them!"

"You didn't!" I called back.

"See you inside!" he shouted, as he disappeared from view.

I stopped the first waiter I found and exchanged my empty glass for a full one. Faces vaguely familiar slid by in the distance, but I felt no urge to draw closer. A young woman with laughing eyes glanced at me, and I remembered when that might have been the first beginnings of a new romance. I stared back at her for a moment, and then, looking away, moved on. At the announcement that it was time to enter the great hall where dinner was to be served, I left the crowd behind me and made my way along the glass-lined lobby to the rest room. Standing on the marble floor, staring at the tiled wall in front of me, I barely noticed when someone used the urinal next to me. As I zipped my fly, however, he spoke my name. I looked back and found myself caught in the gaze of a gray-eyed stranger, looking at me over his shoulder.

"Yes," I replied, reaching down to turn on the faucet, "I'm Joseph Antonelli."

"We've never really met," he explained, moving to the next basin. He turned off the faucet, wiped his hands on a paper towel, and waited while I did the same. "I'm Arthur O'Rourke," he said, as he shook my hand.

The name meant nothing to me, but there was something impressive about him. Tall and thin, with a high forehead, deep-set intelligent eyes, and a narrow, sensitive mouth, he had the generous look of someone always willing to help.

"I believe you know my wife," he said. "Gwendolyn." Arthur O'Rourke, twenty years her senior, was married to the DA.

"Yes, of course," I said, wondering what she had told him about me as I let go of his hand.

"I was surprised when I heard you'd retired," he remarked. "I know Gwendolyn was disappointed. She's always said you were a great lawyer."

"It was kind of her to say so," I replied, as he held the door open for me.

Walking down the hallway together, he asked me

whether there was any chance I might practice law again, quickly adding that it was not something he could ever have done.

"Be a criminal defense attorney?" I asked.

"Oh, no. Be an attorney of any kind. I could never imagine having to stand up in a courtroom," he said. "Gwendolyn seems to thrive on it. I really admire that about her."

He spoke quietly, carried himself with an easy elegance, and had the sensibilities of someone who flinches at the utterance of a harsh word.

"Do you think you might practice law again?" he asked, as we entered the dining hall.

"I'm thinking about it."

He stopped and turned to me. "You should," he said, quite serious. "I always wished there was something I could do really well," he went on, a trace of regret in his voice.

We said good-bye, but before I began the search for my own table, I watched him work his way toward his, an unhurried journey interrupted by acquaintances and well-wishers. I saw his wife in the distance, moving purposefully from table to table, fastening her glittering gaze on each person whose hand she shook, making a deliberate circuit of the room. There were six hundred people here, and I was certain that before coffee was served Gwendolyn Gilliland-O'Rourke would convince each of them that he or she was the only one she really wanted to see.

In the center of the hall, surrounded by dozens of round tables for ten, was a long, narrow, rectangular table where I found Horace and Alma. I took the empty chair in front of my name card between Alma and a woman whose smile seemed uncertain about the difference between cynicism and disdain. Though she was at least seventy, it was not difficult to imagine that she had once been very beautiful and cruel.

"Joseph, let me introduce Madame Natasha Krupskaya, the prima ballerina who has graciously consented to spend the season as adviser to our company."

To my surprise, Alma spoke to her guest in Russian. Madame Krupskaya nodded and, looking up at me, said in slow, halting English, "How do you do?" Turning back to Alma, she laughed and said something in Russian, something that, from the intonation and the gesture she made with her eyes, sounded very much like a question. Alma answered briefly.

Bending close to me, she whispered, "She asked how many ballerinas you've slept with."

I shot a glance at the aging dancer, quite prepared to believe that her own list of lovers would make a volume of innumerable chapters. She ignored me.

"And you said?"

Alma looked at me, her round eyes open wide. "All of them."

Most of the elegantly dressed men and women at the center table were members of the ballet company's board of directors, elected neither because of their capacity for sound advice nor their knowledge of the arts, but because they had money to spend and had been convinced this was a good way to spend it. Old or new, money was always welcome.

Alma shoved her chair back and I started to get up.

"No, I'll just be a minute."

In a seamless motion, she was on her feet and moving toward the stage at the front of the hall.

"And just how many ballerinas have you slept with?" I asked under my breath.

Raising her head, Natasha Krupskaya studied me. "Do you think love should be bounded by convention, Mr. Antonelli?" she asked, in perfect English.

When Alma reached the stage and began to speak, everyone stopped what they were doing. She spoke for less than a minute, offering words of welcome and an amused warning that after dinner no one would be allowed to leave until the speeches had been given. That was all, but the soothing effect of her voice was so pronounced that she was already off the stage, on her way back to the table, before people resumed their conversations.

"You should have been a lawyer," I said, when she sat down next to me. "Juries would have done whatever you wanted them to do."

"You accusing my wife of duplicity?" Horace laughed.

"No. I'm accusing her of charm."

Alma's black eyes glowed. "Is there a difference?"

"Duplicity becomes charm when you are so attracted by the effect you don't care about the cause."

I looked up. Russell Gray, the chairman of the board, was sitting directly across from Alma. In his early forties, twice divorced, he represented some of the oldest money in town. He had long, expressive fingers, the hands of a musician, and fine, delicate features suggesting the kind of ambiguous sexuality that can antagonize men and attract women. His voice was a tremulous whisper, like someone short of breath, and whenever he said something he thought especially interesting, he would tilt his head coquettishly to the side, his eyes still on you.

"Lawyers are duplicitous," he went on, resting his elbows on the white tablecloth and spreading open his hands. "Artists are charming. Alma is an artist."

When she demurred, Gray reminded her that she had been a member of the New York City Ballet.

"Yes, but only for two years."

"Why only two years?" someone asked.

"She met me," Horace explained.

"By far the best thing that could have happened to her," Gray remarked, with a languid wave of his hand.

I was caught off guard by the generosity of the sentiment. He saw the look of surprise on my face.

"Don't you think so, Mr. Antonelli?" Leaning back, he crossed one arm across his chest and pressed his finger against his lip. There was a brief glimmer of satisfaction in his eyes.

"Best thing that could have happened to both of them," I replied.

Perhaps because he found it embarrassing, Horace changed the subject. "I just want everyone to know that Alma isn't the only one with a serious interest in the arts. When I was a kid I wanted to be an actor. That is, I wanted to be an actor until I found out that they always wanted me to play the same role. I was a little militant in those days," he added, as an aside. "I told them: Iago or nothing!"

"But Othello is one of the greatest roles of all time," Gray protested, laughing amicably.

"Not the way I saw it. He should have figured out what was going on."

"That would not have been much of a tragedy," Gray replied.

"No, but it would have been a lot closer to justice, and maybe that would have been a better lesson."

"Maybe," Gray conceded, "but it wouldn't have been better art."

"You mean, not as charming?"

"Yes, in a way."

"Then, more duplicitous?" Horace asked, pressing the point.

Shrugging his thin shoulders, Gray replied, "I don't really know."

Alma had barely touched her salad and had ignored her entrée. Exchanging a glance, she and Gray were on their feet.

"I'm afraid I have to borrow your wife," Gray remarked, walking around the table to take Alma by the hand.

Horace and I watched as they moved from table to table, visiting briefly with everyone who had paid for the privilege of being there.

"What do you think of him?" Horace asked.

"He's all right," I replied indifferently. "Why?"

"No reason. He treats Alma well. I just have a problem with people who never had to work for anything." He shook his head as if to clear his mind. "Doesn't matter. Tell me," he said, his arm over the back of Alma's empty chair, "what did you decide? You want to do this thing?"

Across the dimly lit hall, I noticed Gilliland-O'Rourke, standing relaxed at a table. Draping my arm over the top of Horace's, I pulled my knee up onto the empty chair between us.

"Did you know she was going to be here?"

"Tell you the truth, I never really thought about it. Everybody is here. Why?"

"I ran into her husband. In the men's room, right after I left you in the lobby."

Horace looked out over the packed dining room. "And I ran into Marshall Goodwin."

"It must be strange," I said, "talking to someone who doesn't know that you know things about him."

Horace nodded. "When you're a prosecutor you get to learn all sorts of things about people. You have any idea how many people have allegations made about them? You got to see the police reports about your clients, people formally charged with doing something; I got to see the reports that were made when there wasn't enough evidence to bring charges. Listen," he said, his eyes searching the room, "some of the best-known people here tonight, including a couple of our finer members of the judiciary, have police reports written about them that they know nothing about."

Removing my arm, I raised my knee and wrapped both hands around it. "Without more evidence, that's exactly what could happen to the file I just read."

His hand engulfed my knee. "This isn't just another murder case," he told me, grimly defiant. "You see Gilliland-O'Rourke working the room? She's going to run for governor. This guy is going to become the next DA. I know you have to be sure in your own mind. I *want* you to be sure. But remember something. This isn't one of those cases where you can just decide that maybe he didn't do it. If there is any incredible evidence at all, you take it to trial. If he isn't guilty, let a jury decide. At some point, you have to trust the system."

He looked at me for a moment.

"I always did." Then, trying not to laugh, he added, "Except maybe when you were the defense attorney."

iv

THE FIRST TIME I WENT THERE, I HAD TO FORCE MYSELF
to climb the steps at the entrance of the state prison.
When you visit a client in a county jail, you can get in
and out in a matter of minutes; once you disappear inside the high stone walls of the state penitentiary, you
wonder whether you will ever get out at all.

Under the watchful eye of a young female guard
dressed in regulation gabardine slacks and crisp white
short-sleeved shirt, I signed the visitor's log. In the small
waiting area, several women, along with a couple of
children, stood listlessly biding their time. On an orange
plastic sofa with seats so low her knees were nearly as
high as her shoulders, a bored-looking woman in her
late thirties sat reading a book and chewing gum. She
looked like a regular, one of the wives or girlfriends who
moved to cheap apartments in Salem so they could visit
their men, twice a day during visiting hours. The moment it was one o'clock, she pushed herself up and, her
eyes still on the open page, walked slowly toward the
bank of lockers on the far wall. After she put both the
book and her tattered leather purse inside a locker, she
got into the short line that had begun to form.

Holding my briefcase with both hands in front of me,
I stood in line, gazing down at the linoleum littered with

black scuff marks, waiting my turn to pass through security. The woman who had been reading passed through the metal detector and was stopped. She had to get rid of the gum. A large black woman set off the alarm and stood to the side, removing her earrings.

I handed my briefcase to the guard. While he inspected the contents, I began to take off my shoes. Dress shoes have a thin metal plate inside the sole, and while you can wear them through any airport detector in the world, they never get through the sensitive system used in maximum security prisons. My shoes, keys, fountain pen, and pocket change were handed over. I had forgotten about my belt, and as soon as the buzzer sounded, I reached down, unfastened it, and handed it over as well. In stocking feet, I passed successfully through the narrow wooden archway and was given back my belongings. I put on my belt and shoes.

When everyone had cleared security, a guard led us down a brown carpeted ramp, past a barred window with a view of two wooden picnic tables in a green grass enclosure surrounded by the high walls of the prison and, in the distance, the glass windows of a guard tower. At the bottom, we waited for a cell door to slide open. Far ahead of us, blue-shirted inmates were going about their business, the same way that people move about in the courtyard of a mall.

After only a few steps we stopped again while the guard inserted a heavy metal key into a steel door and ushered us into a rectangular room buried halfway in the ground. Vending machines lined the far wall. On a raised platform next to the rest room, a uniformed officer sat at a wooden desk, his eyes roving up and down the long rows of facing plastic chairs, guarding against illegal narcotics and attempts at illicit contact. When I gave him my name, he picked up a black dialless phone and reported my arrival.

A short distance away, the woman who had been reading a book, the one I was certain was a regular, was sitting across from an inmate with a crooked nose, sandy-colored hair, and the faded look of someone who had been inside for a very long time. There was nothing romantic about the way they looked at each other; they resembled a married couple you might see sitting somewhere on a park bench, content in each other's company. But an hour from now, instead of walking home together, he would go back to his cell and she to her dumpy little apartment. They would eat their separate dinners, and then the phone would ring—the collect call she got every night—and on a recorded line they would gradually get around to the soft obscenities that were as close as they would ever get to intimacy. It might go on like this for years, until he was finally released and, after a few short weeks, passion spent, they discovered that nothing was the way they had always thought it would be.

The air was heavy with sweat and tobacco. When I reminded the guard I was still there, he lifted the receiver and grunted something into it, his eyes moving steadily from one chair to the next.

For a long time I stared at the clock on the wall high above the guard's desk, convinced it was broken, until, unaccountably, the long hand jolted forward and a minute had apparently passed.

"Mr. Antonelli," the guard was saying. Swinging his legs out from behind the desk, he rested his elbows on his knees. "I'm sorry, but he isn't here."

"What do you mean, he isn't here?" I demanded.

He shook his head. "They should have told you out front. He's over in maximum security."

It was not his fault. "You mean," I grumbled, "I have to go all the way back out and then in again?"

"Yeah, afraid so." He picked up the phone again. "I'll get you out of here right away."

I left the concrete labyrinth the same way I had come. The sound of the steel gate closing behind me still jarred on my ears as I opened the glass door in front and hustled down the cement steps to the pavement below.

I drove around to the back and went through the same routine as before, but by myself this time. Only people on official business came to this entrance; no one else was allowed inside. Then the guard led me along a short wide corridor toward a series of open solid doors that led into glass-partitioned visitation booths.

"No," I said, stopping. "Not in there. I sent word I wanted him someplace where I could talk to him face-to-face."

"That's face-to-face," he objected. It was the first time he had spoken. His voice, a high-pitched whine, seemed oddly out of place.

I was not in a mood to explain myself, and now that I was not acting as a defense attorney, I did not have to.

"Put him in a room with a table and chairs."

"You sure?" he asked, the corner of his mouth twisted down. "I wouldn't want to be alone with that guy."

"I'll be all right," I assured him, while he searched through his key ring for the one that opened a solid door a few steps behind us.

Removing a legal pad from my briefcase, I placed it on the table in front of me and scribbled the date in the upper left corner. Then, with nothing else to do, I tapped the pen in a slow, monotonous beat, the sound of it the only tangible proof that time had not come to a complete and final stop.

Through a door on the other side of the room I heard the muffled sound of voices, and then a metal key twisted in the lock. Travis Quentin was shoved into the room. His wrists were handcuffed behind him, and his ankles shackled together. Wrapped twice around his waist, a bulky chain hung between his wrists and down to his ankles and back again, pulling his shoulders back and thrusting his chest forward. He was held up by two guards, one on each arm. They sat him in the chair on the other side of the table.

He looked at me for just a moment, a scowl on his thick, puffy mouth, and then snapped his head toward one of the guards.

"Take these goddamn things off me!" he demanded, lifting himself off the chair far enough to demonstrate what he meant.

The guard looked at me. I began to tap my pen against the tablet. Quentin's round head followed the guard's eyes.

"You want to talk to me, mister, you tell him to take these goddamn things off me." His voice was not quite so loud, and his tone not quite so demanding.

"You've made a mistake," I replied. "I don't want to talk to you, Mr. Quentin. I'm here because you want to talk to me."

Sitting on the edge of the chair, his neck bulged against the pull of the chains. His right eyelid drooped down. He watched me tapping my pen on the yellow legal pad, trying to figure out what I was doing.

In a rough, dry voice he insisted, "Without me, you don't have a case."

The pen tapped like a metronome, measuring the intervals between each time I shook my head back and forth. Abruptly, I stopped and bent my head forward.

"What case, Mr. Quentin? Those allegations you made to keep yourself out of the gas chamber? Do you think anyone is just going to take your word for it?"

"The guy hired me to kill his wife," he said.

He was still struggling against the chain, but his movements were becoming less violent, more like gestures of contempt.

"Would you like me to ask the guards to do something about those?" I asked, with a slight nod toward the heavy metal links draped around his waist.

"What the hell do you think?" he snarled.

Folding my arms across my chest, I sat back and said nothing. We stared at each other for a moment. Finally, he relented. "Yeah, I would."

I glanced at the guard who was standing an arm's length away from him. "You can take them off."

When he finished removing the cumbersome chain, the guard looked at me, uncertain what to do next.

"Take the cuffs off as well," I said.

His wrists free, Quentin brought his thick hands around in front of his throat, formed them into fists, and pushed them hard against each other, stretching his arms until his elbows were thrust forward. He dropped his arms to his sides, shaking the circulation back into his fingers.

With the chain draped over his arms, the one guard motioned to the other. "We'll be right outside," he said, as they opened the door.

"One of you should stay," I said, pointing toward a chair in the corner. My eye moved back to Quentin.

"Just in case we have different recollections later on about what is said here."

"I've already told my story to the state cops that came down to LA. The guy hired me to kill his wife. I killed her. I admitted it. What else do you need to know?" he asked, rubbing his arm.

"I read the reports. There's nothing there."

He still did not understand. "What do you mean? How many times do I have to tell you? He hired me to kill her and I killed her."

Elbows on the edge of the table, I folded my fingers together and rested my chin on my thumbs. I looked straight at him.

"All right. It goes like this. You killed her. He hired you."

"Yeah, right."

"Then he's guilty of conspiracy to commit murder. But no one can be convicted in a conspiracy case on the uncorroborated testimony of a co-conspirator. And that's what I meant when I say there's nothing there. You don't have any evidence that Goodwin was involved. Nothing to back up what you say."

"Well, if he didn't hire me, how did I know who she was or where she'd be?" he asked with a smug grin. "How did I know any of that?"

"You could have found out who she was after you killed her. You stole her purse. It had her wallet, her driver's license, a photograph of her husband."

"Yeah? Then what about the fact he had me in his office alone for more than an hour and the sweet deal he gave me. What the hell's that, just a coincidence?"

"The DA's office dismisses cases all the time. The search wasn't any good. He had you brought in because he wanted to see if he could use you as witness in a drug case. He made a deal with you."

Drawing back from the table, I crossed my ankle over my leg and locked my fingers around my knee.

"They might even argue that you made the deal—offered to testify in a drug case to save yourself from ten years in prison—and then, when you were free, decided to show him that you had the real power. Now, when you're facing the death penalty, you decide it wasn't enough to kill his wife, you're going to say he paid you to do it." Narrowing my eyes, I added, "You have any idea what a good defense attorney can do to a confessed murderer on the stand?"

Shaking my head, I got to my feet and walked away. The guard crouched in the corner, his forearms on his thighs, staring at the floor.

"What did he say to you when you were in his office?" I asked, leaning up against the cinder-block wall.

"Nothing. He asked me if I'd like to plead guilty to possession and do a month in the county jail. I said something like 'Who do I have to kill?' He said something like 'We'll take that up later.' And I knew right then."

My hands in my coat pockets, I crossed one foot in front of the other. "What did you know?"

"He wasn't kidding; it was a deal. He was going to keep me out of prison, and I was going to take care of someone for him. It was the look he had."

"You were there for at least an hour. What did he talk to you about before you knew he wanted you to kill someone?"

"About my record, mostly."

"What about your record?"

"Everything," he replied, with a caustic laugh that rattled in his throat. "From the first time I was arrested. He went right down the list, asking me what happened. He said he wanted to know everything he could about me."

His half-closed right eye twitched unconsciously as he thought about what had happened.

"I kind of liked the guy. I didn't trust him," he added quickly, and let me know by the way he said it that he never trusted anyone. "But I kind of liked him. He reminded me of one of those defense lawyers who tell you how they're going to win your case and you don't know if they're just lying or they're really so stupid they believe it."

He paused for a moment, as if he was weighing something in his mind. Then, a blank look on his face, he shrugged his shoulders.

"At least they don't treat you like the first thing they're going to do after they talk to you is go wash their hands."

Coming back to the table, I turned the chair around and, with one leg on each side of it, draped my arms over the top.

"Was he particularly interested in the manslaughter convictions?"

"Yeah. He wanted to know how I felt about it."

"How you felt about it?"

"Yeah," he replied, his head turning slightly to the side. "He wanted to know if I ever thought about anyone I'd killed."

"What did you tell him?"

"Nothing much." He shrugged as he looked away.

"What did you tell him?" I asked again.

Ignoring me, he scratched the side of his pockmarked face and mumbled something inaudible.

"What did you tell him?" I insisted.

His head snapped around and he glared at me, his eyes filled with a strange, almost kinetic malice.

"I didn't tell him I was sorry, if that's what you're thinking."

"You're not sorry you dropped that boy ten stories off a roof?" I shot back.

"I was just a kid," he said, curious that I should even mention it. "It wasn't anything. Nothing like what I did with Goodwin's wife."

Most criminals disparage their crimes to make them seem smaller, less significant, less worthy of punishment, than they really are. Travis Quentin had no desire to slander his own accomplishments. There could have been no doubt in Marshall Goodwin's mind that in Travis Quentin he was dealing with a man without a conscience.

"After you were taken back to jail, you never had any contact with him again?"

"Never."

"And the day you were released, someone gave you a package? That was how you knew what you were supposed to do?"

"Yeah. I walked out of jail and this woman came up to me. Doesn't say anything, just hands me an envelope and walks away."

"What do you remember about her?"

A stupid, garish grin cut across his face. "She had a body that wouldn't quit."

"What color hair?"

"Hell, I don't know."

"What was she wearing? How was she dressed?"

"Don't remember, but she was dressed good, in some kind of suit."

"A professional woman. Good. How old?"

"Late twenties, early thirties."

"And she didn't say anything? Didn't ask you if you were Travis Quentin? Didn't tell you she was delivering something from the DA's office, something from Goodwin?"

"I told you," he said irritably, "she just handed it to me and left."

"And that's all you can tell me about her?"

"No, that's not all I can tell you," he snarled. "I can tell you who she is."

"A moment ago you couldn't even tell me what color her hair is."

"I don't know what color her hair is. But I know who she is."

Out of patience, I slapped the table with my open hand. "Then why didn't you say something about it before? Why isn't it in the transcript of the interview you had with the police?"

"They never asked me, that's why."

"All right," I said, trying to control myself. "What's her name?"

"I don't know her name."

Glowering at him, I shoved myself up from the chair.

"She was in court the day they arraigned me. I saw her standing at the table just before they brought me in. A real looker, not someone you could forget anytime soon."

"She's a lawyer, a defense lawyer?" I asked, incredulous.

"No," he replied, the lines in his forehead deepening. "She isn't a defense lawyer. She's a prosecutor."

Grabbing the back of the chair with both hands, I stared at him. "You're sure? You're absolutely sure?"

"Like I said, she wasn't somebody you could forget. Not with that body." In the corner, the guard looked up from the floor.

"She had dark hair and big dark eyes. Five feet four or five, slender, right?"

I did not pay any attention to what he said in response. It didn't matter. I knew who it was. I was sure of it.

UNDER A LOWERING SKY I LEFT THE PRISON AND
headed back to Portland. After two hours with Travis
Quentin it was no longer a question whether I would do
what Horace Woolner had asked. That question had
somehow answered itself. I found myself wondering instead about what it was going to be like, starting up for
the second time. In his will, Leopold Rifkin had left me
his house and his extraordinary library because he
thought it was never too late to begin the study of serious things. But Horace was right. Leopold had read his
books and done his work as well. He would not have
expected anything less from me.

As soon as I got home I went into the library and
picked up the phone. Waiting for Horace to answer, my
eye fell on the volume of Aristotle that lay on the corner
of the desk and I remembered how each time I opened
it I was taught again the depths of my ignorance.

Alma answered. "You made another conquest.
Madame Krupskaya keeps asking about you."

I remembered the Russian woman's bright-colored
face, made up like a painted mask. "How old is she,
anyway?"

"Well," she replied, "I don't think it's really true that

she danced for the czar . . ." Her voice faded into the silence of uncertainty.

"She was very interesting," I remarked, trying to be discreet.

Soft laughter, like the hushed giggle of a schoolgirl, penetrated her speech. "Are you interested, Joe?"

"Not yet."

"Not yet!" she burst out. "What does that mean, not yet?"

"I'm too young for her," I explained.

"The age difference—whatever it is—isn't going to change, Joe."

"No, but when I'm eighty or eighty-five it won't matter so much."

"That's what you say now," she teased gently.

"Is Horace around?"

"You mean you didn't call to talk to me?"

She waited just long enough for me to feel awkward. "He's on his way home. He called from court just before you did. Shall I have him call you?"

I asked if she would and then she invited me to dinner. "Sometime soon," she said. "Perhaps I can find someone a little less—what shall I say?—*mature* than Madame Krupskaya."

"I'd love to have dinner, just the three of us."

"Or maybe the four of us," she insisted. "You really have to get out more often, Joe. We worry about you. You need to have a life, Joe. Everyone deserves that," she said, quietly serious.

A half hour later, Horace got right to the point.

"How did it go with Quentin? What's he like?"

"He's a fairly powerful argument against the death penalty, that's what he's like."

Horace read my mind. "Too good for him, huh?"

My gaze lingered on the library shelves lined with dozens of works of moral philosophy. What good would books like these do someone like Quentin? When you were old enough to begin the study of ethics, it was already too late for it to have any effect on what you were.

"Right and wrong don't have any meaning for him." I tried to explain. "Imagine someone who does whatever he feels like doing and then, as soon as he's done it, forgets all about it, the way you might toss a candy wrapper out of your car."

"Did he tell you anything new?"

"I think I know who delivered the package, the one with the information about Goodwin's wife."

"Good. Who?"

"The woman he married, Kristin Maxfield."

"You sure?" he asked, after he muttered an obscenity under his breath.

"Quentin recognized her. He saw her in court the day he was arraigned."

"Doesn't mean she was involved," he remarked.

"Let me ask you something, Horace. Goodwin was in the middle of a trial when they told him his wife had been killed. It was a murder case. Was she the one who took over for him? Was she co-counsel in that case?"

He tried to remember. "Might have been. They usually tried cases together."

I could see it, the two of them sitting across from each other in the conference room, thick three-ring trial manuals lying open on the table between them, the door to the hallway left open. Anyone working late would have seen them there, getting ready for another day in court. I knew what it was like, the constant preparation, the obsession with every detail, the inability to free your mind from it for more than a few moments at a time. On the night Nancy Goodwin died, while they worked, was that what they were thinking about?

"I have to know," Horace said, "one way or the other. Are you going to do it?"

I could still get out of it. If I said no, that would be the end of it, and Horace would never hold it against me. If I said yes, I was in for the duration.

"Yes." After a short pause, I asked, "You knew all along, didn't you?"

"You had to come back," he said. "Sooner or later. You needed to be away for a while, but you were never ready to quit for good. It's in your blood. You'd miss it too much. It's like war. Everybody grows to hate it, but when there hasn't been one for a while, everybody forgets what it's really like and they start to look for the first excuse to start a new one."

I hoped he was wrong and was almost certain he was right. In trial work the only thing that mattered was whether you won or lost. Now, after everything that had happened, I thought it made a difference whether you deserved to win.

DURING THE NEXT FEW HECTIC DAYS I DEALT WITH THE prosaic details of beginning for the second time in my life a new practice, limited, at least for the moment, to a single case. How young and naive I had been the first time I looked for office space, certain I was about to embark on a career in which every defendant was innocent and none of them was ever convicted. How quickly it had all passed. Before I knew it, I was staring out the window of my corner office, a senior partner in the fastest growing firm in the city, watching the sun set on Mount Hood, wondering how things might have been had I remained an anonymous lawyer conferring with a clientele of indigent defendants in a dimly lit two-room office with a used desk and a couple of borrowed chairs. It was, I suppose, a form of middle-age self-indulgence, the vague regret at vanished innocence, the knowledge that the prize is never quite what you thought it was going to be.

I had no desire to make my second beginning like the first, however; the days of Spartan simplicity were over. I rented a four-room suite in a modern building several blocks from the courthouse, filled it with Oriental rugs and expensive furniture, and then realized I had no idea what to do next. Helen Lundgren, my secretary for more than a dozen years, had always taken care of everything. As I now discovered, my dependence had been so habitual that I had not even thought of her until I needed her.

The telephones had just been hooked up, and the first call I made was to my old firm.

"You could have called before this, you know," she scolded. "You're not drinking again, are you? You haven't done anything stupid, have you? You're not . . . ?"

"No, I'm fine. Just fine. I'm opening up a law practice."

"The criminals will be glad to hear it," she said sharply, still certain there was no such thing as a false accusation or an honest mistake.

"I was wondering—hoping, actually. Would you be interested in working for me again? I know you've been with the firm a long time, but I could really use the help."

Her voice sank to a conspiratorial whisper. "You

know what they have me doing here? I prepare estate planning documents. Trusts, things like that. You have any idea how dull that is?" she asked plaintively. "You have any idea how much I miss murder and rape and all the things we used to do? When can I start?"

"How much notice do you have to give?"

"I'll give them what they deserve. I can start tomorrow."

Helen was waiting for me the next morning, one bony knee crossed over the other, if anything even thinner than she had been before. Her hair had a little more gray in it, and there were a few more lines at the corners of her eyes.

"How's your husband?" I asked, as I sat down behind the desk.

"Still the luckiest man alive," she replied briskly.

"I'd sort of hoped you might have changed a little," I said, leaning back in the chair as I tried to suppress a grin.

"No, you didn't," she retorted. "Shall we get to work?"

By the end of the week it at least looked like a law office. Someone Helen found worked all day and, it seemed, straight through the night, constructing bookshelves on two facing walls in the room that now became both a conference room and a library. Without a word between us, Helen made all the arrangements to bring out of storage the lawbooks I owned, and the morning after the shelves were finished she was standing on a stepladder placing each volume of the *Oregon Reporter* in its proper chronological place. Though she always treated my offers to help like an invitation to abuse, I made one anyway.

"If you want something done right," she replied, lift-

ing the next volume with both hands, "you have to do
it yourself." She could retrieve every known homily at
will and recite it as if she had never heard it before.

"When it's convenient," I drawled, as I headed for
my office, "would you put a call in to the DA's office?"

The door closed and the buzzer on my console rang.
"Who do you want there?"

On the front right corner of my desk, a glass bud
vase held a single red rose. Neither the vase nor the
flower had been there the day before.

"Thank you for the flower."

She ignored me. "Who do you want me to get on the
line?"

"Marshall Goodwin."

Goodwin was not in, but two hours later he called
back.

"Joseph Antonelli!" he exclaimed, with the same exuberance he lavished on perfect strangers. "Did I hear
your secretary right? *Law offices of Joseph Antonelli!*
So you're back at it? Great! What can I do for you?"

He seemed surprised when I invited him to lunch,
and even, I thought, a little ill at ease. Was it because of
the line that was drawn so frequently between prosecutors and defense lawyers, a line that discouraged social
contact? Or was it something else?

"There's something I'd really like to talk to you
about," I said, when he hesitated.

"Sure, I'd love to," he replied, reverting to his normal
enthusiasm.

We met the next day at a fish restaurant a block off
Burnside and sat in a wooden booth near the back.
Dressed in a paisley tie and a neatly pressed double-
breasted suit, Goodwin smiled at the waitress as he or-

dered a drink and kept his eye on her while she walked away.

"Nice," he remarked, turning back to me. "Don't you think?"

"A little young," I replied.

"So, tell me," he said, his eyes full of apparent interest. "What made you decide to come back?"

"I thought it was time," I said, looking back at him.

It was a strange feeling—or, rather, it was strange that I seemed to have no feeling at all. I'm not sure what I expected. I had defended dozens of people charged with murder, most of them guilty, almost all of them acquitted. But a trial, even for murder, is like watching a play, one of Shakespeare's histories, in which all the violence takes place offstage. The victim is dead, and no matter how depraved the manner of the death, it happened far away from the ornate civilities of a courtroom. This seemed different and, in a peculiar way, more real. I was face-to-face with someone who might be a murderer and did not even know he was a suspect.

"I never had a chance to tell you," I remarked solemnly, "how sorry I was about what happened to your wife."

He looked away, as if he was not sure how he should respond.

"It was a long time ago," he said finally. Brightening, he changed the subject. "Now, tell me," he asked earnestly. "What are you going to do? I have a hard time imagining you doing anything as dull as civil work. Or are you back to criminal defense?"

"I'm going to prosecute," I replied evenly.

He had just started to take another drink, and he laughed. "You're going to what?"

"I've been appointed a special prosecutor in a murder case," I explained. "You know the statute."

"Oh, sure, sure," he said. "When a county doesn't have anyone with the right expertise or experience. Well, I never thought I'd see you trying to put someone away," he went on, as he lifted his glass. "Welcome to the club."

The waitress returned and, one at a time, dealt onto the table the dishes we had ordered. Goodwin rattled the ice in his empty glass and ordered another. As he raised his hand, I noticed his watch, a thin crushed gold band and a flat jade stone face with two narrow hands to measure the minute and the hour. It was the simple elegance of understated luxury, and I could not take my eyes off it.

"I bought it for myself," he remarked, pulling his sleeve back until the watch was completely exposed. "Last year, when I turned forty, I had it made."

"I didn't realize deputy district attorneys did so well."

"So where is the case you've got?" he asked, pretending to be interested. "Do you have to go out to one of those one-horse counties where they've only got two lawyers in the DA's office?" The smile on his face left no doubt what he thought of anyone who had to work outside the only city in the state that counted.

"No, the case is right here."

"Here? Portland? That's impossible."

"They've reopened the case, Marshall."

"What case?"

"The case of your wife's murder."

I leaned against the hard wooden back of the booth, waiting to see what he would do. He did not react like a husband who had lost his wife but like a lawyer confronted with a technical question of law.

"She was killed in Corvallis. The case would be brought there, not here."

"Your wife was murdered in Corvallis. The conspiracy to have her killed took place right here, in Portland—just a few blocks from here, as a matter of fact."

He studied me through narrowed eyes. "Just a few blocks away? What are you telling me, somebody planned her murder? Why?"

"I thought maybe you could tell me."

He started to shake his head and then stopped. His eyes opened wide. "What do you mean?"

"Travis Quentin confessed. He told the police everything. How you had him brought to your office, how you dropped all the charges against him, how you had an envelope delivered to him the day he got out of the county jail with instructions about where to find her and where to find the money you were paying him."

A look of astonishment spread across his face. "And that's the reason you were appointed a special prosecutor?"

Sliding out of the booth, he threw his napkin down on the table and shook his head.

"You've got a major problem on your hands, Antonelli."

"What's that?"

"I didn't do it."

| vi

"WHAT ELSE WAS HE GOING TO SAY?" I ASKED, AS HOR-
ace glowered at me.

"Why did you let him say anything? What was the
point?"

"I wanted to see his reaction when he heard it for the
first time. Before he had time to think about what he
was going to say."

I was sprawled on a chair in front of Horace's desk.
He was on the other side of the room, pouring a cup of
coffee.

"Sure you don't want some?" he asked, as he sank
into the leather chair behind the desk. Cautiously, he
brought the chipped mug to his mouth. "It's been a long
day." He sighed. "The motion calendar was murder.
Everybody always has to make their record. Sometimes,
I think that's all we do on the bench, read the same
canned briefs, listen to the same tired arguments from a
bunch of hollow-eyed lawyers too scared of making a
mistake to say or write anything original, or even
halfway interesting."

He started to take another sip, and then changed his
mind, his eyes full of malicious wonder.

"You should have seen it," he said. "One of those
guys from the public defender's office—you know the

type: washed-out white guys with terminal depression—
is droning on and on, making an argument on a motion
to suppress, repeating almost verbatim what he had
written in his brief."

With a merciless talent for mimicry, Horace let his
head sag to the side as he dragged his eyes listlessly
around the room, darting them away each time they
were about to land on me.

" 'This issue was decided three years ago in the case
of . . . ,' " he said, imitating an exhausted voice that
spoke only at the end of each labored exhaled breath.
His head snapped up. "I couldn't help myself," he explained. " 'Isn't that the case that was just overruled?' I
asked. For the first time he actually looked at me.
Christ, it was like watching a corpse get a transfusion,
blood rising into his face. I turned to the deputy DA. He
didn't know anything either, but you don't think he was
going to admit it, do you? Hell, no!" he roared.

" 'Is that your recollection, Mr. Krueger?' I asked.
The little weasel! He answers, 'I'm sure your honor's
memory is better than my own.' " Horace shook his
large graying head with sad-eyed derision.

"I turned back to the public defender. 'And what's
your recollection, counselor?' Now, if he had stood his
ground, if he had been prepared, if he really knew what
he was talking about, he could have said, 'No, your
honor, the case has not been overruled, it's still good
law.' Instead, all he can do is fumble around, letting
everyone see he thinks the case he's relying on isn't good
anymore."

Holding his mug with both hands, Horace quietly
sipped some coffee. Under half-closed eyes he stared at
something in the distance.

"There used to be a few lawyers around who didn't

spend all their time worrying about themselves," he said pensively. "Not so many years ago, a DA would have corrected me immediately. That it didn't help his case wouldn't have mattered. We were all supposed to follow the law, and it didn't matter whether correcting someone else's mistake cost you a temporary advantage."

I pulled myself up in the chair. "Things change."

His mouth turned down at the corners as he thought about it a moment. "I haven't seen too many changes that were for the better, have you?"

We were looking at each other, caught in our different memories of the past and the things that had altered our lives forever.

"I suppose not," I replied.

Horace turned away, his hands in his lap, his two dead legs spread apart, watching out the window.

"It's all an illusion," he said presently. "The whole idea of progress. The important things haven't changed. They never will." His voice was barely audible.

"Do you believe him?" Horace asked suddenly.

"Goodwin?"

His face turned slightly to the side, away from the outside light. "You still think he might be telling the truth?"

"I'm not sure I'm ready to take this to trial, Horace," I admitted.

Shifting his weight, he pulled the chair closer to the desk and rested both arms on top of it.

"When I was DA, there were times when I wasn't absolutely sure. Sometimes there was a question, something that bothered me about it." He studied me for a moment. "You never had that problem, did you? You never had to worry about whether the defendant was really guilty. I worried about it all the time. It's the worst thing there is, that fear that you might convict someone for something they didn't do. Everybody can talk all they want about letting the jury decide. You're the one who gets to lie awake in the middle of the night wondering if you made a mistake. Winning is supposed to be the only thing that matters, but let me tell you something: there were a few cases I didn't mind losing."

Searching his eyes, I asked, "You don't have any doubt about Goodwin?"

"I'm not prosecuting this case. You're the one who has to decide."

With both hands, Horace pushed himself out of the chair.

"Sure you don't want some?" he asked, as he walked in his rigid stride toward the metal coffeepot on the other side of the room.

After refilling his cup, he moved toward a black-and-white photograph in a simple black wooden frame hanging on the wall next to where the bookshelves ended.

"That was us," he remarked, tapping his knuckle against it. There were twenty or thirty men and women, each of them wearing an identical T-shirt. "Woolner's Warriors." He laughed. "We were in a softball league. Slow pitch," he explained. "I was the manager, I guess because I could yell louder than anybody else. That's Goodwin, right next to me. He was maybe the best athlete on the team. He could run like a deer." His head moved back and forth like a fighter's. "You know, I liked him. I really did."

I got up and went over to where he stood. "Kristin in it?" I asked, moving closer until the photograph was right in front of me. I found her, second from the left in the back row, about as far away from Goodwin as possible. Everyone in the photograph worked in the district attorney's office, and nearly half of them were women, but there was something in her large dark eyes that drew you toward her and, when you looked away, made you want to look back.

Horace was watching me. "Maybe she's the motive," he suggested tentatively.

I kept staring at her, reluctant to stop. "Kristin could be the motive for a lot of things," I acknowledged, looking away. "But all he had to do was get a divorce. Why have his wife murdered?"

"For the money," Horace replied with a shrug, as he headed back to his desk.

Lingering next to the photograph, my hands shoved into my pockets, I asked, "You ever notice anything about her? Anything about the two of them?"

"Everybody noticed her." Horace snorted. "Tough not to. But between them? No. In fact, if I remember right, she was engaged to somebody."

"Someone in the office?"

"No one I knew. Actually, I don't think I ever met him," he remarked, his face turned up toward the light that fell from the window. "She was almost too good-looking. You know what I mean? Most guys wouldn't think they had a chance with her. When word got around she was engaged, I'd bet you anything everybody just assumed it was some rich guy and once they were married she'd be gone."

Crossing one foot in front of the other, I stared down at my shoes.

"I almost asked her out once," I confessed.

Horace laughed. "Why didn't you?"

"I don't really know," I said, glancing up. "Maybe because she seemed just a little too sure of herself."

"Maybe, when it came to her, *you* weren't so sure of yourself. I remember some of the women you've been with. Most of them weren't all that shy."

"I had the feeling that with her everything was a game."

"She may have gotten herself into a pretty dangerous game this time," Horace said, frowning.

"Maybe she just thought she was delivering a packet of information to a witness," I suggested. "She was working for Marshall, remember."

"It's possible," he replied, without conviction.

With one last glance at her face in the framed group photograph, I walked back across the room. The clouds bunched together, and the glow that had burnished the side of Horace's dark face disappeared. Dim shadows enveloped the room, and the whites of his eyes seemed to hover, ghostlike, in the air. For a brief moment I had the strange, disquieting sense of being watched by someone I did not know.

I started to sit down again and changed my mind. It was getting late and I had to go.

"I need a little more time. There are some details I'd like the police to follow up on."

The sun shot through again, and Horace turned toward the light, slowly rubbing the tips of his fingers back and forth against each other.

"It might be too late," he said. "Gilliland-O'Rourke called late yesterday. I haven't returned it yet." As he motioned for me to sit down, Horace picked up the phone. "Why don't we find out what our old friend wants. . . .

"Gwendolyn!" he exclaimed, as if the sound of her voice was the best thing that had happened to him all day. "How nice of you to call. Should have called you back before this, but I've been in court all day, and you know how that goes."

He pulled the telephone away from his ear and rolled his eyes.

"There's no reason for you to get so upset," he said, wincing. "There was no way they were going to take that chance. . . . It wasn't a question of whether anyone trusted you. You have to understand—"

His mouth still open, he looked at me and then, shaking his head, hung up the phone. "It's like I was saying, some things never change."

"She was upset?"

His head bobbed back and forth, his eyes filled with amusement. "Let's just say she was a little annoyed. Goodwin told her, two days ago, right after he had lunch with you. He had to."

I had not thought about it, but as soon as Horace said it, I knew he was right. If Goodwin had waited until he was formally charged, it would have looked like he had tried to hide something. Whatever the reality, by going to her right away, he could keep up the appearance of outraged innocence. And now Gilliland-O'Rourke was outraged as well.

I looked at Horace. "What do you think she's going to do?"

With a caustic grin, he replied, "You know as well as I do what she's going to do. She's going to do something so far beyond the pale, something that after she does it is going to seem so obvious, we're going to wonder why we hadn't thought of it before. Right?"

"There isn't anything she *can* do," I objected.

With his eyes opened as wide as they would go, Horace looked at me and started to laugh. "You think?"

It was nearly five o'clock and I was already late. I left

the courthouse wondering what Gilliland-O'Rourke could really do, and by the time I arrived at the hotel I had almost convinced myself that she would try to turn things around by charging me with subornation of perjury in the murder trial of Leopold Rifkin.

OLD HABITS DIE HARD, AND SOME HABITS DO NOT DIE at all. I lived alone, but I had not yet acquired any serious interest in celibacy. In the year since Alexandra left me, I had begun to keep occasional company with a woman for whom sex was too exciting ever to be diluted by anything as generous as love. A tall, lanky blonde with a shallow chest, she once told me that from the time she entered college until the day she filed for her third divorce, she had slept with hundreds of different men and had found none of them entirely satisfactory. We used each other for pleasure, and because there were never any expectations, there were never any disappointments. We became, in our fashion, something more than casual acquaintances and something less than good friends.

Lounging on the hotel bed, a sheet pulled up to my chest, I listened to the shower running in the bathroom. She came out with nothing on but a towel wrapped around her hair and sat down next to me.

"I don't have long, Joe."

A trace of some indefinable regret curved along her wide, full mouth, and she leaned toward me and gave me a perfunctory kiss. Perhaps because she had to go, I wanted her to stay.

"We have the room. We could spend the night."

She rolled forward on her hip until I was looking straight up into her brown lucent eyes. The scent of her

breath reminded me of a girl I could not remember,
someone I had known as a boy during a season of weekend evenings spent parked in a car. Her fingers touched
my forehead and then my hair.

"You'd really like to spend the night?" Her voice was
a whisper.

"We could have dinner. . . ."

She put her hand over my mouth and shook her
head, her eyes full of teasing skepticism as she crawled
next to me under the thin white sheet.

We lost ourselves in the trancelike delirium of sex.
When it was over I listened again to the sound of the
shower, and as I watched her get dressed never thought
about asking her to stay. She intrigued me with the way
she moved—everything was accomplished with almost
mechanical efficiency. She looked at me while she put on
her clothes, her hands and legs in constant movement.

"We could spend the night sometime," she said, as
she buttoned her blouse. "But not tonight. I have a
date."

My hands locked behind my head, I asked, "Is it serious?"

She turned away from me and, using the mirror
above the small desk, started to put on her lipstick.

"He wants to get married," she explained indifferently.

"Is that what you want?"

She snapped the cap back on top of the lipstick and
then smacked her lips together.

"I like being married," she said, as she wheeled
around, as if presenting herself for inspection. "How do
I look?" she asked, a doubtful expression on her face.

She was attractive and I told her so.

"You're sweet," she said, as she bent down and, careful not to smear her lipstick, gave me a kiss on the cheek.

"Don't get up." She laughed as she moved away. When she got to the door, she looked back. "Call me next week?"

After the door shut behind her, I lay there, staring at the ceiling, without energy, without desire, lost in a vast emptiness. After a while, I dragged myself off the bed and took a long, hot shower.

Dressed, I tossed the room key on the small desk below the mirror and took one last look around. Crumpled pillows and wrinkled sheets covered the bed, and every towel in the bathroom had ended up on the floor. The room reeked of sex. In two hours we had turned one of the most expensive hotel rooms in the city into a scene from a cheap motel.

As I was leaving the hotel, I changed my mind and dropped in at the bar. It was small, with a few tables scattered along the wall. I sat down on a leather bar stool and ordered a scotch and soda. Through the glass window in front, lettered with the name of the bar, the blue and red neon lights from a movie theater down the street smeared the rain-slick pavement with their own reflection.

At the far end, pictures flashed on a television set. Nursing my drink, I watched for a while, amused at the changing expression of the anchorwoman as she introduced each segmented story, all of them no doubt matters of great urgency and none of them lasting for more than twenty seconds.

"Would you mind turning on the volume?" I asked the bartender suddenly. The district attorney was making a statement.

"Sure," he replied, wiping a glass with a bar towel.

Reaching up, he turned the set loud enough for me to hear what she was saying.

Gwendolyn Gilliland-O'Rourke was getting older. The flame-red hair was turning to a brownish rust, and her green eyes no longer seemed quite so bright. But if she looked a little different, she still sounded the same.

Standing just outside her office, the words OFFICE OF THE DISTRICT ATTORNEY plainly visible, she read from a prepared text the announcement of an arrest.

"After a lengthy investigation, conducted in the utmost secrecy by the state police, Marshall Goodwin, chief deputy district attorney of Multnomah County, has been arrested for the murder of his wife, Nancy Goodwin, a murder that took place two years ago. At my direction," she went on, staring straight into the camera, "Mr. Goodwin was taken into custody this afternoon. Because Mr. Goodwin, who was first appointed by my predecessor, Judge Horace Woolner, has served as chief deputy district attorney, it has been decided that to avoid any suggestion of either favoritism on the one hand or undue severity on the other, a special prosecutor should be appointed to bring the state's case against the defendant. I am pleased to announce that the state will be represented by one of the preeminent defense lawyers in Oregon, Joseph Antonelli."

The camera left her answering the questions of reporters and returned to the newsroom anchorwoman.

"Marshall Goodwin, chief deputy district attorney, considered the logical choice to become district attorney next year when Gilliland-O'Rourke makes her expected bid to become the state's governor, has been arrested on a charge of murder. In a surprising twist, criminal defense attorney Joseph Antonelli will serve as the prosecutor in the case. We tried to contact Mr. Antonelli, but so far we have been unable to reach him."

I got up from the bar and paid the bill. Outside, I turned my collar up and hunched my shoulders, trying to keep dry in the endless drizzle. Across the street, a few people were lining up at the box office of the theater. For a while, I walked aimlessly, marveling at my own stupidity. I could almost see Goodwin marching into Gilliland-O'Rourke's office to tell her he had just learned he was about to be charged with the murder of his wife. And I could see her, one of the most ruthless people I had ever known, giving him all the assurances of a friend and then, as soon as he was gone, making arrangements to have him arrested. I had wanted to see Marshall Goodwin's face when he first heard what Travis Quentin had said because I wanted to be sure that he was guilty. Instead, all I knew now was that I was about to prosecute a case against a man who might very well be innocent.

LIKE TIME ITSELF, THE LAW STOPS FOR NO ONE. WHETHER
it is a drunken vagrant charged with the theft of a cheap
bottle of wine or a pillar of the legal community accused
of murder, anyone who is arrested and taken into custody has to be brought into court within forty-eight
hours. When a deputy sheriff escorted the prisoner to the
counsel table to hear for the first time a formal statement
of the charges that were being brought against him,
Marshall Goodwin seemed more embarrassed by the
way he was dressed. The expensive suits and understated
ties, tapered shirts, and tasseled black shoes had been replaced with the shapeless V-neck blue denim top and
baggy drawstring pants that made every inmate look the
same.

Goodwin did not want to look at anyone, and no one
wanted to look at him. Only the monotonous uniformity of the law saved us from a painful silence.

"Your honor," I began, "my name is Joseph Antonelli. I am here in the capacity of a prosecutor under
special appointment."

Barely visible behind the bench, Judge Stanley
Roberts, a diminutive man who regularly listened with
apparent compassion to pleas for mercy before impos-
ing sentences of remarkable severity, studied the file in

front of him. The overhead lights glistened on the pale skin on the top of his balding head.

He looked up. "I have the order of appointment. Please proceed." As soon as he said it, his eyes darted away.

Though I had heard countless times before the civilized ritual by which the state declares war against one of its own, I had never been called upon to speak the words myself.

"Your honor, we are here in the matter of State *versus* Marshall Goodwin. He is being charged by way of an information with the crime of murder in the first degree. Let the record reflect that I am handing Mr. Goodwin's attorney a copy of the information."

Goodwin had gotten one of the best, and if there were any who doubted how good he was, Richard Lee Jones was more than willing to tell them. Tall and square-shouldered, he moved around a courtroom with flailing arms and flashing eyes, convinced that the sound of his voice could mesmerize any twelve people who had ever formed a jury. One of the last remaining practitioners of old-fashioned courthouse oratory, he seldom got ten minutes into his closing argument before his slick black hair would fall across the corner of his forehead, the way it did in the photograph of Clarence Darrow that he kept on his desk in La Grande, out on the high desert plains east of the Cascades.

He held the document between his thumb and forefinger, as if it were a venomous thing. His mouth was irregular, settled permanently into a long sloping downward curve. A pair of snakeskin boots peeked out from under the cuffed trousers of a perfectly tailored three-piece suit.

Still clutching the paper in his fingers, he pulled his

hand back to his hip and, his other hand on the table, bent forward at the waist.

"For the record, I am Richard Lee Jones." Pausing, he turned his head toward me. "I'll be representing Mr. Goodwin in these proceedings."

"Do you wish to enter a plea at this time?" inquired Judge Roberts.

"Not guilty," he replied, his eyes still on me. "And we'll enter another plea of not guilty to the indictment," he went on, the faint outline of a smile on his mouth, "assuming of course that Mr. Antonelli here can get an indictment."

Abruptly, he turned his gaze away from me and toward the bench.

"Now, your honor, Mr. Goodwin wants nothing more than to clear his name against this outrageous charge. And he can certainly do more to help in his own defense once he's out of custody. Respectfully, we ask that he be released on his own recognizance."

"On a charge of murder, Mr. Jones?" asked the judge, raising an eyebrow. "Bail will be set in the amount of two hundred thousand dollars."

Jones did not seem disappointed. He whispered a few words to his new client before a deputy sheriff put his hand on Goodwin's arm and led him away. Dropping the information into his tan leather briefcase, Jones snapped it shut and turned to go. He stopped just long enough to fix me with one last stare.

"I'll have him out before the end of the day."

Despite Richard Lee Jones, I got the indictment from the grand jury, though there were moments while they listened to the testimony of Travis Quentin when I wondered if I would. Gathered together in a dimly lit room on the top floor of the county courthouse, the members, most of them middle-aged or older, listened in silence as I elicited from the state's chief witness the story of the killing of Nancy Goodwin.

Quentin sat on an armless wooden chair, weighted down by the heavy chains that twisted over his shoulders and around his legs. Two armed guards stood behind him. My place was at a small table directly in front of him, less than ten feet away.

"You murdered Nancy Goodwin two years ago, did you not?"

His arms fastened behind him, Quentin lifted his head and turned it slightly to the side, so that, as was his habit, he was looking at me, one eye lined up behind the other.

"Yeah," he grunted.

"And what was the reason that you took her life?"

His gaze drifted away and settled on one of the members of the grand jury, seated together on his left.

"I was paid to," he explained, as his eye moved on to someone else.

"How much were you paid?" I asked sharply, trying to draw his attention back to me.

His head swung around. "Ten thousand."

"That's not much for a human life, is it?" I asked sternly.

"Not bad for an hour's work," he retorted.

A chair squeaked against the linoleum floor as one juror shifted his weight around; another juror cleared his throat. I watched their faces, but there was no visible sign of shock or outrage or even disbelief. There was instead an almost tangible feeling of resentment, as if, recognizing there was no common bond of humanity that linked them to Quentin, they did not want to be reminded that someone like this was even a possibility.

"And who paid you to murder Nancy Goodwin?" I asked finally.

"Her husband, the district attorney."

"You're referring to Marshall Goodwin, chief deputy district attorney for Multnomah County?"

"Yeah, that's the guy," he answered.

He raised his shackled wrists to his chest, where the chain went taut, and tried to maneuver the iron links to a different spot on his shoulder.

"Couldn't you take these off? I'm not going anywhere," he remarked, nodding at the guards behind him.

I ignored him. "How do you know he paid you?"

He let his hands drop back into his lap, the chains rattling heavily against each other. Sullen-eyed, he stared at me and said nothing.

"How do you know he paid you?" I repeated.

Still, he said nothing.

Pushing back from the table, I crossed my legs and let my hands dangle down along the sides of the chair.

"We have all the time in the world, Mr. Quentin. Take as long as you like," I said quietly. "The chains won't get any lighter."

"It hurts," he said, forcing his head toward his left shoulder.

I looked at one of the guards and nodded. He lifted the chain on Quentin's shoulder and moved it a few inches toward his neck. For an instant, something like gratitude passed over his eyes.

Again I repeated the question, and this time he answered. Methodically, one question at a time, we traced the formation of Marshall Goodwin's contract for murder.

"And when you were released from the county jail, what happened then?"

He described how he was handed a package—a large envelope—and what was inside it. I did not ask him anything about the woman who had given it to him.

When I had asked my last question, I informed the grand jury foreman that I was finished with the witness.

The foreman, a corpulent woman in her thirties with long black eyelashes, looked around.

"Does anyone have any questions they would like to ask the witness?"

It was as if she had suggested an obscene act. Everyone looked away. Finally, an elderly woman slowly raised her hand. I had noticed her earlier, nervously pressing her thin lips together, when Quentin had offered his caustic remark about the money he had made for the murder of Nancy Goodwin.

"Mr. Quentin," she asked, a troubled look in her pale blue eyes, "I would like to know something. Do you feel any remorse about what you've done?"

Quentin paid no attention to her while she asked her question. His eyes followed the movement of his thumbs as they circled back and forth along the chain draped around his waist. As soon as she was finished, his thumbs stopped moving and his head jerked up. His mouth was open, the words already formed, when he saw her, a frail old woman who could never threaten anyone. His mouth closed and, after a moment, he gazed down again at his hands, watching while his thumbs started back into motion.

The two guards helped Quentin up from the wooden chair. As he shuffled his manacled feet along the floor, the chains that bent him over clanged against each other, a strange echo that seemed to come from somewhere deep underground. No one said a word until he was gone.

It was a few minutes past eleven-thirty, and no one objected when it was suggested that we break for lunch before the next witness was called. When I stepped outside the courthouse, the air was clean and fresh, and the sky a cloudless blue. I was meeting Horace for lunch and I had plenty of time. Across the street from the courthouse, I sat on a green wooden bench and watched a squirrel dart across the grass, then suddenly stop and rise up on its haunches, an acorn clutched in its front paws, long whiskers bristling, and then scamper up the side of a twisted oak tree and out along a branch. On the other side of the walkway, a young woman rested her arms on her legs while she talked to a small boy who could only stand up by holding onto her knees.

It was the first warm day of spring. I loosened my tie and took off my coat. The boy let go of his mother's knee, wobbled, and then collapsed, sitting down hard on his bottom. He had that look that only a child can have, wondering whether or not to cry. Beaming at him, his mother began to laugh, and an instant later he laughed too.

Stretching my arm out along the back of the bench, I turned my face toward the sunlight and closed my eyes. When I opened them, I saw the child grip one of his mother's fingers in each of his outstretched hands and, marveling at his own accomplishment, lift first one foot and then the other. How easy it was to let life slip by. I was on the wrong side of fifty, had never married or had a child. During the long years of my ambition, when the only thing important was the next case and the next trial, I had just assumed, when I thought about it at all, that those things would take care of themselves.

With growing confidence, the boy let go of his mother's fingers and started to take a step. To his astonishment, his little legs buckled and he found himself once again sitting on the pavement. This time he did not even think about crying. Rolling over onto his knees, he pushed himself up and rested his arms on his mother's legs, getting ready to try again.

The park was beginning to fill up with people spending their lunch hour out of doors. My coat slung over my shoulder, I walked past the boy and his mother and wondered for just a moment what it would be like to have a wife and a child.

"He'll be running in a week," I heard myself say.

"Probably." She laughed.

She had kind eyes and a pleasant smile, and the boy was so much the center of her universe that though she looked right at me, ten seconds later she could not have described anything about me.

I found Horace waiting for me outside the restaurant. Dressed in a tan suit, a blue and white pinstripe shirt, a large bow tie, and a crumpled gray Irish walking hat, he looked more like a professor of English literature than someone who had spent most of his adult life in the coarsening atmosphere of the criminal courts.

"You're late." He chuckled. "I figured once you were let loose in a grand jury you'd lose all sense of time."

"Actually, we quit early. I've been sitting in the park. Nice suit," I added as we went inside and waited for a table.

"Alma said she'd appreciate it if you didn't put a hole in this one," he said with a straight face. "She picked it out herself."

"Whose idea was the bow tie?"

He measured me through half-closed eyes. "You ever try to tie one of these damn things? It took me half the morning," he remarked with amazement, whether at how long it had taken or that he had been able to do it at all, I could not tell.

We were led to a table on the side next to a window. Outside, the street was jammed with cars and the sidewalks filled with shoppers. Everyone had come downtown, afraid to wait for the next good day.

"Alma buy all your clothes?"

"No," he said firmly. "I buy them. She picks them out. You were just sitting in the park?"

"How is Alma?"

"Busy. That ballet company," he said, shaking his head. "Sometimes I think it's too much. But she loves it. That's the important thing. What were you doing, just sitting in the park? Reading?"

"No, nothing at all. I was just sitting there. I watched a young woman—a girl, really—playing with her son. Maybe a year old, just learning to walk. He'd take a step or two, then fall down seat first, then try again."

Horace nodded. "Made you wish you had a normal life, right? Wife, kids, the whole thing, didn't it?"

"Made me wonder what it would have been like."

"Not too late, you know," he remarked casually, as the waiter approached.

After we ordered, Horace leaned forward.

"Tell me what it was like. You've never been in a grand jury before, have you?"

"Once. Years ago. When I was starting out. I got called as a witness when I was doing court-appointed work. A client of mine didn't show up the day of his trial, so they charged him with failure to appear. They called me in, and the DA who was handling it asked me in front of the grand jury if I had informed my client of the date he was supposed to be in court."

Horace was grinning. "Let me guess. You invoked the lawyer-client privilege?"

"Yeah," I replied. "What did I know?"

"They hold you in contempt?"

"They tried," I said, with a shrug. "Rifkin saved me. He explained to the DA that contempt required a willful refusal to answer and that my refusal was not willful because it was obviously based on ignorance of what the privilege was meant to cover. And then he explained to me that it didn't prevent me from revealing whether my client knew when he was supposed to be in court. He suggested that I go back to the grand jury and tell them what I knew."

"Sounds like Leopold. Only man I ever knew could tell you to your face you were a fool and have you thank him for it."

We were almost finished with lunch when he finally asked the question I knew he had been wanting to ask for days.

"It's your case, and you don't have to tell me if you don't want to, but why haven't you done anything about Kristin? Everybody in the DA's office is treating her like some kind of martyr. Gilliland-O'Rourke told her to take as much time off as she needed. They think she's a victim."

I looked around to make sure no one was close enough to hear. "Horace, I'm not sure they're not both innocent victims."

He began to scratch a figure-eight into the tablecloth with his fork.

"You're still not sure about Goodwin?" he asked, looking at me from under his lowered brow.

"You were right. I made a mistake. I should never

have talked to him. All I accomplished was to let Gilliland-O'Rourke force my hand."

"You have enough for an indictment," Horace remarked, tapping the table with the fork.

"Enough for an indictment, maybe even enough for a conviction, but not nearly enough to convince me I'm doing the right thing," I said, reproaching myself for what I had done. "There's nothing on her," I added in response to his question. "We'll see what she has to say this afternoon."

"You're calling her as a witness?"

"There are a few questions I thought I'd ask."

We left the restaurant and walked along the crowded sidewalk on our way back to the courthouse.

"Alma wants to have you come to dinner," Horace reminded me.

He put his arm around me and his enormous hand enveloped my shoulder, drawing me closer. Gesturing emphatically with his other hand, he insisted with a puckish grin that I really had no choice.

"She wants to have a 'few' people over. You know what that means, don't you? I'm going to have about twelve thousand people milling around and they're all going to be talking about the ballet and the arts and all that kind of stuff, and I'm telling you, Antonelli, you just can't leave me alone with that crowd. So you have to come—as a favor to me."

We were in front of the courthouse. Horace let his hand fall off my shoulder.

"A week from Saturday night. You'll come, won't you?"

Few things seemed to give him so much pleasure as lying about his motives to conceal his generosity. There were dozens of lawyers he could have found to serve as a special prosecutor, all of them eager for the chance to acquire the notoriety a case against a chief deputy district attorney would inevitably bring. He had asked me because he thought I needed to come back to the law and then thanked me for taking the case. And he knew I would never say no to Alma, so they invented occasions to bring me back into the world and made it sound as if I was doing them a favor.

"I'll be there," I promised. "Thanks, Horace."

"No," he said, looking at me with his deceitful eyes, "thank you. You saved me."

We said good-bye at the elevator. "I forgot to mention it," I said as I stepped inside, "but, nice hat, Horace."

As the door shut, he looked at me for a moment and then rolled his eyes, trying not to laugh.

I made it back to the grand jury room right on time. We called our next witness.

Confident and intelligent, shapely and infinitely desirable, Kristin Maxfield Goodwin sat down in the chair recently vacated by a rapist and a murderer, a look of amused impatience on her face.

"I realize these are difficult circumstances, Mrs. Goodwin—"

Her head, held high, tilted slightly higher. "Ms. Maxfield. I kept my maiden name. For professional purposes."

"Of course. Then tell us, Ms. Maxfield—"

"You realize, Mr. Antonelli," she interjected, her large eyes flashing, "that because Marshall Goodwin is my husband, the spousal privilege is at work here, and the privilege can be invoked by either spouse?"

"Are you saying that your husband has invoked the privilege and directed you not to answer the questions of the grand jury?"

She was careful. "I'm not saying anything, Mr. Antonelli. I'm only reminding you that the privilege exists."

"It doesn't really matter," I remarked, as I got to my feet and moved to the side of the room opposite the assembled members of the grand jury. "The questions I have to ask all have to do with matters that took place before your marriage to Mr. Goodwin. As I'm sure I don't need to remind you, the spousal privilege applies only to conversations that take place during a marriage." I paused, and then added, "And not always to all of them."

My shoulders against the wall, I folded my arms across my chest.

"Tell us first, if you would, Ms. Maxfield, where you were the night Nancy Goodwin was murdered."

"I spent most of that evening working in the district attorney's office—in the conference room—preparing for trial."

"You were with Mr. Goodwin, correct?"

"Yes. We were co-counsel."

"Was this the first time you had served as his co-counsel, or was this something you had done rather frequently?"

"We had worked together a number of times, usually in murder cases."

"Did he seem any different that night? Anything seem to be bothering him?"

"No, I don't remember anything. We worked until sometime close to midnight, and then we left."

"Together?"

"We left the building together, if that's what you mean."

"No, that isn't what I mean," I said brusquely, and

took a step toward her. "What I mean is: did you—the two of you—spend the night together?"

With a withering glance, she declared, "We did not!"

"Did you spend the night with anyone?"

"Yes, I did."

"With your fiancé?"

She searched my eyes. "Yes, that's correct."

"And his name was?"

She looked down at her lap and then, licking her lip, looked up. "Conrad. Conrad Atkinson."

"About how long after the death of Nancy Goodwin did you end your engagement to Mr. Atkinson?"

"Two or three months, I think."

"And was this because you had become involved with Mr. Goodwin?"

"No," she insisted. For the first time she looked away from me and toward the members of the grand jury. "I had worked with my husband—Marshall Goodwin— for several years. We had become very good friends, but there was nothing else between us. After his wife died— that was such an awful thing for him to go through—he needed all his friends. I spent as much time as I could, trying to help. It was only much later, after my engagement was broken off, after he had had time to get over the death of his wife, that we first began to go out. Until then, I don't think we had even had dinner together."

"During the time you were working together, did he ever mention to you anything about Travis Quentin?" I moved back to the small table directly in front of her.

"No," she replied, without hesitation.

Draping one arm over the corner of the rickety metal chair, I sat back, crossed my legs, and swung my foot back and forth.

"You ever laid eyes on Travis Quentin?" I asked, watching the pendulum-like movement of my shoe.

"Not that I'm aware of."

I looked up. "Not that you're aware of? Are you saying you didn't deliver to Travis Quentin a sealed manila envelope on the day he was released from the county jail?"

If she had had more time to think about it she might have said, I remember being asked to deliver some legal documents to a potential witness who was just being released. Instead, with only an instant to make up her mind, she denied it.

"No, I did not."

I fixed her with an incredulous look and let her wonder how I had found out and how much more I knew.

BEFORE NIGHT FELL ON THE DAY OF HIS FIRST APPEAR-
ance, Marshall Goodwin posted bail and walked out of
the county jail, not exactly a free man but free enough.
He could go where he wished, so long as he did not
leave the state, and he could do anything he liked except
break the law. The only real limitation imposed by his
release agreement was the obligation to maintain contact with his attorney and make his scheduled court appearances.

Arraignment on the grand jury indictment had been
scheduled for nine-thirty. When I arrived at nine-fifteen,
the corridor outside was filled with television crews setting up their equipment. Inside the courtroom, where
cameras were not allowed, dozens of carelessly dressed
journalists filled the benches that during most criminal
proceedings held a handful of spectators, if they held
anyone at all.

Right at nine-thirty, Judge Stanley Roberts entered
from a door behind the bench and, arranging his robe,
took his accustomed place. The subdued cough, the
whispered word, the shuffle of feet sliding over the floor,
the crinkling sound of a turned page in a reporter's
notebook—everything came to a sudden final stop.

"Good morning, gentlemen," he said, without expression. His gaze drifted briefly to the vacant chair between us. "Is there anything you would like to tell me, Mr. Jones?"

"I'm sure Mr. Goodwin will be here any moment, your honor," Jones replied, calm and confident.

We waited like the members of a wedding, wondering if the bride had changed her mind. Standing at the counsel table, I held my hands in front of me and stared down at the floor while I used my thumb to push my shirt cuff above my wristwatch. On the bench, Stanley Roberts rested the side of his round head in the hollow of his hand and methodically tapped the end of a ballpoint pen against a legal pad: two quick beats, followed by a slight pause, and then two more, over and over again, like the sound of a human heart filling up the silence of a lonely life. Below him, the court reporter, hunched over her machine, reached down to rub her ankle while she stifled a yawn.

The tapping stopped. Richard Lee Jones, both hands shoved down into his pants pockets, looked up, a raised eyebrow the only expression on his otherwise blank face.

"I don't imagine you thought it necessary to impress upon your client the importance of punctuality?" Roberts asked, irritation written all over his small mouth.

"I'm sure he'll be here, your honor," Jones replied, evading a direct answer.

Ominously, the two-beat tapping began again. A moment later, the judge glanced down at his watch.

"We were scheduled to start at nine-thirty, Mr. Jones. It's now nine-forty. How much longer do you suggest we wait?"

Any answer he gave would be wrong. In a gesture of uncertainty, Jones shook his head and lowered his eyes.

"In that case, I think we have all waited long enough," Jones announced.

Just as he started to get up, the door at the back of the courtroom swung open. It was as if Goodwin had been waiting outside, determined to push things every bit as far as he could. Dressed in a dark blue suit and a red-and-gold striped tie, he strode up the aisle.

"Sorry I'm late, your honor," he said breezily, as he stood next to his attorney. "Traffic," he explained with a brash smile.

Biting the inside of his lip, Roberts studied him. "How many times have you appeared in my court?"

The averted eye, the downcast look, the hopeless aspect of the prisoner who stood, wretched and trembling, in the drab uniformity of oversize clothes, had vanished entirely. Dressed like a lawyer, he acted like the one we all remembered. With a jaunty grin, he replied, "Only once as an inmate, your honor!"

The anger in the judge's eyes abated. Whatever he might say, he was not going to do anything. Goodwin had won.

"You know better than to be late," he said, while Goodwin nodded dutifully. "If it happens again, you might find yourself back in the county jail. And I'm sure you've had enough of that," he added.

Chin up, Goodwin agreed. "I certainly have, your honor."

"All right, then," Roberts remarked, mollified. "Let's get to the business at hand. Mr. Antonelli?"

"Your honor, we are here once again in the case of State *versus* Marshall Goodwin. The grand jury has

now returned an indictment charging Mr. Goodwin
with the murder of Nancy Goodwin."

Laconically, Jones extended his hand and announced
that the defense would waive a formal reading of the indictment. I handed him the copy, and he put it face
down on the table without looking at it.

"The defense enters a plea of not guilty, your honor,
and requests that the case be set for jury trial."

Roberts made the requisite notations in the court file.
Out of the corner of my eye, I saw Goodwin exchange
a wink with the court clerk, a cheerful, kindhearted
woman who had worked at the courthouse longer than
most of the judges.

Clearing his throat, Roberts put the file to the side
and, leaning forward, folded his hands together. He had
written something on a piece of paper.

"It is a very serious matter when anyone is accused
of a crime," he began to read, "especially one as serious
as this. The defendant in this or any other case has the
right—the absolute right, I might add—to a fair trial
and to the presumption of innocence. The public, on the
other hand, also has a right—the right to the impartial
administration of justice. We have an obligation to
avoid even the appearance of partiality. The defendant
in this case holds a position of great public trust and in
that position has worked on a daily basis with every
judge in this county. For that reason, we have all agreed
that someone from outside the county, someone from
outside the judicial district, should preside from this
point forward with all proceedings relating to this case,
including, of course, the trial itself."

With the court file under his arm, Roberts got to his
feet. "As soon as a judge has been chosen, counsel will
be informed."

He started to turn away, then stopped. Looking directly at Goodwin, he said, "I trust it will not be inappropriate for me to say that I hope everything will come out the way it should."

It would be difficult to invent a more neutral statement of goodwill.

As slowly as I could, I gathered up the documents I had brought with me and methodically placed them in the proper order inside the case file. When I was finished, I sat down and jotted some meaningless notes on a blank legal pad. I was killing time, waiting until Goodwin and his lawyer had left. As far as possible, I wanted to avoid the press, but I also wanted to see how Richard Lee Jones was going to try his case to the public.

For more than a decade, Jones had given shameless self-promotion a bad name. How much of what he said he really believed, and how much of it was a conscious attempt to attract attention, was a question that perhaps not even he could have answered. Like every young lawyer who has to start out on his own, Jones had taken every case he could get. It was his own unique achievement, from the first, to lose nearly every case he had. Juries hated him. He called witnesses for the prosecution liars and prosecutors negligent incompetents; he routinely accused the police of either losing evidence that would have helped the defense or manufacturing evidence that helped the state. Before he had tried a half-dozen cases, he was already famous for closing arguments that seemed to take longer than the trial itself.

His record of consecutive losses might have continued to accumulate, had it not been for a remark by the district's only circuit court judge. One Monday afternoon, as the court was about to begin work on the criminal docket, the judge looked out over the courtroom.

"Those of you who are here today to be arraigned on criminal charges are entitled to be represented by an attorney. If you can't afford an attorney, the court will appoint one. We have several fine attorneys in private practice who have made themselves available for that purpose. When your name is called, you'll come up here"—he nodded toward the long wooden table inside the bar—"and Mr. Davies, the district attorney, will recite the charges that have been brought against you. If you want to enter a plea of not guilty, if you want to go to trial, I'll appoint someone to represent you.

"But if you decide you would like to plead guilty and get it over with, you still have a right to have a lawyer help you get the best deal possible. In that case, I'll appoint Mr. Jones over there," he said, tossing his head toward the side of the courtroom where young Richard Lee was sitting alone. "Mr. Jones, I can assure you, is about as good at making sure that the guilty get what they deserve as anyone I've ever seen."

It was a story that Jones told on himself. Whether it was true or just part of the legend he had tried to create about himself, no one could deny that, from then on, Richard Lee Jones began to treat everyone with at least a formal show of respect. His string of losses stopped, and he began to win. But underneath it all, he never stopped believing that he could take any side and win any argument, and that if he lost it was only because someone had cheated.

Everyone who had tried a case against him was willing to concede he was a very good trial attorney; Jones himself insisted he was the best there was. Everyone else was a pretender, a charlatan, a fool. In almost every trial followed by the national media, Richard Lee Jones would appear on camera and, with the solemn regret of a parent who has to reprove a recalcitrant child, offer his opinion that the lawyers in the case had failed to do their job.

Closing the courtroom door quietly behind me, I moved as unobtrusively as I could along the outer edge of the crowd that swarmed around Jones and his client and his client's wife. Caught in the hot glare of the television lights, their three faces reflected all the self-confidence of instant celebrity. They were the center of attention, and they knew it.

As he listened to a reporter's question, Jones readied himself. "You ask me what kind of case the state has against my client? I'll tell you in a word: none. There is no case," he continued, rolling his head from side to side, as if he still could not understand how anyone could have done something so shameful as charge his client with murder. "A man confesses to the murder of Marshall Goodwin's wife, Nancy Goodwin. Does he make this confession because he can't live with himself anymore? Because of the guilt he feels for doing such a terrible thing? No. He confesses only after he's killed a few more people and he's trying to find a way to stay out of the gas chamber."

Another reporter yelled out, "But he says Goodwin paid him to do it!"

"He says a lot of things," Jones replied, with a dismissive wave of his hand. "If you were facing the death penalty, you'd probably get pretty inventive yourself. He's a confessed murderer, and there isn't any evidence of any sort to back up anything he said."

The same reporter shot back, "If there isn't any evidence, how come your client has been indicted?"

A knowing look creased Jones's closed mouth. "It's curious, isn't it," he said, with an expression that hinted darkly at something. "I mean, it's curious that with nothing else than the self-serving statement of a killer, they would think to bring a case against anyone, much less someone as respected as the chief deputy district attorney of the largest county in the state."

Tilting his head, his eyes darted from one television camera to the next.

"Now, I don't know why they did it. But isn't it a little strange that instead of turning this over to the present district attorney, the police went to a sitting circuit-court judge who just happens to be the former district attorney? I wouldn't want to suggest that there might be something political going on here, but it does seem a little odd, doesn't it?"

"Are you saying that Judge Woolner is trying to get Gilliland-O'Rourke by charging her chief deputy with murder?" an anonymous voice shouted from somewhere deep within the densely packed throng of reporters.

Jones denied any improper intention. "I can only recite the facts. I'll leave it to you to figure out what they mean."

While Jones answered questions, I kept my eye on Kristin, watching the way she reacted to each thing that was said. She was the perfect audience, quick, responsive, sharing the mood of those around her before they knew themselves exactly how they felt. Holding her husband's hand, she gazed out over the crowd, laughing with everyone else at something Jones had just said. Then she saw me, and in a brief moment of uncertainty her laughter stopped.

"If that's true," someone asked, directing the question to Goodwin, "why did the district attorney issue the order for your arrest?"

Taking a half step forward, Marshall answered, "She was just doing her job. As soon as I learned I was going to be charged, I told her." He lowered his eyes, and then, wearing an even more serious expression, looked up and insisted it had been his idea. "I told the district attorney that the only way to preserve our reputation as a completely impartial office was to have me arrested herself. The last thing I wanted," he said, looking straight into the camera, "the last thing either of us wanted, was to have anyone think we play favorites among the people the law requires us to prosecute."

He made it sound as if he had arrested himself.

I had started to head down the corridor toward the door when someone whispered my name, and a hand grasped my arm.

"Well, Antonelli, did you ever think you'd have a chance to try a case against the greatest lawyer the world has ever known?"

With a round, smooth face, piercing black eyes, and a waistline that wobbled when he walked, Harper Bryce looked like a snowman beginning to melt. Folding up his reporter's notebook, he tucked it into the pocket of his sports jacket and put his pencil above his ear.

"Haven't seen you in a while," he said, when I did not answer.

We reached the door and stepped outside.

"I haven't been around for a while."

"Why did you come back?"

I was careful. "It was time."

He nodded as if the words meant something.

"You want to tell me what's really going on with this thing? You don't want me to just write what that egomaniac just said, do you?" His voice was deep and fluid and came at you in short, abbreviated bursts, as if he threw out a few words at a time and then waited to see how they worked before he tried again.

"Aren't all lawyers egomaniacs?" I asked. It was something he had once written.

"That's right." He snorted. "Some more, some less."

"Richard Lee Jones?"

He laughed. "The common measure does not apply."

I could not resist. I stopped and looked at him. "Me?"

Tugging on his tie, breathing heavily, he seemed to think about it. With a shrewd smile, he studied me for a moment and then shook his head.

"I never could figure you out. Sometimes I thought you had more ego than Emperor Jones himself. Other times you seemed so lost in what you were doing, I wondered if you had any ego at all. There are people, you know," he went on, as we strolled along the sidewalk, "who get so wrapped up in what they do, they lose themselves in it, forget themselves completely. Wish I was a little like that," he added wistfully.

But Harper Bryce *was* like that; he was forever losing himself in whatever story he was trying to tell. He had been covering the courthouse for longer than I could remember and had watched more trials than any lawyer I knew. A frequent visitor to the half-empty courtrooms where most litigation takes place, Bryce was fascinated by the way ordinary people, confronted with the loss of either their money or their liberty, could eschew the truth so completely. It was a fault from which he himself was not entirely free. Whenever he reported on one of my cases, the facts were often wrong, the testimony of witnesses was often embellished, and yet, when you looked at it as a whole, the impression it conveyed was usually right. Perhaps there was more of the artist in him than he cared to admit.

We continued walking and did not say anything more until we got to the next corner and waited for the light to change.

"What did you think of that performance back there?" he asked.

The light turned green. "I'm not going to comment on anything," I said, as we stepped off the curb together. "Not on the record, anyway."

"Agreed," he said, with a chuckle. "Everything off the record."

He was starting to have trouble keeping up. Pulling on my sleeve, he stopped.

"If you don't mind my asking, where are we going?"

"I'm going to my office," I replied. "You want to come along?"

"How far is it?"

"Just another block."

He seemed relieved. "You have a few minutes to talk?"

"You mean, off the record?"

"Is there any other way?"

When we walked in, Helen was standing barefoot on a chair, hanging a framed picture on the wall next to her desk. It was something by Monet, a laser reproduction that supposedly duplicated perfectly each brush stroke on the original. Embarrassed, she hopped down and put on her shoes. I introduced her to Bryce, and her mind filed him in the proper category.

"Harper Bryce, reporter and columnist," she said, as her fingers disappeared into his plush, uncallused hand.

Bryce had a certain courtly charm, and in the presence of women you almost expected him to pronounce his carefully chosen words with the slow grace of a Southerner. As it was, Helen forgot her usual cheerful cynicism and began to buzz around, trying to be helpful. She brought us two fresh cups of coffee and shut the door to my office.

I tried to explain her eagerness. "You're one of the few people she's ever seen me with who isn't accused of a crime."

"I suppose that means I'll have to wait another week before I murder my editor," he said, and sipped his coffee.

We talked for more than an hour, and when I read the paper the next morning I had what I needed. The story of Marshall Goodwin's arraignment on a charge of arranging the murder of his wife was treated almost as a preface to the revelation that, "according to sources close to the investigation," the chief deputy district attorney had not acted alone. "A second person, whose identity has not yet been disclosed, faces almost certain indictment as a co-conspirator with Marshall Goodwin in the murder-for-hire scheme. Joseph Antonelli, appointed as special prosecutor in the case, would neither confirm nor deny these reports."

After reading what Bryce had written, I was not entirely surprised to receive a call telling me that Gwendolyn Gilliland-O'Rourke wanted to see me. When I arrived, the receptionist ushered me right in.

I had not been in the DA's office since Horace Woolner had resigned to become a circuit court judge. The room had a completely different look about it. With his obsessive fear of disorder, Horace had made certain nothing was ever out of place; the jacket Gilliland-

O'Rourke had left draped over the arm of the sofa would never have been found anywhere except on the hook behind the door or the coat rack in the corner. Horace worked on one file at a time and kept all the others stacked neatly at the front of his desk; documents were littered all over Gilliland-O'Rourke's varnished antique writing table, some of them spotted with petals that had fallen from a vase filled with cut flowers.

The most striking change, however, was the difference in what they wanted to remember. Horace had kept a picture of his wife on his desk; among the gallery of photographs that now covered the walls I could not find a single one of Arthur O'Rourke. They were all of Gwendolyn next to someone else, a governor, a senator, a member of the state legislature, the last defeated candidate for county clerk, anyone who had ever held an office or thought about running for one.

Standing next to the writing table, she gave me her hand and then, gesturing toward the brocaded chair on the other side, took it away.

"Congratulations," she remarked as she sat down. "You've managed to go from defending the guilty to prosecuting the innocent. Not many lawyers can make that claim."

Except for the ballet dinner, where I had watched her move from table to table, intent on greeting everyone in the room, I had not seen her in person since the day the jury brought back its verdict in the case of Leopold Rifkin. She watched me as I sat back against the chair, her eyes, usually inviting and often flirtatious, filled with ice-cold anger. Picking up the newspaper that had been lying, folded in half, on the corner of the table, she tossed it toward me.

"What do you think you're doing?" she demanded to know. "You're going to indict someone besides Marshall?"

Ignoring her, I let my eye wander around the room until it came to rest on one of the photographs grouped together on the wall immediately to my right. Only a few years out of law school, Gwendolyn was wearing a black judicial robe, her right hand raised, taking the oath of office as the youngest district court judge in the state. She looked as if she could hardly wait to get started.

I looked back at her.

"It was a long time ago," she said curtly. "You haven't answered my question. Are you planning to indict someone else?"

"So because it was a long time ago, you'd prefer we both pretend nothing ever happened between us?"

Her green eyes flashed. "I'm the DA. Horace Woolner had no business doing what he did, and you have no business trying to keep me in the dark. You might regret it."

Raising my chin, I stared back at her. "You care to explain that?"

"I don't think I need to. We both know what you did in the Rifkin trial."

"I got an acquittal for a man we both know was innocent."

"You got a small-time thief to claim he witnessed a murder he never saw," she replied, with a show of defiance.

"If you thought you could prove that, you would have," I retorted.

"I'm sorry," she said, her voice less strident, if still far from friendly. "I shouldn't have said that."

"You should never have prosecuted him," I said, my own voice less hostile. "He wasn't guilty. You had to have known that."

She looked away, a slight twitch at the side of her mouth. Then, a moment later, her eyes came back around.

"Do you really think that you have more evidence against Marshall Goodwin than I had against Leopold Rifkin?"

"I knew Leopold wasn't guilty. Are you convinced Goodwin is innocent?"

"Are you convinced he's guilty?" When I did not answer, she went on. "Marshall has a clear track to become district attorney. Why would he take a chance like that, risk everything?"

She had spent her life calculating her own advantage, and she assumed everyone else did the same thing. Everything, even murder, was a matter of measuring the benefits against the costs.

"I notice you didn't say he must be innocent because he'd never do such a thing."

"Either way," she said with a shrug.

I put one hand on the arm of the chair and bent toward her.

"Either way—if you don't think he did it—why did you have him arrested?"

Her explanation parroted part of Goodwin's. "This office can't afford to have people think we treat anyone differently from anyone else."

Glancing away, she added, as something strictly between ourselves, "It's bad enough that it looks like the chief deputy was a murderer and we didn't know it."

Drawing herself up, she took a deep breath, as if bracing herself for more bad news.

"Now tell me, who else do you think was involved?"

There was no reason to tell her, and there would have been a certain pleasure in refusing her something she wanted to have. She was looking at me, waiting, her lips pressed together, intent on giving away nothing of how she felt.

"We're looking into the possibility that Kristin Maxfield may have been involved."

"I see," she said, as she rose from her chair and walked me to the door. "I suppose we'll just deal with that when the time comes."

The door closed behind me. Gilliland-O'Rourke did not know any more than I did whether Marshall Goodwin was guilty, or whether, if he was, Kristin Maxfield had been involved. And I had the odd feeling that she did not really care.

THERE WAS ONE MORE WAY TO TIGHTEN THE SCREW. I
told the detectives who were in charge of the investigation to bring Kristin Maxfield in for questioning. She
was not amused.

"Would you like to have an attorney present?" she
was asked.

"I am an attorney," she reminded them.

She was sitting on one side of a small rectangular
table in a room used for interrogations. Facing her on
the other side were the two detectives, one of them,
Rudy McLaughlin, just a few years away from retire-
ment, his partner, Mark Haskell, a good ten years
younger. I stood behind a one-way glass and watched
while they took her through a series of questions designed to suggest we knew more than we did.

McLaughlin took the lead. "You testified in front of
the grand jury that you didn't deliver anything to Travis
Quentin the day he was released from the county jail."

She listened to the question without apparent interest, gazing down at her hands folded in her lap. When
he finished, she looked up, her eyes glancing off his before they came to rest on her own reflection in the glass.

"Yes," she said finally, turning her attention on the
detective.

Haskell, the younger detective, jumped in. "Travis Quentin says you did."

"I wouldn't know Travis Quentin if he walked in this room." Her eyes drifted back to the glass.

It was McLaughlin's turn. "We know you were both in on it together. The only thing we don't know is why."

"Why?" she asked, lifting her soft dark eyelashes. "That's a good question. Why would I do a thing like that?"

Unfazed, McLaughlin went on. "We know your husband did it because of money, what he would have lost in a divorce. But we don't know why you helped him."

Before she could respond, Haskell added, "Maybe you didn't know you were helping him. Maybe you just thought you were taking Quentin some legal papers, something like that. Maybe you thought it had something to do with Quentin being a witness in that drug bust."

She denied everything, and she never once lost her composure.

Finally, she asked, "Am I under arrest? Because if I'm not, I think I've answered all the questions I care to."

"No, you're not under arrest," McLaughlin told her. "Tell me," he went on, when she got up to go, "do you really believe your husband is innocent, that he didn't have anything to do with the murder of his wife?"

She stood in front of the see-through mirror, checking her makeup.

"Any questions you have about my husband you had better take up with his lawyer."

I went back to my office and waited for her to call.

"DID YOU ENJOY THE LITTLE SHOW THIS AFTERNOON?" Kristin Maxfield asked.

Settling easily into the chair in front of my desk, she fixed her eyes on mine as she crossed her legs. She had on the same clothes she had worn during the interview, but her blouse was no longer buttoned all the way up and her jacket was open at the front.

I did not answer her question.

"Perhaps you could tell me why I was dragged in there like that?"

"I was under the impression you came in voluntarily."

"Let's not split hairs. I was told the police wanted to ask me a few questions. Did you think I was going to refuse to come in? Why don't you just tell me exactly what it is you're after." Pausing, she moistened her lips with her tongue. "Then maybe I can help you. Then maybe you'll realize you're going in the wrong direction with all of this."

"The wrong direction? I don't think I'm going in the wrong direction. I think your husband hired Travis Quentin to kill his wife." I waited for an instant and then added, "And I think you helped him do it."

Her eyes never left me, her expression never changed. Coolly analytical, she asked, "Knowingly?"

It was a question only a prosecutor or a criminal defense lawyer would think to ask. Anyone else would have just denied they had done anything wrong; she wanted to draw a distinction between things that were punishable and things that were not.

Folding my arms, I slouched back into the corner of my chair.

"Does your husband know you're here?"

Opening her purse, she searched through it. "Do you mind if I smoke?" she asked, as she opened a gold cigarette case.

I looked around for something to use as an ashtray. A metal tin half filled with paper clips was the best I could do. Emptying it into the center drawer, I reached across and put it on the desk directly in front of her. She lit the cigarette, took one drag, and flicked the ash into the tin.

"No, Marshall doesn't know I'm here." She picked up the cigarette, took one more drag, and snuffed it out. "And he won't, either," she added, looking at me with her large, candid eyes.

Lacing my fingers together behind my head, I rocked slowly back and forth in the tall leather swivel chair. "What is it you want to tell me?"

"What is it you want to know?"

I shook my head. "I already know."

"No, you don't," she said, shaking hers. "You may think you do, but you don't, not really."

I stopped rocking and sat still. "I know you delivered an envelope to Travis Quentin the day he was released."

"Let's just suppose—for the sake of argument—that I did. It could have been completely innocent."

I brought my hands down and gently grasped the arms of the chair. "Was it?"

"Again—just assuming it happened, and assuming it was an innocent act—it would still be a crucial part of your case, wouldn't it? As a matter of fact, it's only if it *was* an innocent act that it could be a crucial part of your case. Isn't that true?"

As we looked at each other in the dying light of the late afternoon, I knew what she was doing and why she was there. My elbow on the arm of the chair, I stroked the side of my chin while I picked up the thread of the conversation.

"Because if it was not an innocent act you would be

a co-conspirator, and no one can be convicted on the uncorroborated testimony of another co-conspirator."

"Assuming—for the sake of argument—that it really happened," she said.

Her voice seemed to come from somewhere far away. Then a slight movement of her head signaled a different mood.

"Do you remember when we first met?" she asked, a subtle teasing sparkle in her eye.

"It was right after you started, wasn't it? You were handling misdemeanor cases in district court."

She was laughing at me with her eyes, dismissing my feeble effort to disguise what I felt by a bare recitation of the ordinary circumstances that had brought us together.

"I wondered why you never asked me out." Her eyes flashed and then dimmed and then flashed again. "I would have said yes." She waited a moment, allowing me to wonder what I had missed, before she added, "Or is that the reason you didn't ask?"

"I thought you were a little young for me," I lied.

It was as if she had known what I was going to say before I said it. Her smile did not change, not by so much as a fraction of an inch, but there was now a touch of cynicism about it, the silent mockery of my ill-disguised duplicity.

"I was older than Alexandra."

"What do you know about Alexandra?"

"Only what they say."

"And what do they say?" I asked quietly, determined not to look away.

"That you were in love with her, and that she left you."

There was neither a trace of sympathy nor a hint of

understanding in her voice. She was describing something that could never have happened to her.

"And what about you? You were engaged to one man but you broke it off to marry another. He must have been in love with you, and you left him."

For the first time, she laughed out loud. "Oh, I don't think he was really in love with me, not the way I think you were in love with her. No," she went on, her laughter fading away, "I don't think anyone has ever been in love with me the way you were in love with Alexandra. No one I ever left moved into a monastery."

"Please. I just decided it was time to do something else. I stopped practicing law and spent a year reading the kind of things I'd never really had time for. It isn't that extraordinary, you know. A lot of people, when they get to a certain age, take a sabbatical, try to look at things from a different angle."

I caught myself. It had been a long time since I had been in the presence of a woman who looked at me as if the only thing she wanted was to listen to whatever I would tell her about myself.

"I took a year off. And now I'm back."

"As a prosecutor."

"Yes, exactly," I said abruptly. I sat straight up in the chair. "Which is of course the reason you came to see me." In the silence of the room the echo of my voice came back to me, taunting me with the pretentious sound of my awkward formality.

"Yes, of course," she agreed, a cryptic smile on her mouth.

She lowered her eyes. When she looked up again, the smile was still there, but fainter than before.

"Do you know what first attracted me to Marshall?

His ambition. I don't mean his desire to succeed. I mean how remarkably self-absorbed, how utterly selfish he was."

"He masks it rather well," I remarked, watching the way she moved her head just a little from one side to the other each time she paused for breath.

"Marshall acts like he's everyone's best friend. But he only does that because he wants to be admired," she said. "And he wants to be admired," she added with a mocking glance, "because he thinks he's the most admirable person he's ever known. I can assure you, Joseph Antonelli, that Marshall is his own favorite subject. He seldom talks about anything else."

She saw I was not entirely convinced.

"The first time I ever had dinner with him—we barely knew each other—he told me he was going to be governor. I think he said that before we even ordered. And he said it as if he was certain I would consider it just about the least surprising thing I'd ever heard."

"Did Gilliland-O'Rourke know her chief deputy wanted the same thing she did?"

"He wouldn't have cared. That's what I found so attractive about him. He didn't care about anyone except himself. Everyone else was simply someone to use."

I was watching her, trying to understand what she wanted.

"Does that surprise you, Antonelli? That I liked that about him? That he went after what he wanted and didn't give a second thought to who it might hurt?"

She looked at me, waiting for me to answer, daring me to follow her to a place where convention had no meaning and the rules were whatever you wanted them to be.

"I thought you were like that," she said, softening her glance. "When we first met. I still think you're like that."

Picking up my fountain pen from the desk, I held it at both ends and began to roll it back and forth in my fingers. "You think I'm like your husband?"

A flash of disapproval shot through her eyes. "That isn't what I said."

I watched the barrel of the pen spin first one way and then the other.

"I heard what you said. Maybe you're right about me, or rather maybe you *were* right about what I was like then. Maybe you're still right," I said, with a shrug. "But it doesn't really make much difference, does it?"

"It might," she said cryptically. "It sort of depends on what you want, doesn't it?"

I put down the pen and looked at her. "No, it really depends on what *you* want. Now, why don't you tell me what that is? What do you want, Kristin?"

"I don't want to be indicted for something I had nothing to do with," she said emphatically.

Leaning back, my elbows on the arms of the chair, I spread my fingers apart and pressed the tips of both index fingers against my mouth.

"Okay," I said finally, "it's a deal."

"A deal?"

"Yes. You tell me everything you know, and everything you did, and you won't be indicted. And you can start by telling me you delivered that envelope to Travis Quentin."

"All right. I did that. Marshall told me Quentin had agreed to testify in a drug case. The envelope was supposed to contain a copy of some of the police reports, the ones that covered people Quentin knew something about."

"Why did he ask you to do it, instead of the police department?"

"He said the fewer people who knew Quentin might be a state's witness the better. You have to remember, I was basically Marshall's assistant. If someone had to go get a police report, or interview a witness, or look up a citation, I was it. There wasn't anything unusual in what he asked me to do."

"If that's all there was to it, why did you lie to the grand jury?"

Reaching into her purse, she removed the cigarette case. Pensively, she took out a cigarette and tapped it against the cover after she snapped it shut. As she lit it, she slipped the case back into her purse.

"I had to protect my husband," she said, following with her eyes the ribbon of smoke that curled up from the cigarette. She took one long drag and then, with a twisting action of her hand, crushed it out.

"There wasn't anything going on between the two of you then?"

She looked up from the crumpled cigarette, lying next to the other one like two broken bodies.

"No," she said firmly. "He wanted there to be, but I was engaged to someone else."

She lied to protect her husband, and she would not sleep with one man while she was involved with another. For a moment we just sat there, sharing the solitude of two people who understood the truth hovering behind her lie.

"When did it start? You and Marshall?"

"That night," she said, watching me with a strange intensity. "The night his wife was away. The night she was murdered."

She had lied twice to the grand jury.

I got up and walked past her to the window. In the street below, strangers crowded together in the aimless order of circumstance, hurrying home. I could sense her turning around in her chair, watching me from across the room. My eye still on the passing scene, I said quietly, "When you were engaged to someone else."

Unhurried, her words drifted across, filling up the space between us. "Yes, but by then I knew it was over between us. What happened with Marshall had nothing to do with it."

She had been trained to make distinctions and to use them to her advantage.

"And the reason you lied to the grand jury about that?"

When she did not answer, I looked back over my shoulder. She was sitting sideways on the front edge of the chair, one leg crossed over the other, the hem of her skirt halfway up her thigh.

"I didn't lie," she said simply. "I didn't spend the night with him."

"But you said you spent the night with . . ." I knew the answer before I reached the end of the question. "I see. You were with Marshall, and then you spent the night with your fiancé."

I turned away and watched the thinning crowd below.

"Where?" I asked after a while.

"Does it matter?" She laughed quietly.

"It might."

"In the parking structure. In the back seat of his car."

The lights were getting dim, and the dwindling crowd cast shadows in the street.

"So while Travis Quentin was raping his wife, Marshall Goodwin was with you, in the back seat of his car." I turned around and faced her directly. "Tell me, do you think the timing was accidental?"

Her eyes never left me. "How would I know that?"

"One way is if you were certain your husband had nothing to do with her murder. Because if he didn't, he wouldn't have had any idea what was happening to her in a motel room a hundred miles away while he was so engaged with you, would he?"

Moving away from the window, I stood right next to her.

"Don't you believe in your husband's innocence?"

Her head was tilted back as she looked up at me. "He says he didn't do it," she replied evenly.

"Do you believe him?"

"I'm his wife," she said, without emotion.

"So was Nancy Goodwin," I said. I went back to my chair and glanced at the clock on the corner of the desk. "It's getting late. You probably have to go."

"No," she said, shaking her head, "I don't. I can stay as long as you want. We could have dinner, if you like."

"That's probably not a great idea," I replied. "There's just a few more things I'd like to know. Why that night? Nothing had gone on between you before. What happened? Or had you been falling in love with him for a long time?"

"Love? I told you I was attracted to him. I liked the way he took what he wanted. That night he told me he wanted me."

"Did it bother you that he was married?"

She almost laughed. "Was it supposed to?"

Beautiful and cold, sensual and elusive. For much of my life I had found women like this fascinating and irresistible.

"How did you feel? When you found out that you had been making love with him while his wife was being murdered?"

"I never really thought about it," she replied, in a voice that betrayed a certain impatience. "I really don't see what any of this has to do with anything. I've admitted I slept with him."

"Yes, while you were still engaged. What was his name again—your fiancé?"

"Conrad Atkinson."

"Were you in love with him?"

"Conrad was charming. Very good-looking," she added. "And very intelligent."

"You didn't answer my question," I reminded her, following the movement of the fountain pen I had begun to push back and forth again. "Did you love him?"

It was nearly dark outside, and the lamplight seemed to draw everything together until the only things visible were the desk, the chair, and the blue Persian rug.

Her voice was smooth. "Whether I was in love with Conrad Atkinson—or, for that matter, anyone else—is quite frankly none of your business."

I brought the fountain pen to a stop and looked up. Everything about her was of a piece: the defiant independence, the belligerent smile, the taunting self-certainty about what she would do and what she would not.

Pushing away from the desk, I stared hard at her. "None of my business? You lied to the grand jury. You were under oath and you lied. Now you come here and tell me that you don't want to be indicted for something you didn't do. And then you tell me, when I ask you whether you were in love with the man you were engaged to marry, that it's quite frankly none of my business."

"It doesn't have anything to do with what you need to know," she insisted.

"I'll decide what I need to know! I already know what happened. I want to know why. I want to know why Nancy Goodwin was killed! I want to know why your husband had her killed!"

"I don't know anything beyond what I've told you," she replied calmly. "I delivered an envelope to Travis Quentin when he was released from jail, but I didn't know what was in it. I became physically involved with Marshall the night his wife was killed, but I didn't know she was dead until I heard about it the next day, when they brought the news to him while we were in court."

She knew more than that. I shot out of the chair. "And when was the next time?"

"The next time?"

"Yes. The next time you were together. How long after she was dead?"

She did not have an answer she wanted to give. Her mouth opened and closed. She looked at me, without expression, waiting for me to ask her something else.

I was leaning forward as far as I could go, resting my weight on my hands. "Was it the next night? The night after that?"

Whatever debate had been going on within her, she spoke as if there were nothing out of the ordinary about what had happened.

"He told me he didn't want to be alone."

I waited for the rest, but that was all she said.

"When did he tell you that?"

Her eyes were fixed on mine. "The day of the funeral. The day they buried his wife. That night."

My head dropped between my shoulders and I stared down at the dark blank surface of the desk, feeling sorrier for Nancy Goodwin than I may ever have felt for anyone in my life. A wave of fatigue rolled over me, and I sank down into the chair, pressing the bridge of my nose.

"I thought he was lonely," I heard her say.

It seemed strange. The thought that Marshall Goodwin had been having sex with another woman while someone he had hired was killing his wife had not bothered me nearly so much as the knowledge that he did it all over again the day she was buried. Was it because what he had done in the back seat of his car had become a part of the overall brutality of the murder, while the second time seemed like a gratuitous obscenity? There was a difference between murder and desecration.

"You thought he was lonely," I said, opening my eyes. "Do you think a jury will think that? Or do you think they'll decide that anyone so indifferent to his own wife's death is likely to have had some involvement in her murder?"

SHE FLOATED FROM ONE GUEST TO ANOTHER, WEAVING her way across the crowded living room, her eyes settling for a moment on each person with whom she stopped to exchange a word, a laugh, a smile. Finally, Alma was standing in front of me. She said something I could not hear. Laughing, she repeated it, but her words were lost in the noise around us. She rose up on her toes, slipped her thin arm around my neck, and kissed the side of my face.

"In the kitchen!" she shouted into my ear.

Her hand fell away, coming to rest on my shoulder, as she searched my eyes to see if I understood. As I nodded helplessly, she stepped back, her fingers sweeping along my coat sleeve until they reached my hand. She squeezed it and then, letting go, moved back into the crowd.

On the other side of the dining room, empty of furniture except for the table, moved up against the wall, a woman carrying a tray stacked with platters of steaming food shouldered her way through a swinging door. She put everything down, arranging each dish, and went back for more.

Horace was standing over the stove, an enormous gas range with a stainless steel hood that towered up to

117

the ceiling. Groaning, he scraped another load of chicken wings from the grill and, with a cautionary look, handed the hot pan to the woman I had seen earlier.

As soon as he saw me, he set down his metal tongs and shook my hand. The perspiration that streaked his face had run down his neck and soaked his shirt collar. Laughing, he gathered up the ends of the white chef's apron he was wearing and used it to wipe his eyes.

"I didn't know you could cook, Horace," I said, as he reached for a half-full bottle of beer on the counter next to the range.

His eyes stayed on me while he drank. With a loud sigh, he put down the empty bottle.

"Cook, sew, I have all the domestic virtues," he remarked with a wry grin. He nodded toward the dishwasher, which was already humming with its first load. "I learned a long time ago to stay ahead of the game," he explained.

The kitchen door flew open and the maid was suddenly standing before us, clutching the empty tray.

"That should just about do it, Gloria," Horace said. "Just this last batch," he added, swinging his eyes around to the chicken still roasting on the grill.

"The salads, Mr. Woolner," she reminded him.

Horace rolled his eyes and shook his head. "I'd forget my legs if they weren't strapped on."

Without a word, she followed him to the double-door stainless steel refrigerator and held up her tray. He put two large ceramic bowls on it and hesitated with a third bowl in his hand.

"I can take it," she assured him.

Dropping his chin, he raised an eyebrow.

"Really." She laughed, struggling to keep the two bowls balanced on the tray.

Horace looked over her head and caught my eye. I put my drink down on the counter. Horace pulled the bowl he was holding away from her.

"Mr. Antonelli here is a librarian and he could use the exercise," he explained, as he placed his hand gently on her shoulder and turned her toward the door.

She went on her way. Horace handed me two bowls from the refrigerator and took the last two himself.

We were an incongruous parade, a short white maid, followed by a fairly tall white man in a dark suit, both of us dwarfed by a black man the size of a tree. The crowd seemed to be larger and more tightly packed together, everyone talking at the same time. We could have walked in naked and no one would have noticed.

As soon as I found room on the table, Horace's hand grabbed my shirt and pulled me away. I followed him back into the kitchen.

"What'd I tell you?" he asked, as he took off the apron and, crumpling it up, tossed it without looking inside the pantry. "Alma's idea of a dinner party. Here, look at this!" he exclaimed as he led me over to the kitchen window.

The Woolners' condominium was in a high-rise building at the southern edge of the city, less than six blocks from the courthouse, with a view of downtown Portland and the river that had once marked its boundary and now divided it in half.

"What do you see down there? You see any people? Of course you don't. Every last son-of-a-bitch in the goddamn city is here tonight. Open house at the Woolners'. Three homeless guys showed up about an hour ago. Threw their ass right out. You gotta draw the line somewhere."

He reached inside the refrigerator, got another bottle of beer, and opened it. He took a long swig, and then he started to relax.

"It's a hell of a party, don't you think?" he asked eagerly. "Alma loves this kind of thing," he added, his voice sinking into a husky whisper.

Slowly, he settled down. His breathing became quieter, more measured. Behind me, through the closed kitchen door, the din raged on.

"Let's get out of here," Horace suggested. "I could use some air. You can tell me all about your new life as a prosecutor."

We took an elevator down to the lobby. The doorman jumped to his feet and held open the glass front door. Horace nodded as we passed.

On the side of the building closest to the river, an iron bench faced a small two-tiered fountain that stood on top of a mound of earth covered with flowers. We sat down and watched the broad river below, running north under the steel bridges until it merged with the Columbia and ran with it to the sea. The outline of Mount Hood shimmered in the silver light of the moon. The only sound was a distant hum from the freeway running along the other side of the river.

My gaze ran from the river to the mountain and back again. I remembered the night I took Alexandra to Leopold Rifkin's home, the night we ended up on the walkway next to the river, not far from where I was now. It was the night I knew I was in love with her, the night I told her I wanted to marry her.

"You want to know who your judge is going to be?"

It took me a moment to realize Horace had spoken.

"What?" I asked, turning away from the river and all the things it had left behind.

There were times Horace could read my mind.

"You still think about her, don't you?"

"Not as much as I used to," I said, shrugging.

He pretended to believe me. "Somebody else will come along." He stopped himself with a short, rueful laugh. "That's a lie. If something happened to Alma? I don't think somebody else would come along. It couldn't happen. There isn't anybody else for me. Without her . . ." His voice trailed off, and the thought, wrapped up in silence, finished itself.

"You said something about a judge?"

His eyes widened and he began to chuckle. "It's your lucky day, counselor. You get a black judge, Irma Holloway, from down in Eugene. You know how many black people there are in this state?"

"No."

"I'll tell you how many." Furrowing his forehead, he spread open his left hand and began to count on his fingers. "Let's see. There's me, of course. Then there's Irma, and then there's—oh, hell, what's that guy's name?" He looked across at me. "You know, that guy that always shows up on TV as the obligatory 'black spokesman'? Irma must have voted for him, 'cause I know I didn't. Now, who else?"

"What about Alma?"

He pulled back his closed mouth and narrowed his eyes. "Never been too sure. She's only half. Her father was white. Anyway, my point is that with hardly any minority population at all, you have these black judges. You imagine what it would have been like, not here, but someplace like Mississippi or Alabama, an all-white jury sitting there, and the door swings open and a black judge comes walking in? Twelve heart attacks! But not here. Most every jury I have is all white, and no one ever thinks twice about it. At least I don't think they do. You ever try a case in front of her?"

"No, I don't think so."

His eyebrows shot straight up. "You'd remember if you had. You look cross-eyed in her courtroom, she'd just as soon come off the bench and knock you upside the head. Little bitty thing too. Skinny, scrawny, with big bad eyes looking at you like you did something wrong and she's the only one who knows it. I can just see her standing up on her tiptoes, grabbing some jerk-faced kid by the ear, pulling him off somewhere, and just beating the hell out of him. Reminds me of my own mother," he said, laughing. "Just like her."

"Is she good?"

His eyebrows shot up again, and he looked at me, sizing me up. "You'll enjoy it. I'm not so sure about Richard Lee Jones." A grin spread across his face. "He's a real piece of work, isn't he?"

His feet spread to the width of his shoulders, Horace hunched forward, resting his arms on his artificial legs. Reaching down, he picked up a pebble and, flicking his wrist, sent it flashing into the darkness. He reached for another one, raised up, turned his shoulder, and sent this one winging over the top of the fountain. Draping both elbows over the bench behind him, Horace sat back and stared into the night.

"Is it working out?" he asked. "Are you able to work during the day and study in the evening?"

"Let's just say that Aristotle was hard enough when there wasn't anything else I had to think about," I replied, with a rueful laugh.

He turned to me with a grin. "So tell me, what have you learned from Aristotle that's going to help you with this case?"

I thought about it for a moment.

"Nothing from Aristotle, at least not directly, but there is something in Hobbes. You know that famous phrase, life in a state of nature as 'solitary, poor, nasty, brutish, and short'? The only thing anyone really cares about is survival—self-preservation—because if you don't look out for yourself no one else will, not if they have to decide between their life and yours. That's what Goodwin's wife, Kristin Maxfield, reminds me of. She came to see me. She doesn't care about anything except saving herself. She admitted she lied to the grand jury. She did deliver the package to Quentin."

I told Horace everything. When I was finished, he got to his feet and put his hands on the small of his back.

"You're sure about Goodwin now, aren't you?"

"After what she told me, there doesn't seem much room for doubt."

"Did she tell you that Gilliland-O'Rourke put her on administrative leave?"

"No. Gwendolyn doesn't take any chances, does she?"

He stared down at the ground, shoving the gravel with his foot. "Don't think she won't try to get even for all of this. We've embarrassed her. She won't forget it."

He looked up at me, a troubled look in his eyes. "But forget Gwendolyn. There's something wrong here." Drawing his shoulders back, he glanced over my head at the building where, twelve stories above, the party was still going on. "Kristin is still lying. There's something going on, I can feel it. She didn't have to tell you she had sex with him the night of the murder. And she sure as hell didn't have to tell you she had sex with him the night of the funeral." His eyes came back to mine. "Why do you think she did that?"

I read the answer in his eyes, a reminder of what was just below the surface of my thoughts.

"Because sex is intimacy, and by telling me about it she creates something between us, a kind of trust."

"Yeah, and remember something else. You can't betray anyone who doesn't trust you first, can you?"

I stood up, and we began to walk back toward the lobby.

"Have you talked to her former fiancé?"

"Not yet."

"Might be a good idea. He probably has a few interesting things to say about her. I wonder if he knew she was never in love with him."

"She's never been in love with anybody," I remarked, as we approached the awning-covered sidewalk.

Inside, the doorman was standing next to the front desk, twirling a silver key chain, lost in a daydream. Horace slapped the glass door with his open hand, and then roared at the startled expression on the doorman's face.

"There's another line in Hobbes," I said in the elevator, "but I'm not sure if it reminds me more of Kristin or Gilliland-O'Rourke."

Horace looked at me, waiting.

"Life is 'a perpetual and restless desire of power after power, that ceaseth only in death.' "

"Ceaseth," Horace repeated, laughing at the way it sounded.

"You have to understand," I said, as the elevator

door slid open, "in the seventeenth century everyone talked with a lisp."

Horace opened the door to the condominium, and we were hit by a wall of noise. It was louder than when we left, much louder. Music blared from a set of speakers. Something was going on in the middle of the living room, and the crowd had moved back until a space was clear in the center. Her hair flying behind her, Alma was dancing with one of the young men from the ballet troupe. She executed one turn after another on her bare feet, her hand barely touching his, looking for all the world as if she never touched the ground at all.

She came close to him and, with a fleeting, sensual glance, spun away and then, in a single effortless motion, came back to him as he bent low, rolled over his shoulders, and landed where she had begun.

Joining in the applause, Horace watched as Alma pulled back both arms and dropped low into the pose every ballerina strikes when the music finally comes to an end. As the applause died away, a distant look came into his eyes. I had seen it before, on the faces of men watching their daughters graduate from college or giving them away in marriage, the look of someone who knows that most of what they have to look forward to are the memories of things that have already happened. I had seen that look on dozens of fathers; I could not remember ever having seen it on the face of a husband.

Someone turned down the music, and the crowd surged back toward the center. Reaching out, Horace grabbed my arm and held it.

"You can't leave. You have to stay till the end. All right?" he asked, holding my arm fast until I agreed.

I wanted a drink, but the bar had been set up next to the fireplace on the other side of the living room. It was easier to get something out of the refrigerator.

Leaning against the kitchen counter, someone vaguely familiar was smiling into the drink he was holding with both hands, listening politely to the slurred speech of a willowy young woman standing next to him. When he heard the door swing shut, he looked up at me, grateful for the interruption.

"Joseph Antonelli! That's right, isn't it?" he asked affably. He reached out his hand and stepped forward. The young woman, who had been hanging on his shoulder, struggled to catch her balance.

"Russell Gray," he reminded me, as we shook hands. His hands were soft, supple, like kid gloves that have never been worn. "We met at the ballet dinner."

"Of course." I apologized. "We had a little discussion about the difference between lawyers and artists."

"Did we? I don't remember. Well, it doesn't really matter. I'm sure you got the best of it."

We stood there for a moment, neither one of us saying anything.

"Oh, I'm sorry," he said with an embarrassed laugh. "Let me introduce you." He looked at the young woman and waited for her to help.

It was my turn. "I'm Joseph Antonelli," I said.

"I'm Susan," she replied, and wandered off.

"Do you know her?" I asked Gray.

"Never saw her before in my life."

An open bottle of wine was on the counter next to the sink. I found a glass in the cupboard. Pouring it half full, I took a drink.

Gray stared into his own glass, moving the ice with a slight movement of his wrist.

"It's surprising we hadn't met before. Portland isn't a big place."

"I think we probably move in different circles," I remarked.

The circle of my acquaintance had narrowed until there was hardly anyone left in it, and I knew next to nothing about the world of old money, where I imagined everyone did what they wanted and never worried about what it would cost.

He accepted the distinction between us as if it was commonplace. "Yes, but we both know Alma—and Horace too—and they speak very highly of you."

I had never heard of Russell Gray until a couple of weeks ago. Horace had never even mentioned him to me until the night of the ballet dinner, when we sat together at the same table.

"In any event," Gray said, changing the subject, "you seem to have gotten yourself involved in an interesting little business since the last time we met—the affair with Marshall Goodwin, of course."

"Yes, I'm prosecuting the case." I started to explain, but Gray was not listening.

"It's really extraordinary," he said. "To think that Kristin left Conrad for a man who murdered his wife!"

"You know Kristin?" I asked.

"She was engaged to one of my best friends. I've known Conrad for years. Everyone was shocked when she broke it off."

"Do you know why she did?"

He sighed. "I'm not sure. I think she just told him she was in love with somebody else."

"How did he take it?"

"Conrad? Oh, he was quite upset. Who wouldn't be? But he got over it." He went back to the case. "Goodwin actually had his wife murdered? That's really quite unbelievable. I don't understand that sort of thing. I've been married twice and divorced twice. These things happen. You don't go around killing someone because you don't want to be with her or she doesn't want to be with you. Nothing lasts forever."

He looked up at me.

"This will sound dreadful, I know. But when Kristin broke off the engagement, I was actually glad for both of them. I had thought she was only after Conrad's money. When she married Goodwin, it seemed to prove that money wasn't really the most important thing for her after all."

"What was?"

"Why, love, of course. What else?"

"Yes," I said. "Exactly. What else?"

The door swung open and the maid came in, the platter she carried stacked with dirty dishes. I poured what was left of the bottle into my glass, and when I turned back Gray had disappeared. I saw him later, just before he left, standing at the doorway, saying good night to Alma. She kissed his cheek, the way she had kissed me, and then stood there, watching him go.

A half hour later almost everyone had gone. I helped Horace move the dining room table back into place and then, our work done, we sat down and made a start at finishing off what remained to drink. While we were at it, Alma came in, a languid look in her eyes. "That was a wonderful party," she said, and stood next to Horace, her arms resting on his shoulders.

IT WAS ALMOST FOUR IN THE MORNING WHEN I GOT home, and I had had too much to drink to sleep. I got out of my clothes, took a long hot shower, threw on a robe, made a cup of coffee, and went into the library. Sitting at the desk, I thought about what Russell Gray had said, the offhand remark that nothing lasts forever, and the easy assumption that it was true. Right in front of me was the volume of Aristotle through which I had for months now been making a slow, sometimes tortuous progress, trying to follow as best I could words written more than two thousand years ago. Some things last longer than others.

AMONG OTHER THINGS LEFT IN THE LIBRARY OF LEOPOLD
Rifkin are the numerous volumes of Diodorus Siculus, a
Roman citizen born in Sicily who spent thirty years in the
century before Christ writing a universal history of the
world. Somewhere near the beginning he remarks that
only the ancient Egyptians knew how to protect the law
from the scandalous conduct of lawyers. All criminal
proceedings were conducted in silence, and everything
was done in writing. At the end, when all the writings
had been examined, the judge placed a carved image of
Truth upon one of the two pleas, without ever once
speaking a word. The Egyptians, according to Diodorus,
were convinced "that if the advocates were allowed to
speak they would greatly becloud the justice of a case; for
they knew that the clever devices of orators, the cunning
witchery of their delivery, and the tears of the accused
would influence many to overlook the severity of the
laws and the strictness of truth." In Egypt, perjury, like
murder, was punishable by death.

Sitting at the counsel table in a small sixth-floor
county courtroom on a bright summer day, I waited for
the defense to finish with the first juror on voir dire,
wondering what the Egyptians would have made of all
this. Richard Lee Jones, who had almost certainly never

heard of Diodorus Siculus, was doing everything he could to convince an elderly woman he had never met that he was the most friendly, trustworthy person she would ever know. I had spent twenty-five years of my life having this same conversation and could only hope that it had not seemed as false and contrived to others as it now did to me.

Jones had taken the seat at the end of the counsel table closest to the jury box, but even that was not close enough. He pulled his chair back from the table and, placing his elbows on his knees, bent his lanky frame as far forward as he could. Parted on the left, his shiny black hair fell over his forehead as usual.

"You understand that, because this is a criminal case, the defendant is presumed to be innocent of everything they've charged him with?"

According to her jury questionnaire, Mildred Willis was a seventy-four-year-old widow with three children and seven grandchildren. She had moved to Oregon as a child and later worked as a telephone operator. Since her marriage she had not held a job outside the home. Painfully thin, with white hair and kindly blue eyes, she was the only female juror wearing a dress. She took her time when she answered a question.

"Yes, I understand that."

"And you understand that this presumption of innocence follows the defendant"—Jones paused long enough to sit up and glance back at his client—"Marshall Goodwin, throughout the trial? Not just part of the trial but all of it. Right up to the time when you go into the jury room and start deliberations. You understand that, don't you?"

She thought about it. "Yes," she said, "I understand that too."

The jury box was directly across from the bench, where the quick-tempered Judge Irma Holloway was concentrating on every word. It was an unusual arrangement. In most courtrooms, the jury is seated to the side and the counsel table is in front of the bench. Here, it was almost impossible to keep an eye on the jury while you were debating an issue before the judge or examining a witness on the stand.

For the first time in my life, I was sitting at a counsel table during a trial alone. I had no one to worry about, nothing to be responsible for, nothing except a woman who had been dead for more than two years and a belief that evil should never go unpunished.

Jones went on and on, asking questions about her children and her grandchildren, what she watched on television and what books and magazines she liked to read. It was like watching in a concave mirror a distorted reflection of myself. Finally, I got to my feet.

"Mr. Antonelli?" Judge Holloway asked in her piercing voice. "Do you rise for the purpose of making an objection?"

I pretended surprise. "No, your honor. I rise to get the circulation back in my legs."

While the spectators and reporters laughed and several jurors smiled, Richard Lee Jones wheeled out of his chair and objected vociferously.

"Your honor, I didn't disrupt the prosecution while he interviewed this juror. I would think common courtesy—"

"Loses out to physical necessity," I said, under my breath.

With a brisk nod, Judge Holloway got to her feet.

"In chambers, gentlemen."

It was not as easy as it sounded. The judge had a private entrance through a doorway directly behind the tall black leather swivel chair at the bench. We had to make our way past eight rows of spectator benches to a doorway at the back corner of the courtroom, down the gray linoleum corridor to the clerk's office, and through the law library, to the door that finally opened onto the private chambers of Judge Robert M. Beloit.

A garrulous, backslapping fool, Beloit had rescued himself from a failing law practice by convincing the governor, a former fraternity brother, to appoint him to a circuit court vacancy. A lifetime member of the National Rifle Association, he was always on the lookout for something new to kill, and his office was decorated with just a few of what he had managed to find over the years. An elk, a bighorn sheep, and a cougar stared straight ahead, as if they had crashed through the wall and were only momentarily dazed. We were meeting in chambers to discuss a legal procedure in a murder trial, surrounded by the proud, soulful eyes of a dead menagerie.

Irma Holloway sat straight up on the edge of the chair. Behind her high, sharp cheekbones, large eyes, and pinched mouth, she was a bundle of nervous energy on the verge of erupting at any moment.

She looked at us as we settled into the two wooden Windsor chairs in front of the desk. Then her gaze lifted to the dead-eyed animals that covered the two facing walls. She slid back in the chair, slowly shaking her head.

"Are you a hunter, Mr. Jones?" she asked, a thin, polite smile on her mouth.

"Yes, I am, your honor. Most everybody out where I come from is."

She turned to me. "And you, Mr. Antonelli?"

"No," I replied. "It was never anything I wanted to do."

A smirk started across Jones's face, and Judge Holloway rounded on him.

"You don't approve, Mr. Jones?"

"It's not up to me, your honor," he said, shrugging his shoulders. He pushed his boots out in front of him until his legs were straight and then crossed one ankle over the other. "I don't care if Antonelli doesn't want to hunt. Though I could have done without that condescending tone of his. Far as I'm concerned, Antonelli can do whatever he wants. It's a free country. Except," he added, a warning in his voice, "I don't think he really has any business getting in my way while I'm talking to someone during voir dire. All I've got to say," he went on, glaring at me through half-closed eyes, "is that it better not happen again."

"And all *I've* got to say, Mr. Jones," she said, fixing him with a lethal stare, "is that unless you want to wind up like one of these animals, your head mounted on the wall, you'd better never tell me what to do again!"

"I didn't—"

"You don't come in here—I don't care what lunatic normally sits in these chambers—and start telling me what the other lawyer in this case better do or not do. You get my meaning, Mr. Jones? I didn't call you in here to hear what you think. I called you in here so you'd both know," she added, shooting a glance at me, "that in my courtroom I make the rules and you follow them, and pity the fool who first forgets it! You understand?"

Jones stared back at her, a grudging smile his only response.

"You both understand?" she demanded, her eyes switching to me.

I nodded.

"Now, let's get this straight." Leaning forward, she began to shake her finger. "This is a courtroom. It is not Drama One-oh-one. Leave the theatrics at home."

Jones settled back in the chair.

"I don't just mean Antonelli, here. That's the last time he gets to his feet and pulls that kind of stunt. But let me tell you," she went on, bending farther across the desk, "it's also the last time you turn the examination of a prospective juror into a miniseries on that person's life."

"I have a right to explore avenues of possible prejudice in a juror. This isn't some drunk-drive case, your honor."

"You want to argue the point, Mr. Jones? Save it for the appellate courts. I'm putting a ten-minute limit on how long either one of you can ask questions of each prospective juror."

Jones was beside himself. "Ten minutes? That's an impossible limitation."

"If you can't do it in the time allowed, Mr. Jones, I'll do it for you. The court has the power to take voir dire out of the hands of the lawyers if they're not doing it properly."

With a shudder, she cast one last disgusted look at the heads mounted on the wall. "Somebody should shoot *him*," she muttered under her breath. Her eyes came back to us. "All right. Let's get back to work."

Jones stopped me in the hallway. Pulling himself up to his full height, he stood close to me, backing me against the wall.

"I'm going to bury you, Antonelli. You never were as good as me."

I moved along the wall. When I was free of him, I stopped, reached out to him, and laid my hand on his shoulder. "Listen, if it'll make you feel any better, I'll tell you right now that I've never thought I was as good as you."

I began to walk toward the courtroom door.

"I mean, let's face it," I said, as I opened it and waited for him to pass. "If you were only *half* as good as you tell everyone, you'd still be a hell of a lot better than anyone else who has ever tried a case."

His face went crimson and he bit his lip. We were inside the courtroom and everyone was watching. We moved up the short aisle that ran between the spectator benches and the wall. Jones stayed a step ahead of me, and when he reached the gate in the wooden railing he held it open, nodding politely as if we were friendly adversaries.

With a few last inconsequential questions, the defense finished with the elderly Mildred Willis. It was now the prosecution's turn to begin the examination of the next juror called into the box.

Content and exhausted, Dolores Lightner, the mother of two small children, sat with her arms wrapped around her bulging belly, waiting patiently for her third. Whether from an instinct of kindness or a fear that anyone that close to birth would find it difficult to condemn someone to death, I made up my mind to get rid of her.

"I see from the form you filled out that you have two children?"

Her smile had motherhood written all over it. "Yes," she replied. Though I had not asked, she added proudly, "A girl, three, and a boy, one and a half."

From my place at the far right end of the counsel table, I smiled back. "And you're expecting your next child how soon?"

"Eight weeks," she replied shyly.

I rose from my chair. "Your honor, in view of Mrs. Lightner's condition, perhaps she might be excused?"

Jones was on his feet. Before he could say anything, Holloway held up her hand.

"Mrs. Lightner," said the judge, in a quiet, compassionate tone, "do you think you would be able to serve? As I said before jury selection began, the defendant has been charged with murder. And I'm afraid that some of the evidence may be graphic and quite unpleasant. When I was pregnant," she added, "it's not something I would have wanted to do."

Emphatically shaking her head, the young pregnant mother of two insisted she was perfectly able to serve and wanted to do so.

"I don't want my children growing up in a world where someone gets away with murder," she insisted seriously. "I believe in an eye for an eye," she added.

"Did you have something you wanted to say, Mr. Jones?" Holloway asked without expression.

He made the best of it he could. "No, your honor. I just wanted to make sure she had a chance to decide for herself whether or not she could serve."

"The court appreciates your concern," she remarked dryly. "Mr. Antonelli, you may continue your examination."

After Mrs. Lightner, we moved on to the other jurors, repeating ourselves over and over again. When we finished with the twelve jurors called into the box, we began to use our peremptory challenges, replacing one juror with another and taking the new one through the same questions we had asked before.

No one really picks a jury. You start with the twelve they give you, chosen at random from two dozen that are brought into the courtroom, and go from there. Every lawyer has a theory about what kind of jury to get and what kind to avoid, but you never really have the choice. It is like playing poker: when you throw away two cards, you do not get to ask the dealer for the two that would give you the hand you want. The defense got rid of Dolores Lightner, and in her place we got an overweight thirty-five-year-old motorcycle mechanic with a Harley-Davidson tattoo on his arm.

We had been doing this for days, and I was bored with it. I waited until he had squeezed into the chair.

"Would you like to be on this jury, Mr. Armstrong?"

"Sure." He shrugged. "Why not?"

"Do you think you can be a fair and impartial juror?"

"Yeah, I guess."

Sinking back into my chair, I waved my hand listlessly. "Pass this juror for cause, your honor."

Finally we had a jury. The judge instructed the clerk to swear them in. As I watched the eight women and four men listening as the clerk read the oath, I found myself wondering if I had not underestimated Richard Lee Jones's ability to ingratiate himself. He worked a kind of magic with his voice. He had talked to them, every one of them, slowly, patiently, as if they were children who could only understand things put into the simplest of terms. I had thought it was patronizing, yet instead of resenting it they seemed almost grateful. I was not worried anymore about whether Marshall Goodwin was guilty. Now that the trial had started, the only fear I had left was the fear I might lose. It did not matter what side I was on; whenever I stepped into a courtroom all I could think about was winning.

THE NEXT MORNING, AS I MADE MY WAY THROUGH THE crowd that had begun to assemble in the corridor outside the courtroom door, I heard a familiar voice.

Dressed in a wrinkled summer-weight suit, Harper Bryce was at my elbow.

"I've got a bet down that says no matter how long you go on opening, Jones goes longer."

"As long as you don't bet that he'll have more to say."

Television crews were setting up their equipment. A young woman with lacquered hair and a microphone dangling in her hand was pacing back and forth, rehearsing her twelve-second lead. Drinking coffee from plastic cups, several reporters lounged next to the wall, while they read in the morning papers the stories they had written last night.

"Any chance we could have another conversation?" inquired Bryce casually, as we reached the door.

"Whenever you like."

"How about after court today?"

"I'm not sure about today," I said vaguely, "but sometime soon. Same rules as before, right?"

Nodding, he reached in front of me and opened the door.

"It's always a pleasure, Mr. Antonelli," he said.

I was twenty minutes early, but the courtroom was almost full. Everyone wanted to hear what was going to be said in the two opening statements, in which each side would lay out what they thought they could prove or were certain they could refute. Alone at the counsel table, I pulled out the yellow legal pad on which I had written my notes.

Jones and his client had come in and were sitting at the opposite end of the table. The court reporter was inserting new tape into the stenotype machine. I reached into my briefcase, removed a document from a file folder, and passed it across.

Goodwin glanced down at the paper, his face still animated from the conversation he had been having with his lawyer. As soon as he saw me, the lively expression faded. He turned back to Richard Lee Jones, and I heard his voice, eager and dismissive, start up again.

Short and chubby, with large, astonished eyes and a small, bewildered mouth, the court clerk stumbled in like someone not quite sure she has come to the right place and, almost as if it were an apology, announced, "All rise."

With a quick nod, Irma Holloway acknowledged our presence at the counsel table and took her seat on the bench. "Bring in the jury," she ordered with a peremptory wave of her hand, as she glanced down at the court file.

"I have a matter for the court, your honor," said Jones.

The clerk froze in her tracks, looked up at the bench, and waited for instruction.

Knitting her fingers together, the judge rested her hands on top of the file and gazed at Jones expectantly. "Yes?"

"Your honor, the counsel for the state has just handed us an amended witness list. The amendment consists of a single name, the name of the defendant's wife." He went on, speaking in slow, sweeping phrases. "The defense would like the opportunity to file a formal motion in opposition to the use of spousal testimony by the prosecution, and we would further request oral argument on that motion."

I was on my feet, waiting for him to finish.

Holloway turned her attention to me. "Mr. Antonelli?"

"The decision was made only yesterday to call the defendant's wife, Kristin Maxfield, as a witness for the prosecution. I doubt if she has yet been put under subpoena. If Mr. Jones means, by his reference to spousal testimony, those statements protected by the spousal privilege, I can assure the court that is not the kind of testimony we hope to elicit. I would add, your honor, that Mr. Jones cannot possibly claim that the decision to call the defendant's wife is a surprise. He is certainly aware that Mrs. Goodwin was not only interviewed by the police but testified before the grand jury that returned the indictment in this case."

"Well, I *am* surprised!" Jones exclaimed.

Angrily, Holloway turned on him. "Mr. Jones, in this courtroom you will speak when I ask you to and not one moment before. Now, what is it you want to say?"

He went on as if he had not heard a word she had said.

"I'm surprised that Mr. Antonelli is so desperate to win that he's thrown away all respect for a married woman's privacy. Leaving aside the question of whether Mrs. Goodwin's testimony does or doesn't fall within the legal prohibition on spousal communications, there is, after all, something called common decency. I can't imagine any lawyer asking a woman to help him convict her husband. I just can't imagine that, your honor, and we're requesting a formal hearing to make sure it doesn't happen here."

Holloway fixed him with a withering stare. "Save it for closing argument, counselor. Your motion is denied. At the time the witness testifies, you can of course raise any objections you might have." She paused, lifting her thin eyebrows. "Any objection, that is, that has some basis in the law."

Turning away, she found the clerk still waiting to be told what to do.

"You may bring them in now," she said.

A few minutes later, the clerk returned, followed by a shuffling parade of a dozen men and women chosen for the anonymous notoriety of deciding if Marshall Goodwin had murdered his wife. As they settled themselves into the jury box, the elderly Mildred Willis exchanged a brief smile with the juror next to her, the motorcycle mechanic. They seemed to like each other.

| xii

IRMA HOLLOWAY WAS A STUDY IN FORMALITY. "LADIES and gentlemen," she began, in a steady voice, "we begin with opening statements from the two attorneys. The prosecutor will go first and the defense will follow. Opening statements are for the purpose of providing you with a preview of the evidence each side expects to produce during the course of the trial."

With a look of the utmost seriousness, she went on to explain.

"There are only two kinds of evidence. There is the evidence given by the testimony of witnesses, witnesses sworn under oath to tell the truth. And there is the evidence provided by things themselves, things that frequently serve as what we call exhibits. Simple examples would be a weapon that was used in the commission of a crime, blood samples, or fingerprints."

Pausing, she looked from one end of the jury box to the other.

"The opening statements of the lawyers are not evidence. I want you all to be clear about this. You are not here to be persuaded by the speeches the lawyers give, you are here to decide whether or not the evidence in this case—and only the evidence—proves beyond a reasonable doubt that the defendant has done what is alleged in the indictment."

With one decisive nod, like the last hammer stroke that drives in the nail, she folded her hands together, gazed straight ahead, and invited me to begin.

"Mr. Antonelli."

I walked close to the jury box and let my eye go from face to face until I had looked at them all.

"This is a terrible case. You will wish you were somewhere else when you hear some of the things that will be said in this courtroom and see some of the photographs of what happened two years ago, when Nancy Goodwin was raped and murdered in a motel room a hundred miles away. I'm not going to ask you to imagine what it must have been like for her—what she must have felt, what she must have thought—when, with her mouth taped shut, she saw the blade of the knife and felt a hand grab her by the hair and pull back her head—when, just before he slashed her throat, she heard the killer say that her husband, Marshall Goodwin, had paid him to do it. No one can really imagine what that must have been like. No one needs to. The act itself is brutal enough."

I went back to the beginning and started over. Dispassionately and concisely, I described the sequence of events that led from the discovery of Nancy Goodwin's body to the voluntary confession of the man who had killed her.

"The law insists, quite properly, that no one can be convicted of a crime on the testimony of a co-conspirator alone. The law requires additional evidence: first, that a crime was actually committed and, second, that the defendant was involved. The law does not require that this additional evidence be the testimony of an eyewitness, or evidence which by itself would be sufficient to convict. We will provide all the evidence necessary to corroborate the testimony of the killer, Travis Quentin. We will prove beyond a reasonable doubt that the defendant, Marshall Goodwin, had a private conversation with Quentin, dropped the serious criminal charges that were pending against him, gave him precise instructions on the time and place his wife would be alone, and, in addition, gave him ten thousand dollars in cash as payment for murder."

I spoke for less than thirty minutes; Richard Lee Jones spoke for more than an hour. The glittering blue-and-gray snakeskin boots he had worn at the arraignment were now replaced by plain brown ones. With sorrow and contempt, he recited a tale of police incompetence and official misconduct with such earnest conviction that by the time he got to the end he had probably talked himself into believing it.

The premise was straightforward, and once you accepted it everything else seemed to make sense. Moving slowly back and forth in front of the jury box, stopping just long enough to fix them with looks of studied sincerity, Jones insisted that the police had bungled the initial investigation by failing to secure the crime scene in a way that would have preserved evidence left behind by the killer.

"Imagine what it must have been like to find out that the wife of the chief deputy district attorney of the largest county in the state has been murdered and you've managed to destroy any chance there might have been to find her killer. Now imagine what it must have felt like when someone saved you all that embarrassment not only by confessing to the crime but also claiming that lurking behind this whole thing, masterminding it, was none other than this evil genius, the chief deputy district attorney himself!

"Imagine how eager they all were," he said, shoving his shoulders forward as he began to pace, "the local police, the state police, all of them—to get this thing behind them. You think for a minute they doubted what this confessed killer told them? They were too busy writing it all down to wonder whether they maybe should listen with just a little doubt, just a little suspicion, to the accusations of someone trying to save himself from the gas chamber."

Suddenly, he stopped and looked at me over his shoulder.

"Mr. Antonelli failed to mention that, didn't he?" he asked, turning back to the jury. "He merely said something about a plea bargain. Some plea bargain! Their chief witness—their only witness—confessed to killing Nancy Goodwin *only* after he'd been arrested for killing a couple more people down in California. The deal he made was that if they gave him life instead of death— and isn't that a deal anyone would be pretty desperate to make?—he'd tell them not only about the murder but about who paid him to do it. And he promised them— you can bet on it—someone big, someone really big, someone prominent, someone the rest of us read about in the newspapers."

Pausing, he studied them with a shrewd eye.

"We all do that, don't we? I do it myself. We see somebody getting ahead, getting somewhere we never got and know we never will, and we believe the first bad thing we hear about them. And then when someone like that is brought down, someone famous, someone we may think is just a little too self-important, whatever we say in public and whatever we say out loud, inside ourselves, where no one else will ever know, we cheer a little, don't we?"

He had them, every last one of those twelve jurors. They followed him with their eyes, bound to him by a shared confession of human weakness.

"That's what this case is all about," he assured them. "Travis Quentin wants to save his life, so he makes up a story. The police want to save their reputation, so they choose to believe that story. Everyone wants to be in on the kill, the chance to bring someone down, so they line up for the chance."

He was standing at the far end of the jury box, his hand on the railing as he stared down at the floor. Then he slowly looked up, until across the distance his eyes met mine.

"This case is poisoned with politics," he warned. "Everybody knows that Marshall Goodwin was about to become district attorney. And now they have the chance to stop him."

I was on my feet, ready to object, but Judge Holloway was ahead of me. "You make one more unsupported accusation like that, Mr. Jones, and you'll be held in contempt!"

Without a word, Jones turned his back on her and faced the jury box. She never saw the caustic look that told everyone that, as far as he was concerned, the force of her reaction had only proved him right.

"Marshall Goodwin has not only had to endure the agony of losing the woman he loved in a vicious murder. Now he's had to undergo the humiliation of being accused of her death. No one can bring Nancy Goodwin back, but at the end of this trial he can at least walk out of this courtroom with the knowledge that no one could honestly believe he had anything to do with it."

Still angry, Judge Holloway watched with the rest of us while Richard Lee Jones swaggered back to his place at the counsel table.

EVERYTHING HAD TO BE PROVEN, EVEN THE FACT THAT Nancy Goodwin was dead. A long list of witnesses took the stand to tell their part of the story: the maid who found her, the police officers who investigated the scene, the coroner who performed the autopsy. Photographs taken from every angle of the hotel room and the gruesome pictures taken later of Nancy Goodwin's body were passed through the reluctant hands of the jurors and made permanent exhibits in the record. This necessary prelude to the heart of the case lasted the better part of a week. Then it was time to hear the testimony of the man who had raped and killed her.

On more than one occasion I had defended an inmate charged with an act of violence, and I knew firsthand there were few things more likely to prejudice a jury than a prisoner brought into court bound and chained. It didn't occur to me to have Quentin appear any other way. I wanted the jury to see for themselves how dangerous he was and how utterly depraved a man had to be to hire someone like Travis Quentin to kill his wife.

When I called his name as the state's next witness, the door at the back opened and two burly uniformed guards escorted Quentin into court. Locking his knees together was a heavy iron chain, wrapped several times around his legs, looped over his neck, crossed back over his chest, and fastened with a padlock at his waist. Stretching the chain as far as it would go, he could barely raise his right hand to his shoulder as he stood in front of the witness stand and listened to the clerk administer the oath. With the help of the two guards, he sat down, two strands of the chain sagging heavily in his lap.

Though he was my witness, I attacked him.

"How many people have you murdered, Mr. Quentin?"

He pulled his head slightly to the side, lining me up with his eyes. He did not answer.

Moving behind the counsel table, I walked over to the side of the jury box. With my hand on the end of the railing, I rephrased the question.

"Let's make it simpler. In the last two years?"

He sneered. "Three, I guess. The two in California, the one up here."

"You guess three. By the one up here, you mean Nancy Goodwin, correct?"

"Yeah, I guess that was her name."

"You killed her in a motel room in Corvallis, correct?"

His eyes stayed focused on mine. "Yeah, that's right."

"You cut her throat?"

Jones was out of his chair. "Your honor, for some reason Mr. Antonelli here keeps leading his own witness." He turned toward the jury and added, "Maybe he's forgotten he's the prosecutor in this case."

There was a ripple of laughter from the benches, silenced by a single crack of Irma Holloway's gavel.

In no hurry, Jones turned back to the bench. Judge Holloway was waiting for him.

"The questions put by Mr. Antonelli to the witness, while a little unorthodox, are, in light of the circumstances surrounding the witness's appearance, an acceptable departure from the usual form of direct examination. On the other hand, Mr. Jones, there is no equally compelling reason to allow an exception to the required form for raising an objection. If you don't know what that form is, the court clerk will be glad to show you the way to the law library during the next recess. Are we clear now, counselor?"

She did not wait for an answer.

"Mr. Antonelli," she said, turning for the first time to me. "Please continue."

Slowly, deliberately, I repeated the question. "You cut her throat with a knife, didn't you?"

Quentin had no mind for abstractions. The colloquy between the defense attorney and the judge had nothing to do with him, and with lowered eyes he had passed the time weaving his thumb in and out of the chain around his wrists. When he heard my voice, he lifted his dull eyes.

"Yeah, that's what happened," he muttered.

"You've made a full confession to the police, haven't you?"

"Yeah."

"I want you to be completely honest about this, Mr. Quentin. The only reason you confessed to the murder of Nancy Goodwin is because you were otherwise facing the possibility of the gas chamber for the murders you committed in California, correct?"

Putting one shoulder forward, he tried to move the chain away from the side of his neck.

"It was part of a deal. I told them everything I knew about the killing in Corvallis, and I was sentenced to life."

"Without possibility of parole, correct?"

"Yeah." His lips parted, exposing crooked yellow teeth. "I'm not getting out."

"And you've also now entered a plea of guilty on the

charge of murder in the first degree here in Oregon for
the murder of Nancy Goodwin, haven't you?"

"Yeah. Couple months back."

"What about sentencing?"

"Doesn't really matter, does it? I'm spending the rest
of my life in prison in California."

"We both know it matters, Mr. Quentin. If you don't
testify truthfully in this case, you could get the death
penalty, couldn't you?"

His mouth barely moved when he replied in the af-
firmative.

"In other words, Mr. Quentin, you're here to tell the
truth about what happened two years ago, because if
you don't it could cost you your life?"

He started to nod, then stopped, as if he had just
thought of something.

"Not quite as good as they say it is, though," he said,
grinning stupidly. "It's not like the truth will set me
free."

I moved my hand from the jury box railing and approached the witness stand.

"Now let's go back to the beginning. I want you to
describe to the jury everything that happened from the
time you were first taken to the district attorney's office
until the time you murdered Nancy Goodwin."

Prodded by an occasional question, Travis Quentin
told his story with the detachment of a man who cared
nothing about what he had done. When he reached the
end, I had only one question left to ask.

"Did anyone tell you that Nancy Goodwin was four
months pregnant when you killed her?"

He shook his head. "No."

I was standing at the far corner of the counsel table,
just across from the defendant and his lawyer.

"Marshall Goodwin never bothered to mention that?"

"I didn't know anything about it," he said, tugging at the chain that was cutting into his shoulder. "Until she told me."

"She told you?" I repeated helplessly.

"Yeah," he said. "But people say a lot of things when they think they're going to die."

Richard Lee Jones began asking the first question of his cross-examination before he had finished getting out of his chair. "Now, if I understand all this, Mr. Quentin, everything you said really comes down to some pretty simple arithmetic, doesn't it?"

Quentin had no idea what he was talking about, and neither did anyone else.

"What I mean, Mr. Quentin, is this," he said, stalking along the railing of the jury box. "You murder this woman—Nancy Goodwin—in Corvallis." He stopped still and stared hard at him. "Right?"

"Yeah."

Jones started pacing. "Then you murder two more people down in Los Angeles." He stopped again. "Right?"

He did not wait for the answer but started walking again, long ungainly strides, in front of the jury. "That makes three people you killed." He held his foot in place, glancing quickly across at the witness. "Right?"

Turning until he faced Quentin directly, he drew himself up to his full height.

"But then you figure out," he said, squinting at him, "that killing three people gets you the gas chamber, but by killing just one more you save your own life. That about it, Mr. Quentin? The truth is," Jones spat out, "you've made this whole thing up, start to finish, haven't you?"

Quentin drew his head to the side and waited, an ominous look in his eye.

"You killed three people—lately. I think that was the way your lawyer put it."

"Your honor," I protested, jumping to my feet.

"I'm warning you, Mr. Jones," Judge Holloway said.

"The way the prosecutor put it," Jones went on, as if he had not heard a word, "you kill two people in California, know you're going to the gas chamber, and so you confess to another murder, one here in Oregon, and because that isn't going to get you anything by itself, you kill again—or, rather, you try to, don't you? You tell the police you were paid to kill that woman—and the man who paid you was her husband. That's what I mean by trying to get away with three murders by committing a fourth. Because that's what you're trying to do, isn't it—murder Marshall Goodwin here just as surely as you murdered his wife?"

"Your honor," I objected, "if there's a question somewhere in that speech, I for one would be glad to hear it."

Jones was too quick. "I'm sorry, your honor," he said, with his best imitation of a bashful smile. "I got a little carried away."

He turned back to the witness.

"You testified that you were given an envelope that contained instructions, correct?"

"Yeah." Quentin grunted.

"The name of the motel where Nancy Goodwin would be staying?"

"Yeah."

"When she'd be there?"

"Yeah."

"Well, then, Mr. Quentin, where is it? Where is the envelope, with these very precise instructions that told you where to go and when to be there? Where is it?"

Quentin shrugged. "Burned it."

Placing his boot on the step below the witness stand, Jones rested his hand on the corner of the bench in front of the judge.

"Did you burn the money too?" he asked, pushing his face forward until he was almost nose-to-nose with Quentin.

It only seemed like a mistake. As hard as he could, Quentin threw his head forward, trying to hit him. Jones backed away, avoiding the blow. With a look of triumph, he moved back toward the counsel table.

"And you testified that Marshall Goodwin, the chief deputy district attorney, brought you to his office and announced to you that he was dropping all the charges against you—not because you agreed to be a witness in a drug case but because he might want a little favor later on. Is that about it, Mr. Quentin?"

"No, that's not about it! He hired me to kill his wife. He paid me ten thousand dollars to do it!" Quentin yelled angrily. "And if you don't believe me, ask his wife, the one he's married to now. Ask her! She's the one who brought me the envelope the day I got out of jail!"

For an instant, Jones stared at him. Then, forcing a smile, he turned to the jury. "That's a very good idea," he said.

He turned back to the witness, shook his head, and looked away again.

"No further questions, your honor," he said, as he sat down.

The questioning of Travis Quentin had taken most of the day, but there was still enough time left to show the jury that Richard Lee Jones was bluffing. As soon as the guards had helped Quentin out of the courtroom, I called the next witness for the prosecution.

Wearing round eyeglasses, her hair pulled close to her head and wound in back into a large round bun, she looked like a librarian leading a life of stringent repression.

"Would you please state your name for the record."

Her head held high, she carefully enunciated the words. "Kristin Maxfield Goodwin."

She crossed her legs, the hem of her beige linen skirt well below her knee.

I took her through the necessary preliminaries quickly. She answered each question directly, easily, in complete control of herself.

"And did you, Ms. Maxfield, on the day Travis Quentin was released from the county jail, deliver to him a sealed manila envelope?"

She did not hesitate. "No, I did not."

| xiii

UNDER A BLAZING SKY, HARPER BRYCE, STRUGGLING TO keep up, followed me from the courthouse back to my office. Collapsing in the chair on the other side of my desk, he unbuttoned his suit coat and let his hands fall to his sides.

"How about a nice hot cup of coffee?" I asked, as I tossed my jacket over the back of a chair.

He grasped the arm of the chair, pulled himself up, and muttered, "Thanks, anyway."

Helen had already left. I went into the outer office and from a small refrigerator got a soft drink. I poured coffee for myself.

Lifting his eyes in a gesture of gratitude and partial forgiveness, Bryce held the cold can in both hands before he snapped it open. "That was one of the more entertaining days I've spent in the Multnomah County Courthouse," he said.

Setting the case file on top of the desk, I put my briefcase on the floor. "Glad you enjoyed it."

Crossing one ankle over the other, I stretched my legs over the corner of the desk. I took a long deep breath and let it out slowly, trying to clear my mind of all the fragmentary images and discordant sounds colliding against one another, the irrepressible memories of a trial day that seemed as if it had gone on for a week.

Bryce thought he knew what I was thinking about.

"She surprised you, didn't she?"

His question brought my eyes back into focus. Gazing at the scuffed tips of my black wingtip shoes, I remarked, "Now, why would you think a thing like that?" Turning my head, I looked at him across the desk. "Do you really think I'd call a witness if I wasn't certain what she was going to say?"

"You call the wife of the defendant to corroborate the testimony of her husband's chief accuser. How certain could you be?"

"You want the truth?"

"Not if you can invent a more colorful lie."

He pulled his reporter's notebook out of his side pocket and turned the pages until he came to a blank space on which he could write. "You were about to tell me how surprised you were," he said, looking up.

"No I wasn't," I replied. I took a drink of coffee. "Remind me. What made you think I was surprised?"

Bryce took notes like a court reporter. Flipping backward through the dog-eared notebook, he found the place he was looking for.

"All right," he mumbled to himself. "I'll skip over all the preliminaries. . . . Yeah, here it is," he announced, his small, heavy-lidded eyes alert.

"*Question: 'And did you, Ms. Maxfield, on the day Travis Quentin was released from county jail, deliver to him a sealed envelope?' Answer: 'No, I did not.'* " He glanced up, a suspicious look on his face. "That answer didn't surprise you?"

I made no reply, and he looked down at what he had written.

"*Question: 'Is that what you told the grand jury?'* *Answer: 'Yes.' Question: 'Is that the truth?' Answer:* *'Yes, it is.'* "

Bryce turned the page.

"*Question: 'When did you first become romantically involved with Marshall Goodwin?' Answer: 'That's really none of your business.'* "

Bryce glanced at me, his eyebrows arched into a question mark. "None of your business? As I recall, she said it with a considerable degree of anger—righteous indignation, even. And, if I remember, you started to get a little angry yourself."

He went back to the notebook. "*Question: 'Did you have sex with the defendant the night his wife was murdered?' Answer: 'No, of course not.'* "

I held up my hand. "That's enough. I was there. I remember what happened."

"I just want to know—off the record—you thought she was going to say something else on the stand, didn't you?"

The truth was I did not know what she was going to say, but it had not been too difficult to understand why, despite what she had told me in private, she had continued to lie.

"Let's suppose you and I decide to commit a crime, a murder. Let's just say we decide to kill that editor of yours."

"That's not a crime," he interjected. "That's a public service."

"We don't want to do it ourselves, so we hire someone. We'll call him *Mr. Smith,*" I continued.

Bryce could not help himself. "Jones being too obvious."

"Only, Smith gets caught and, to save himself, confesses." I swung my feet to the floor, put both hands on the desk, and bent forward. "Smith knows I hired him. All he knows about you is that you gave him the envelope that told him where to go to commit the murder and where to go to get the money. He tells the police I hired him, and they put me on trial for murder." I searched his eyes for a moment. "Now, tell me, what do you do?"

"You mean, what do I do when I'm called as a witness?"

"Called as a witness by the prosecution and asked if you in fact delivered the envelope."

"Why don't I just tell the truth and say I did. That's all the prosecution knows about my involvement." He thought of something else. "And if I'm Kristin Maxfield I can say it was just part of my job. I didn't know what was inside it."

He waited for my response.

"Why do you think I'd lie about it? Why do you think she lied about it? That's what you think, isn't it?"

I leaned closer. "Who do you have to fear? Who's the one person—the only person—who can hurt you?"

"You are. If I help the prosecution convict you, you're going to help them get me."

"And there's something else. By denying you made the delivery, you directly contradict the testimony of the killer. You're doing everything you can to help me. If I get convicted anyway, I'm still going to remember what you tried to do for me, aren't I? But with your testimony, I've got a pretty good chance of winning, and if they can't convict me, what do you think the chance is they'll ever go after you?"

Removing a white linen handkerchief from his inside pocket, Bryce mopped the last remaining beads of perspiration from his brow.

"That's all very interesting, but you haven't exactly told me the truth in this little parable, have you? You haven't explained why the prosecution would ever be stupid enough to call me as a witness in the first place."

I turned up my hands. "Everybody makes mistakes."

"Can I quote you on that?" he asked, with casual sarcasm. "What's the real reason?" he persisted. "Why did you call her? She's already told the same story to the police and the grand jury. What made you think she'd tell a different story on the stand?"

"When the trial is over," I said, getting to my feet, "we'll talk again."

Bryce rose awkwardly from the chair, touching the corner of the desk to steady his balance.

"It's an interesting game you're playing with her—or she's playing with you. Whose turn is it to make the next move?"

My hand on his shoulder, I walked him through the outer office to the door. "You know what I've discovered I missed most about trial work? The constant surprise. No matter how much you work at it, no matter how much you think about it, nothing ever goes quite the way you imagined it would. Sometimes the best thing you can do is just watch the way things happen, wait and see what someone does, and then decide what you're going to do."

As we shook hands, he looked me in the eye. "And have you decided what you're going to do?"

"I'll see you tomorrow morning."

"Wouldn't miss it," he replied cheerfully.

I HAD SAID NOTHING TO BRYCE ABOUT KRISTIN MAX-field's surreptitious visit and her calculated confession of what she had done and what had happened between her and Marshall Goodwin. Nor had I made any allusion to our private conversation when I questioned her on the stand. Only Horace Woolner knew what had happened that day she came to see me, and he did not understand why I had not used it.

"Instinct," I told him.

It was a little after nine o'clock at night. We were sitting in my library.

"Instinct?" He grunted. "What do you mean, instinct?" He spread his legs and rested his forearms on them, and stirred the ice in his glass with the tip of his index finger.

"Did you ever play chess?"

He gave me a sidelong glance. "Yeah, a little. Not for a long time."

"I wasn't worth a damn," I admitted, breathing in the scotch. "I used to read about great chess masters and how they anticipated dozens of moves ahead. I kept trying to do that, stare at all the pieces on the board, try to envision each possible move. I couldn't see anything, nothing, not one move. I could see what was on the board, but I couldn't see anything else."

I made a vague gesture toward the stacks of books that swirled up all around us.

"Then I read something Napoleon once said, advice he gave a general who had sent this long list of possible plans he was considering. Napoleon wrote back, 'If you want to take Vienna, take Vienna!' I was trying to explain to Bryce that you can't anticipate every contingency, that once you start doing something, that move affects everything else. That's what Napoleon meant."

Horace was thinking of something else. "Bryce? Harper Bryce? Every time I see him, I want to imitate Peter Lorre."

I laughed. "Peter Lorre? What the hell for?"

"*The Maltese Falcon*. Sydney Greenstreet. He and Bryce are about the same size. They even look a little alike, especially sitting down. Every time I see him, I think of that, and I hear Peter Lorre's crazy wheedling voice asking Humphrey Bogart to tell them where that goddamn falcon is. He's a hell of a card player, by the way."

"I've got a murder trial on my hands, and you want to talk about Peter Lorre?"

"You've got a murder trial on your hands, and you want to talk about Napoleon?" he countered. "Instinct," he reminded me.

"I didn't have time to think about it, but as soon as she denied it, I knew what she was doing and why. So I let her go all the way with it."

"But you still haven't told me why you didn't ask her about what she had said to you."

"I almost did. I almost said, 'Isn't it true, Ms. Maxfield, that just a few weeks ago you told me directly that you had in fact delivered the envelope to Travis Quentin and that you had lied about it to the grand jury?'"

Horace nodded briskly. "Why didn't you? She would have denied it, but that would have put her in direct contradiction not just with Quentin's testimony but with you. The jury would then get to decide between her credibility and yours, not just between hers and a murderer's."

"Perhaps I should have," I conceded, "but I decided to let Goodwin think he could still count on her. I don't think he knows she came to see me, and even if he does, I'm pretty sure he doesn't know what she told me."

Settling back into the deep cushioned chair, Horace held the glass of scotch at eye level, examining the way the liquid swirled each time he rattled the ice. His eyebrows rose and a dubious smile appeared momentarily on his mouth.

"You mean about the sex," he remarked, lifting the glass a little higher. "See the way these different shades of color form, twisting like threads? A long time ago, when a man had been with a woman he didn't know very well, the first thing he'd do when he got home was piss in a glass and then hold it up to the light—just like this—and watch it to see if anything like these threads started to form. It was the first sign of gonorrhea."

"Thank you for sharing that, Horace," I said. "I may never drink scotch again," I added, as I got to my feet.

He stopped laughing just long enough to finish what was left in the glass. "Why not? You didn't piss in it, did you?"

It was time to change the subject. "Can I get you another drink?"

"No, one's enough, thanks." He put the empty glass on the table next to the one I had left. "So, you're going to let it all play out and then recall her as a witness?"

"Maybe," I said, moving around to the other side of the desk. I stood behind the chair, my arms resting on top of it. "Then again, I may not have to. Jones may call her first."

Chuckling, Horace asked, "Tell me about him. What do you think about the great Richard Lee Jones?"

"He's a fraud, but he's good. He talks to those people on the jury like they're important. He makes contact with each one of them, makes them feel unique."

Shoving the chair away from me, I put both hands on top of the desk and stared at Horace, sitting in shadowed lamplight across the room.

"He gives them the impression that he's on their side. When he was giving his opening, he never used the word 'you' when he was talking about what they were going to see and hear during the case. He always phrased things so that it came out 'we.' It wasn't 'You're going to hear from the state's witness,' it was 'The state is going to try to tell us . . .' "

"I never tried a case against him," Horace remarked. "I've watched him, though. I agree with what you said, but he goes too far with it. He tries to make everything 'us against them.' He gets away with it, because everybody is scared of him. The truth of it is, most judges don't know enough law to stand their ground when someone challenges them, and the only reason they're not challenged more often is because most lawyers don't have the guts to stand up to a judge."

Struggling to get his legs under him, Horace finally managed to push himself up.

"Maybe I will have another drink. Just half of one," he corrected himself. "What you really have going on out there," he observed, as I poured a little scotch into his glass, "are a bunch of weak-willed lawyers and fee-bleminded judges too scared of what they don't know to have any idea of what to do with someone who pretends he does."

This formulation seemed to please him and he punctuated it with a short thrust of his head, as if to say, So there!

I sat down in the desk chair and stretched out my legs as far as they would go. "I'm not sure 'feebleminded' is a word I would have thought to apply to your friend Irma Holloway."

The studied severity on his expressive face shattered. Towering above me on the other side of the desk, he crowed, "Told you, didn't I? You imagine what it would have been like, being a kid in a class she taught?" With a visible shudder, he went on. "By the end of the year, you wouldn't be able to close your fingers around a pencil. She would have beaten your knuckles black and blue, made your hand stiff as a board."

He almost seemed to regret that he had never had the opportunity.

As he spoke about her, his gestures grew more animated and his voice seemed to rise several octaves in the scale. "She's just a mean old witch, isn't she?"

He plopped himself happily into a chair he had picked up with one hand and moved to the side corner of the desk, excitement dancing in his eyes.

"It's what white people forget," he explained. "They're always talking about black crime and black welfare and all the unwed black teenage mothers. Well, let me tell you something. Those same black mothers demand respect, and you better believe they get it. You ever see some black kid—tough, mean, like as kill you as look at you? Watch that little prick with his mother. 'Yes, momma; no, momma.' Show me a white woman gets as much respect."

Horace kept talking, on and on, about black kids and white kids and anything else that entered his mind. When he finished the drink I had given him, I offered him another, and when he was through with that, he helped himself to the next one.

"What about the trial?" he asked, interrupting his own monologue.

I remembered something he had said when I first agreed to prosecute the case. "It is like war. Once it starts, the only thing you think about is how to win. And, you're right, Horace, when you've been away from it a while, you really do miss it."

For a moment he searched my eyes. "Then you're sure he did it?" he asked finally.

I had forgotten it had ever been a question. "He's guilty, Horace. I know it."

Somewhere in the summer night a single cricket sang its lonely two-note song. A breeze kicked up, and the air whispered around us.

Walking toward the open French doors, his shoes echoing on the gleaming hardwood floor, Horace stared into the night and shook his head, the way someone does who has resigned himself to things he cannot change.

"Alma probably won't be home before midnight," he said, turning his head just far enough to see me. "From now till the end of summer. Damn near every night, there's something she has to do with the ballet." He glanced at his watch. "Didn't realize it was this late. I better go. You probably still have a lot to do."

"Sit down. Don't go. There's nothing I have to do. I'm ready for tomorrow."

He looked at me and scratched the back of his neck. "A few more minutes," he said quietly.

He sat down again in the chair by the desk.

"If you know he's guilty," he asked presently, "do you know why he did it?"

I crossed one leg over the other and began to tap the edge of a gilded wastebasket with the heel of my loafer.

"Remember when I told you the way Kristin described him?"

Horace looked at me from under his brow. "You mean, how he took whatever he wanted and didn't care who it hurt?"

"Exactly. And she liked that about him. A lot."

I remembered the way she looked when she told me, as if she could still feel the thrill that had rippled through her.

"That was all that mattered—what he wanted. He wanted her, and my guess is both of them wanted it all: money, power, fame. And to get it he did what he had to, or what he had the chance to do. And just like Travis Quentin, once he'd done it, he could forget about it."

There was a trace of doubt in his eyes, a decent skepticism.

"I think that's what happened, Horace. I think he just put it out of mind, as if he had done nothing more serious than get a divorce."

I shrugged and shook my head, in silent commentary on what had become the widespread depravity of the world around us, before continuing.

"We don't have any trouble believing it when someone like Travis Quentin murders and rapes. He doesn't have a conscience. He does what he wants when he wants, and never thinks about the consequences. It isn't that he doesn't *understand* the difference between right and wrong; he doesn't *believe* in the difference. He doesn't believe in anything. We don't want to think someone like Marshall Goodwin, intelligent, well-educated, with a good job and a promising future, could be involved in a murder, but when you strip it all away he's just like Quentin. He doesn't believe in anything either, except the importance of having what he wants. And my guess is it's the same with Kristin." I paused, and then added, "They're not alone, are they."

Waving at the stack of books lined up on the shelves, I tried to explain what I meant.

"There's something Nietzsche wrote: 'The morning paper has replaced the morning prayer.' People used to believe in God, in a moral code that never changed; now no one believes in anything except that everything is always changing and nothing is always either right or wrong."

Horace stared down at the floor. "Goodwin gave a speech last year at the bar association dinner. He was talking about making it more difficult for violent offenders to get out of prison. Then he described what had happened to his wife. He choked up. Everyone did." After a pause, Horace added, "It was one of the most emotional speeches I ever heard, and even now I don't think it was entirely fraudulent. It was worse than that. I think he separated the two things; put his own role in her death out of his mind completely. The only thing that was left, the only thing he still remembered, was that someone had murdered his wife. Maybe you're right, maybe he killed her because it was the easiest way to get a new start with a new woman and some money from a life insurance policy."

He nodded and rubbed his chin.

"But it's not true that no one believes in anything anymore. Some people still believe in things like honor and duty and telling the truth."

A few minutes past midnight, I stood on the front porch and waved good-bye to him as he drove off. Under a cloudless sky, the headlights swept across the lawn as the car curved down the driveway to the entrance below. The iron gate closed behind him, and a faint echo sounded through the clear solitude of the night.

I shut the front door and had just reached the library when the telephone rang. It was Alma.

"I'm sorry to call so late, Joe, but I was a little worried." There was a slight pause, as if she was changing positions or trying to find the exact words she wanted to use. "Horace said he was going to drop by. Is he still there?"

"He just left. He should be home in a few minutes."

She sounded relieved. "That's good," she said in a subdued voice.

"He said he didn't expect you home much before midnight. The ballet and all," I added.

"Well, I'm sorry to call so late," she repeated with her customary pleasant little laugh. "I must sound like the worried wife trying to find her husband."

Alma loved what she did, and Horace loved her too much not to want her to do it, but without her he never seemed to know what to do with himself, and I could not help but feel a little sorry for him. Sometimes love can be the loneliest thing of all.

xiv

WITH A CURSORY NOD TOWARD THE JURY, IRMA HOL-
loway sat down on the front edge of her tall leather
chair. Inclining her head to the side, she held it in place
with the tips of her fingers, and invited me to call the
state's next witness.

"The state calls Bernard Quimby."

Balding, with a full round face and an odd tendency
to blink nervously while he listened to a question and
stare wide-eyed while he answered it, Quimby was with
the insurance company that had paid the claim on
Nancy Goodwin's life.

Standing behind the counsel table, I took him
through the inquiry needed to establish the monetary re-
wards for murder.

"How much was the life of Nancy Goodwin insured
for?"

Staring across at the jury, Quimby replied, "A million
dollars."

"And who was the beneficiary of the policy?" I
asked. His lashes beat rapidly, like the wings of a hummingbird. "Are you nervous?" I asked sympathetically,
before he could answer.

"No," he replied, with a tense shake of his head.
"Well, yes, a little, I suppose," he conceded.

"All right," I repeated, "who was the beneficiary?"

Though it did not stop, the beating slowed.

"Well, actually that's a little complicated." He began to fidget with his thumbs. "You see, the policy was taken out on the lives of both Mrs. Goodwin and her husband." He hesitated, then cast a brief glance in the direction of the defendant. "The beneficiary was the child she was expecting," he added.

I tried to help. "In other words, they took out the policy together, to provide insurance for the child in case something happened to them?"

He looked up. "Yes," he said, "that's right. But you see, there were different contingencies. What happened if both died, if one died, if both of them and the child died." He went on, preparing an endless recitation of the infinite possibilities of insurable misfortunes.

"Yes, I think we understand. Just tell us this. In the event as it happened—Nancy Goodwin and her unborn child both deceased—who was to get the money?"

"Her husband," he answered.

"You mean the defendant in this case, Marshall Goodwin?"

He nodded. "Yes."

"And was that money—one million dollars—paid to Marshall Goodwin?" I asked, turning toward the jury.

"Our company prides itself on paying claims promptly."

"How promptly did you pay this one?" I asked, barely moving my head.

"I believe within thirty days of her death."

The testimony of Bernard Quimby was the beginning of a long march through financial details that, taken together, supplied a motive for murder and helped corroborate the testimony of the killer. Bank statements, credit card receipts, and investment reports were all explained, authenticated, and entered into the record. It was a full accounting of two years' worth of expenditures that seemed lavish at the beginning and had become ordinary and routine at the end. Two weeks after the death of his wife, Goodwin traded in their two cars, an eight-year-old Chevrolet and a three-year-old Ford, on a new Jaguar. He sold the three-bedroom two-bath ranch-style home in a suburban development where they had lived the last five years of their married life and leased a townhouse high on a hill on the western edge of the city. People deal with grief in their own way.

They had waited nearly a year to marry, but Goodwin and Kristin had started making plans for their life together almost immediately. They acquired a secluded half acre with rock outcroppings, a stand of ancient fir trees, and a distant view of the nighttime lights of the city. The architect first visited the site three months after the murder. He remembered they were as excited as a pair of newlyweds, pestering him with questions about how long it would take to build.

Designed for constant alteration, the house was a masterpiece of contemporary innovation. Enormous glass walls let in the changing light, and by the use of temporary partitions, the rooms inside could be expanded or diminished or made to disappear altogether whenever there was a desire for something different.

Various charitable organizations had preserved copies of receipts that had been given Goodwin for clothing he had given away, as he replaced one wardrobe with a much larger one. The closet in the master bedroom of his new house was nearly as big as the bedroom he had shared with his first wife in the old one.

These revelations of Marshall Goodwin's self-indulgent excess were treated by his attorney with a show of indifference. Each exercise in cross-examination was a variation on a single theme. Stretching his hands far apart, Richard Lee Jones would bunch up his lips, narrow his eyes, and shake his head in endless bafflement.

"So, what you're saying," he asked the architect, a slightly built man with a high forehead, a straight, thin nose, and intelligent blue eyes, "is that Mr. Goodwin commissioned you to design a new house. Is that about it?"

"Yes, that's right," the architect replied, a trace of uncertainty in his eyes as he tried to understand where this was going.

Using his leg to shove back the chair as he drew himself up, Jones struck the air with his hand, an abrupt and awkward movement, like someone who reaches out to catch a fly without any expectation of success. Lumbering across to the stand, he eyed the witness suspiciously.

"Tell me, Mr. Dietrich, do you have a specialized clientele?"

"I don't think I know what you mean."

Jones turned to the jury. "I mean, Mr. Dietrich, do you design houses only for murderers? Because if you don't," he sneered, "I'm at a complete loss to see why you've been asked to testify here today."

He did the same thing in a different way with the car dealer who sold Goodwin the Jaguar. "To the best of your knowledge," he asked, searching the eyes of the witness as if he was looking for the first sign of guilt, "how many of the people you sold cars to last year killed someone to get the money to pay for them?"

"Why, no one," the witness blurted out, before I could lodge an objection.

The proprietor of the exclusive men's store where Goodwin had spent almost as much as he used to earn in a year was asked a less threatening question.

"You sell men's clothing, correct?"

"Yes."

"To men?" he asked, as if he wanted to be absolutely sure.

"Yes."

"Good for you," Jones said exuberantly. "For a moment there, I thought you must be involved in something illegal, the way Mr. Antonelli was asking you questions."

He began every cross-examination looking at the witness and ended it facing the jury. And they looked back at him, followed him where he went, and listened to what he said and the way he said it.

After days of this, I was down to the last two witnesses for the prosecution.

Rebecca Easton ran a small neighborhood branch of a large interstate bank, in which Marshall and Nancy Goodwin had kept their account. She was in her mid-forties, with black hair cut straight across her forehead, and was dressed in a red blazer, white blouse, and a black pleated skirt. The enormous circular frames of her glasses gave her dark eyes a slightly startled look.

In response to my question, the bank manager produced first a deposit slip and then a canceled check. The deposit slip was in the amount of thirty-five hundred dollars. This, as her testimony demonstrated, was money moved from a small savings account at the same bank. With this addition, the balance in the Goodwin checking account was brought up to slightly more than eleven thousand dollars.

"And on that same day, did Mr. Goodwin cash a check at your bank?"

"Yes, for ten thousand dollars."

"And was that check drawn on his own account—I should say, the account he shared with his wife?"

"Yes, the account was a joint account. Marshall and Nancy Goodwin. Either person," she explained, "could make deposits or withdrawals."

I was standing at the front corner of the counsel table, closest to the witness stand.

"So one person," I asked, as if there might actually be someone who did not know, "can write a check on an account like this, even if, for example, all the money has been put in by the other person?"

"Yes, exactly. The parties have equal access to the account."

I stared down at the floor, as if it still was not quite as clear as I needed it to be. Perplexed, I looked up.

"So it would actually be possible—if two people have an account together—for one person to hire someone to kill the other and use their money to pay for it?"

She never had a chance to answer. Judge Holloway, her eyes sizzling, brought her gavel down hard with one hand while pointing a finger at me with the other.

"You want to be held in contempt?" she threatened.

I stood straight and said firmly, "I apologize to the court for whatever I may have said. It certainly was not my intention to go beyond the bounds of what I'm allowed to ask."

It was a formal apology that acknowledged nothing in the way of wrongdoing.

"It was deliberately inflammatory, your honor," Jones protested, a scowl descending over the rough-edged features of his face.

She looked at him sharply. "As opposed, I assume, to the strictly accidental nature of *your* attempts to inflame the jury?"

The scowl deepened, the shank of unruly hair dangled close to his eyes. Squinting up at her, he started to say something, seemed to think better of it, and just shook his head in a gesture of sorrowful contempt.

She was quick to see his meaning. "Careful, Mr. Jones," she warned. "This isn't some one-horse courtroom out in the desert somewhere."

He would not look away, and neither would she.

"Counsel will please approach," she said peremptorily.

Shoulder to shoulder, we stood at the side of the bench and bent forward so no one else could hear.

Raking me with her eyes, she hissed, "You've played that game in here for the last time, Mr. Antonelli. If you want to testify, go put a subpoena on yourself."

She turned to Jones.

"You listen to me, Mr. Richard Lee Jones. You ever give me a look like that again, you'll have reason to regret it. Now, both of you, get out there and act like the gentlemen I know you are."

Like chastened children, we resumed our places, consoling ourselves with the secret pleasure we had taken in the punishment inflicted on the other.

Rebecca Easton, her hands folded neatly in her lap, had waited patiently in the witness chair, trying to ignore the angry colloquy taking place on the other side of the bench.

I began as if nothing had happened.

"Mrs. Easton, what I was trying to ask you is whether each person on a joint account has the power to withdraw money from it, no matter which one of them may have put the money in?"

"Yes, of course."

"Now, I'd like to go back to this one transaction. What is the date on the canceled check, made out to cash, by which Marshall Goodwin withdrew ten thousand dollars from that joint account?"

The date was two days before the date on which Travis Quentin had been released from the county jail.

My head bowed, I walked toward the jury box, my arms folded across my chest.

"And do you have a record of the way in which that ten thousand dollars was given to Mr. Goodwin?" I asked, as I stopped in front of the railing and raised my eyes.

"I'm sorry," she replied. "I don't understand."

Turning just far enough to see her, I said, "What denominations were the bills he was given?"

She understood. "Hundred-dollar bills."

I looked back at the jury, my eyes darting from one to the other until I had gazed briefly at them all. Travis Quentin had testified that both the money he had found in the envelope and the money he picked up later at a bus station locker had been in hundred-dollar bills.

"No further questions, your honor."

"Cross-examination, Mr. Jones?" inquired the judge.

Without any questions he could usefully ask, Jones sought to discredit the bank manager's testimony by simply dismissing its importance out of hand. With a shrug of his shoulders, he shook his head and then, rising halfway out of his chair, as if that was all the time he wanted to waste, flapped his hand like someone trying to speed things up. "No, your honor," he sighed, and sank back into the chair.

I had only one witness left. "The state calls Conrad Atkinson," I announced laconically. Out of the corner of my eye, I saw Goodwin whisper something into Jones's ear.

Lean and graceful, Atkinson moved up the aisle with the easy self-assurance of someone who neither doubts his own importance nor thinks it worth mentioning to anyone else. His gray pinstripe suit coat, square across the shoulders and curved inward at the waist, was tailored perfectly.

He sat on the front edge of the witness chair, one leg on the floor, the other crossed over it, and leaned his right elbow on the arm of the chair.

I had only a few questions to ask him, and he answered each of them directly and without embarrassment.

"Mr. Atkinson, you were once engaged to Kristin Maxfield, now Kristin Goodwin?"

"Yes, I was."

"You were in love with her?"

"Yes."

"And she was in love with you?"

"No, I don't think so." He said it the way he would have expressed a doubt that the stock market will always go up.

"She was engaged to you and you don't think she was in love with you?"

An indulgent look creased his well-tanned face.

"Kristin was—how shall I say?—along for the ride. With Kristin you always had the sense that she'd always be there for you—unless you ran into difficulties or"— he lowered his voice—"she found something better."

Bolting out of his chair, Jones began to wave his gangly arms. "Your honor," he bellowed, "I really don't see where any of this is taking us."

Neither did Irma Holloway. "Mr. Antonelli, are we going somewhere with this?"

"Yes, your honor."

She fixed me with a prickly stare. "Then could we get there soon?"

Immediately, I went to the night of Nancy Goodwin's death. "Were you engaged to Kristin Maxfield when that happened?"

"Yes, I was."

"Were you living together?"

"Yes, we were. She kept her own place, but we had been living together at my house for about six months."

"And did she spend that night with you?"

"I suppose it depends on how you define *night*," he replied, with a wistful look.

I was standing in front of him, a few feet from my end of the counsel table. I tilted my head and waited.

"She was involved in a trial. With Goodwin there," he added, nodding briefly toward the defendant. "And I knew she was probably going to be working late. In fact, she'd told me she probably wouldn't be home before eleven or so."

"And what time did she come home?"

"It was after four in the morning. Closer to five, actually. She didn't bother coming to bed. She showered, changed clothes, said something about having to get back to the office, and next thing I knew she was gone."

"How much longer did the two of you continue to live together?" I asked, as I turned and began to pace in front of the counsel table.

"Not long. I had thought for some time she might be

seeing someone else, and that night pretty well convinced me."

I stopped directly in front of Goodwin and looked out over his head at the crowd that was shoved tight together on the courtroom benches. In the back row, Kristin Maxfield was listening to every word.

"Thank you, Mr. Atkinson," I said, with a brief smile. "No more questions, your honor."

Scrambling to his feet, Richard Lee Jones went right up to the witness stand.

"So, Mr. Atkinson, you *thought* your fiancée was seeing another man?"

Atkinson uncrossed his legs and, both feet on the floor, squared up and stared straight into Jones's face.

"Yes, that's correct."

"And to confirm this suspicion, you hired a private detective?" he asked.

"No, of course not."

Spinning away, Jones faced the jury from across the room and exclaimed, "You think your fiancée is seeing another man, and you don't try to find out if it's true or if it's just your own imagination and your own—insecurities?" He wheeled back to the witness. "Why is that, Mr. Atkinson? Surely, someone with your means could afford to investigate?"

"It's not difficult to know when someone you're with is thinking about someone else."

"That must not have been a very pleasant experience. Must have made you jealous."

"You're right. It was not pleasant."

Jones's voice sank to a whisper. "Not pleasant at all. And now you have a chance to get even, don't you?"

Amused, Atkinson replied, "By telling the truth?"

Drawing himself up, Jones asked sharply, "The truth

is, you don't know if she was seeing anyone or not, do you?"

"No, I suppose I don't. Not in the sense that you mean."

"And the truth is, even if she was seeing anyone, you don't know who that someone was, do you?"

"No, but—"

"The truth is, Mr. Atkinson, the only thing you know for sure is that—as you were telling Mr. Antonelli just minutes ago—you were in love with a woman who wasn't in love with you. A woman," he added, lowering his forehead, "who broke off your engagement. Isn't that correct, Mr. Atkinson?"

"I told her it was better if we didn't see each other for a while," he explained.

"And she told you," Jones countered quickly, "that it was better if you didn't see each other at all. Isn't that right?"

"Re-direct?" Judge Holloway asked me, as Jones settled into his chair with a smug look.

"Mr. Atkinson, would you happen to recall the funeral of Nancy Goodwin?" I stole a glance at Kristin Maxfield, sitting expressionless in the back of the courtroom.

"Yes, I remember Kristin saying she felt an obligation to go. I think everyone in her office went."

"Yes, of course," I said sympathetically. "You were still living together then?"

"Yes."

"You weren't invited to go with her?"

"No."

"Do you remember what time she returned?"

"No, I'm afraid I don't. It was sometime early the next morning."

"Do you mean by that a little after midnight?" I asked casually, as if I were certain of the time.

"No, Mr. Antonelli, I mean sometime after the sun was already up. I remember I had already showered and dressed when I heard her car come up the drive."

"How did she explain staying out all night?"

He made a wry face. "I don't think it occurred to her that she needed to explain anything."

A contemptuous wave of his hand was Jones's only response when asked if he wanted to cross-examine the witness again.

Conrad Atkinson left the stand and, with everyone watching, hesitated before he pushed open the door to the hall. Slowly, he turned his head and searched the faces in the last row until he found the one he was looking for. Kristin Maxfield refused to look back, and the door swung shut behind him. For a brief, tantalizing moment, everyone watching had the feeling that they knew more about these two strangers than they did about most of their friends.

"Mr. Antonelli?" Judge Holloway prodded. "Are you ready to call your next witness?"

There is a certain formality by which we mark off the important intervals of our lives. Births, marriages—death itself—each have their ceremonies, the rituals by which we try to make more lasting the memory of the things we do not want to forget because they change forever the way we are. The law follows forms of its own. I had no more witnesses I wanted to call, and there was only one allowable way to announce that I had finished putting on the case against the defendant.

"Your honor," I said, with all the gravity I could summon, "the prosecution rests."

There was no acknowledgment beyond a rapid,

barely noticeable nod, as the judge directed her attention to the other side. "Mr. Jones? Is the defense ready to proceed?"

Jones never seemed to lead with the same part of his body. Sometimes his head popped up, sometimes his hand shot into the air, and sometimes, as now, one shoulder seemed to clear the way as he clumsily extricated himself from his chair.

"Well, your honor," he drawled. "It's getting a little late and, with the court's permission, I would just as soon begin tomorrow morning." He paused and looked around the packed courtroom. "I'm going to put Marshall Goodwin on the stand," he announced, as if he had just accepted a dare, "and his testimony is certainly going to take a lot longer than the time we have left today."

After he had given everyone a chance to take in the significance of what he had just said, he added, "And there is a matter for the court, your honor."

It was nearly four o'clock. With the usual admonitions against discussing the case, Holloway sent the jury home. In front of their twelve vacant chairs and a courtroom still jammed with spectators and reporters, Jones moved to have the case against his client thrown out.

There is a formula for this as well, repeated in every criminal trial in which I have ever been involved. This was the first time I had not recited it myself.

"Your honor, the defense moves for a judgment of acquittal on the ground and for the reason that, based on the evidence provided by the prosecution, no rational trier of fact could possibly find the defendant guilty beyond a reasonable doubt."

In plain English, this means a jury would have to be crazy to convict. Every defense lawyer makes this same motion at the end of the prosecution's case. It has to be made. It is the only way to preserve for appeal the possibility that the case against the defendant was not legally sufficient. There are even times when you actually believe it. Jones seemed to believe it now.

"No one can be convicted on the testimony of a co-conspirator alone, your honor!" he cried. "The testimony of Travis Quentin by itself has no weight whatsoever. Even if he had never committed another crime in his life—even if he was not a savage assassin who kills for the pure fun of it but had never before been in trouble with the law, his testimony could not be used to convict the defendant. There has to be independent proof that the crime in question occurred and that the defendant committed that crime. And what the state has provided beyond the testimony of Travis Quentin has been nothing more than a long exercise in futility. They haven't produced a single witness to verify what Quentin did. Not one. There is no evidence. There is no case. There is nothing to take to the jury."

His face flushed and dank with perspiration, Richard Lee Jones looked up at the bench.

"This court has no choice but to grant this motion and enter a judgment of acquittal," he told her.

Irma Holloway's lips were pressed together, drawing the skin over her sharp cheekbones and lending her an expression of impartial severity. When Jones finished and she looked at me, her eyes, cold and aloof, shielded whatever was going on in her mind. I thought I might lose.

"Your honor," I began, clearing my throat, "Mr. Jones is right. No one can be convicted on the uncorroborated testimony of a co-conspirator. The testimony of Travis Quentin, however, has been corroborated, not just once but in several important particulars. Quentin testified he was paid ten thousand dollars in hundred-dollar bills. The manager of the bank where the defendant had his account testified that Mr. Goodwin withdrew that precise amount in hundred-dollar bills just days before Quentin received it. Now," I went on quickly, "the defendant may be able to show that the money was used for an entirely different purpose, an innocent purpose, and that all this was just an unfortunate coincidence. But the question now is whether the state's evidence, if uncontradicted, is sufficient to take to the jury. The state believes it is."

In quick, abrupt movements, Holloway checked to see if either of us had anything more to add.

"The state has met its burden to put on a prima facie case," she announced. "Motion denied. We begin again in the morning."

She rose from her place on the bench, gazed for a moment at the faceless courtroom crowd, and then turned toward the door behind her and vanished from view.

AS I STOOD ACROSS THE STREET FROM MY OFFICE, WAIT-
ing for the light to change, three shirtless men, chiding
one another for falling behind, shoveled molten black
asphalt into a pothole a few feet from the curb. July had
given way to August, and even in the late afternoon the
sidewalk burned with the reflected glare of the sun.

Inside the air-conditioned building, the perspiration
began to cool on my face, leaving a thin, dry film on my
skin. Helen looked at me and then glanced toward the
open door to my office.

"I didn't know what else to do with her," she whispered, "so I put her in there."

I dropped the overstuffed case file on her neat desk
and headed for the men's room. "If she asks, tell her I'll
be back in a few minutes."

Cupping my hands under the basin faucet, I threw
cold water on my face and slapped it against the back
of my neck. I unfastened my trousers, rearranged the
tails of my shirt, combed my wet hair, and tightened my
tie. After adjusting my suit coat, I moved the heels of my
hands over my eyes and past my temples, trying to draw
away the fatigue on my face.

In the shadows of the lowered blinds, her eyes followed me as I entered the office and walked over to sit

in the chair behind my desk. I looked at her steadily and said nothing. With my elbows on the arms of the chair, I crossed one leg over the other, pressed my fingertips together, and began to rock slowly back and forth.

"Are you angry with me?" she asked.

"Should I be?"

"I could understand it, if you were."

She pulled the hem of her skirt slightly higher as she shifted in the chair. Stretching her arm, locked straight, across the back corner of the chair, she tilted her head in the same direction.

"Your testimony didn't hurt," I remarked with a shrug, as if nothing she could do would make any difference, one way or the other.

"It didn't help," she insisted. She had a look I had seen before, the look on the face of the first girl you fell in love with when she told you she couldn't see you anymore, the look that told you she was not trying to hurt you but did not mind too much if she did.

"It didn't help either one of us," I replied pointedly.

She looked along the length of her arm until her eyes came to rest on her hand, where she spent a moment inspecting her nails. "Do you think I didn't consider that?"

She moved her hand to the arm of the chair.

"You knew it wasn't as simple as that," she remarked, searching my eyes. "You knew I couldn't just turn on him."

"Perhaps I just assumed that under oath you'd tell the truth."

"I told you I'd tell *you* the truth, and I did. You never said anything about having me tell it at trial."

I sat perfectly still. "That's the kind of distinction only a lawyer would make."

"That's the kind of distinction you and I understand."

"It won't be a distinction anyone will care very much about in a perjury trial."

"You think he's going to be convicted, don't you," she asked.

There was a touch of uncertainty in her voice, a hesitancy that seemed to point to something beyond what might happen to her husband.

Raising my eyes, I said confidently, "I don't have any doubt about it."

"You surprised me when you just let my answers go like that. Why didn't you ask me about what I'd said to you here, in this office, when we talked before?"

"Maybe because I understood that you weren't going to tell the truth about anything so long as you thought there was still a chance that Marshall might get off."

"I told you I couldn't just turn on him."

I stood up. "Well, now that you've explained yourself," I said, rather impatiently, "perhaps you'll excuse me. I still have a great deal of work to do."

She tried to conceal her surprise. "I thought you might want to talk about what comes next," she said.

"There isn't anything to talk about," I assured her, as I walked around the desk and helped her out of the chair. "You were there. The defense begins its case tomorrow. I've finished with mine."

In the outer office, Helen was putting the case file in order, as she always did. Opening the door to the hallway, I walked Kristin Maxfield to the elevator.

"Tell me one thing," I said to her, as the elevator door opened. It was empty, and Kristin stepped inside. "Did you have anything to do with the death of his wife?"

She swore that she had not. "And until the trial," she added, her eyes fixed on mine, "I didn't think Marshall had either. I thought the envelope I gave to Quentin held papers about the drug case."

I let go of the door and stepped back as it began to slide shut.

"If you had told the truth at trial," I said, just before the two brass doors met, "I might be able to believe you now."

LATE THAT NIGHT, WITH COOL AIR DRIFTING IN THROUGH the open french doors, I put aside the voluminous case file and gazed at the library shelves, wondering where among all those books I could find anything as intriguing as the subtle duplicities of a wife worried that she might have missed her best chance to betray her husband. It was time to bring another player into the game. I picked up the telephone and called the hotel where Richard Lee Jones was staying. We agreed to meet a half hour before court convened the next morning.

TWO FLOORS BELOW THE COURTROOM WHERE WE WERE trying the case, in a tiny conference room where the press would never find us, Jones listened while I made an offer.

"We'll drop the charge to murder in the second degree. He saves his life and, more than that, he'll eventually be eligible for parole."

He took it as a sign of weakness. Leaning across the small table, he tried to face me down. "When that jury comes back, he's going to walk out of there a free man."

"Listen to me," I replied. "This is serious. The only

reason I'm making this offer is because he isn't the only one I want. I want her, too. Your client agrees to testify against her. . . ."

"His wife?"

"Who do you think I'm talking about?"

Jones got to his feet and glared at me. "You just finished putting on your case, and now you make an offer? All of a sudden you don't want this case to go to the jury?" He could not help himself. "And you used to be so good with juries. What happened, lose your nerve?" He turned to go.

"Please convey my offer to your client," I remarked, as if it was a matter of no great importance. "So there's no misunderstanding about this, the offer will stay open until you rest your case." His hand was on the door, turning the knob. "Unless I make a deal with his wife first. If that happens, there's no offer at all."

The door had opened.

"She's been to see me twice already," I remarked dryly. "But perhaps you already know that." And I went out in front of him.

If I had in any way shaken Jones's confidence, it did not show when he rose from behind the counsel table and, turning to the jury, called Marshall Goodwin to the stand.

Goodwin moved to the end of the counsel table, cast an easy smile toward the jury, and then walked briskly across the front of the courtroom to the witness stand. With an open, almost cheerful countenance, he listened with one hand raised while the clerk rapidly recited the oath.

Wearing a dark tie and a conservative suit, shiny black shoes, and a white long-collared shirt, Goodwin was a model of understated propriety and an eager self-confident witness. He had an answer for everything.

Jones began with the only question that mattered.

"Mr. Goodwin, did you have anything—anything at all—to do with the death of your wife Nancy two years ago?"

Goodwin bent slightly forward, grasped both arms of the chair, and, gazing directly across at the jury, said in a firm, clear voice, "No, I did not."

I did not know if they believed him yet, but watching their eyes I knew they wanted to. Goodwin had the kind of boyish blue-eyed charm that always made people want to believe him. It had been his strength as a lawyer, and perhaps the source of his weakness as a man. Because everything always came easily, it made him believe he could have anything he wanted.

Richard Lee Jones's voice seemed to become more compassionate, more understanding, with each question he asked. His eyes settled on his client in silent approval of each answer Marshall Goodwin gave.

Hour after hour, with steady, clear-eyed sincerity, Goodwin presented the autobiography of someone falsely accused. For the better part of two whole days, Jones led him through the story of his life and marriage and the tragic consequences of Nancy Goodwin's death. Asked about his reaction when he was first informed of his wife's murder, Goodwin broke down and cried.

"Now you've had to sit here and listen while the prosecution tried to convince us to draw certain inferences about your conduct," Jones said, with a sidelong glance at me. "Why don't we just clear the air once and for all about this. Just tell us. When was the first time you ever slept with your present wife, Kristin Maxfield?"

Stark and sensual, stunning in its raw simplicity, the question riveted the attention of the courtroom. The court reporter let her hands rest on the keys as she turned to look.

"Three months before we were married," Goodwin answered, staring level-eyed at the jury.

"And you were married a little less than a year after your first wife was killed?" Jones asked earnestly.

"Yes." Goodwin sighed. "That's correct."

Jones moved from sex to money. "Do you deny that you withdrew ten thousand dollars from your bank account?"

Goodwin treated it as if that was the last thing he would ever want to do. "No, of course not."

"But why would you do that when you apparently had to first transfer money—I believe it was something like thirty-five hundred dollars—from your savings account to cover a withdrawal of that size?"

"We had decided, Nancy and I, to invest the money in a mutual fund. We started talking about it when she found out she was pregnant." With a faraway look, he added, "We decided we had to do everything we could to make sure we started saving money instead of spending it."

Apparently still confused, Jones inquired, "Why didn't you just write a check?"

"I couldn't remember the name of the brokerage firm," Goodwin replied, embarrassed. "It was downtown, near my office, and I had an appointment there later in the day."

"And did you invest the money that day?"

"No. Something came up and I had to be in court. I put the money in a safe in the office."

"Did you ever invest it?"

"There wasn't time. The next day I started a murder trial. The money was safe. I wasn't worried about it. And then . . . well, after my wife was killed, there were some expenses." He spoke quietly, his eyes drifting to the floor.

"One last thing. Did you request that the money you withdrew be given you in hundred-dollar bills?"

"No," he replied, glancing up. "The teller just gave it to me that way. It's easier to count and easier to handle."

It was a few minutes past four when Jones finally finished. Judge Holloway asked if I wanted to wait until morning to begin cross-examination. Behind me I heard the rustling of people getting ready to leave.

"No, your honor," I said, glancing up at the clock. "I only have a few questions to ask this witness. It shouldn't take long."

The fingertips of my left hand rested on the table. I shoved my other hand into my pocket and cocked my head.

"Tell me, Mr. Goodwin. If your present wife, Kristin Maxfield, wasn't sleeping with you until three months before your marriage, who *was* she sleeping with?"

Before Jones was halfway out of his seat, Judge Holloway was hammering the courtroom back into submission and demanding to know what I thought I was doing. I was not in the mood to be apologetic.

"I'm beginning my examination of this witness with questions about statements made by him during the direct examination conducted by his attorney," I said firmly, returning her gaze.

She looked at me a moment longer; then, convinced I was serious, she nodded her head thoughtfully and allowed me to continue.

Raising my chin, I looked hard at Goodwin.

"You testified that the first time you slept with Kristin Maxfield was three months before you married her. Is that correct?" I asked rapidly.

With one hand on the arm of the witness chair, Goodwin shoved himself forward, as if he was more than willing to meet any challenge thrown his way.

"Yes, that's correct," he replied, his words sailing at me as fast as mine had come at him.

"You heard Conrad Atkinson testify that she moved out of his house within days of the death of your wife, did you not?"

"Yes."

"You heard Conrad Atkinson testify that the night of your wife's death, the night you were working with Kristin Maxfield in the conference room of the district attorney's office, she came home only long enough to shower and change and leave for work, did you not?"

"Yes."

"You heard Conrad Atkinson testify that he had for some time prior to that night suspected that his fiancée, Kristin Maxfield, was seeing someone else, did you not?"

"Yes."

Moving around to the front of the counsel table, I sat against it, moving one leg along the edge until my foot dangled a few inches above the floor.

"The other person wasn't you?"

"You're assuming Mr. Atkinson was correct."

"I'm not assuming anything. I'm simply asking you whether you were romantically involved with your second wife while you were still married to your first. It's a simple question. Why don't you just answer it?"

"I was never sexually involved with her. I won't deny I found her attractive."

I slid off the edge of the table and began to pace back and forth in front of the jury box, scratching the back of my head.

"You weren't 'sexually involved' with her?" I asked, stopping still. "Is that what you said?"

"Yes."

"But I didn't ask if you had been sexually involved with her while your wife was still alive. I asked if you had been romantically involved. Would you like to have the court reporter read it back?"

He shook his head. "No. I thought that's what you meant."

"I see. You thought romantically meant sexually. I see. Very well. So, then, by your definition, you were not 'romantically' involved with Kristin Maxfield until three months before you married her?"

A look of uncertainty passed over his face. "Well, no, I would not say that exactly. We had started to see each other, spend a lot of time together. I think I was probably falling in love with her sometime earlier."

"Were you falling in love with her the night you were working together in the conference room, the night your wife was being murdered a hundred miles away?"

"No, of course not. I've already told you that."

Turning my back on him, I faced the jury. "Tell me, Mr. Goodwin, what time did you leave your office that night, the night your wife was killed?"

"Sometime after eleven, I think."

"And did you leave alone?"

"Yes."

Looking at him over my shoulder, I asked, surprised, "You didn't leave with Kristin, walk her to her car?"

"Yes, I'm sorry," he said hastily. "I thought you meant—"

"I know what you thought I meant." Raising my eyebrows, I smiled sympathetically. "Romantically involved," I repeated, waiting while the two words echoed in the expectant silence of the courtroom.

"Nothing happened between the two of you that night?"

"No," he insisted.

"So you weren't with her at all after—what?—eleven, eleven-thirty?"

"Yes, that's right."

"You didn't see her again after eleven, eleven-thirty, until you saw her again the next morning at work?"

"Correct."

"And has your present wife ever told you where, or with whom, she spent that night?"

Jones exploded out of his chair. "He's asking questions about conversation between spouses. There's an absolute privilege involved here, your honor, and I demand the court do something about it."

Irma Holloway shook her finger, scratching the air. "If you want to make an objection, make an objection; if you want to make a speech, go out on the courthouse steps. Mr. Antonelli," she continued, without a pause, "the privilege protects spousal communications."

"Leaving aside the question of whether the defendant is now invoking that privilege, your honor," I replied, stopping just long enough to return Jones's sneer with one of my own, "I'll limit the question to communications that took place before the defendant's marriage to Kristin Maxfield."

"Very well." She looked down at the witness stand where, seemingly unperturbed, Goodwin sat waiting. "You may answer the question."

"Could you repeat the question, please?" he asked.

"Did she ever tell you where she spent that night?"

Jones was back on his feet. "Objection, your honor," he said with a slight bow, making a mockery of the formality she demanded. "Hearsay."

"I'll rephrase the question," I said, before she could rule. "Did you ever, at any time prior to your marriage to her, have a conversation with Kristin Maxfield about where she spent that night?"

"No, it never came up."

"It never came up," I repeated, as if the words themselves were ashamed to be heard.

"What kind of car did you have then, the night your wife was murdered? Four-door or two-door?"

"Two-door."

"But it had a back seat, correct?"

"Yes."

"You parked it at the parking structure across from your office that night?"

"I always parked it in that parking structure."

"And that night you had sex with Kristin Maxfield in the back seat of that car, did you not?" I was staring right at him, taunting him with the knowledge that I knew what they had done and where they had done it, something only Kristin could have told me. His eyes went blank. "And I suppose you didn't have sex with her a second time on the same day your first wife was buried?"

"No, I told you," he insisted. "It never happened!"

"Your first wife, Nancy Goodwin, was a talented woman, wasn't she?"

It caught him off guard. "Yes, she was," he replied, suddenly subdued. "Very talented."

"And you've already testified that it was her idea to take out the insurance policy, correct?"

"Yes," he said, watching me, trying to figure out where I was going with this.

"And she agreed that you ought to move money out of your checking account at the bank into a mutual fund. That is what you testified, is it not?"

"Yes."

"Is it fair to say that she was a full partner in all the major financial decisions that were made while you were married?"

He did not hesitate. "Yes. Completely. If anything, she knew more about that sort of thing than I did."

I lowered my eyes and walked slowly toward the jury box. Standing in front of the last juror in the front row, I rested my hand on the railing.

"That's quite odd, isn't it?" I asked, looking back.

He had no idea what I meant. "Odd?"

"Yes, odd that when you weren't able to deliver the ten thousand dollars in cash to the brokerage firm, you decided to leave it in a safe at work—while you began a murder trial that was scheduled to last for weeks—instead of entrusting the money and the errand to your wife."

He started to answer, but I cut him off with a wave of my hand.

"No further questions, your honor."

| xvi

THE MORNING LIGHT STREAMED THROUGH THE SOLITARY
wooden casement window and over the double set of
bound briefs. Sipping coffee from a maroon plastic cup,
Horace Woolner viewed them with a jaundiced eye.

"These are motions to set aside rulings on motions to
set aside rulings on motions to set aside. It's been going
on so long no one can remember the beginning, and I
don't think anyone really expects to see the end. It's like
that case in *Bleak House*, Jarndyce *versus* Jarndyce.
Dickens. You remember?" He laughed. "It goes on for
years. Years! And then, finally it's over and there's nothing left. Not a cent. All the money they were fighting for
has gone to pay the lawyers."

Open in the front, the black judicial robe draped over
his shoulders was bunched up under his legs where he
had sat down without bothering to straighten it.

"We were told to read *Bleak House* the summer before I started my first year in law school. You know," he
said, raising an eyebrow the way he did whenever he
was about to commit a particularly excessive exaggera-
tion, "the damn thing must be about three million pages
long. They must have paid Dickens by the word."

It was seven-forty-five in the morning. Since the beginning of the trial, it had become something of a set-

tled practice for us to meet in his chambers for a cup of coffee at the start of the day. Horace began his day earlier than any other judge in the building. He liked to schedule oral arguments on complicated civil matters at eight, on the theory that the longer they had been awake the more lawyers were likely to talk. It was a phenomenon that had no obvious application to himself.

Pointing at the two briefs laid side by side in front of him, he asked, "You know what this is about? Two brothers suing each other over the business they inherited from their father. There's no business left, you understand. It went under years ago, but each of them is convinced it was the other one's fault. And someone has to pay, don't they? Which is perfectly fine with the lawyers, who measure the world in billable hours.

"Sometimes I miss being DA," he said, as he stood up. "There's something clean-cut about criminal law." He poured himself another cup of coffee. "Want some more?"

I shook my head and waited until he sat down.

"Are you all right, Horace?"

He looked at me, surprised. "Sure, why not?"

"Because it's not even eight o'clock in the morning, and you're wired."

"I'm always like this," he protested. "I wake up early."

"You go to bed late."

"Yeah, and I wake up early," he insisted. "I've never slept much."

It was a little too glib, a little too evasive.

"You worried about something?" I asked, searching his eyes.

There was a slight pause, a brief hesitation, as if there was something he wanted to say but knew, even as he thought about it, that he was not going to.

"The only thing I'm worried about is whether you're going to be able to convict Marshall Goodwin," he said finally. "I hear he did pretty well the last two days."

With both hands wrapped around the cup, he lifted it to his mouth but did not drink.

"Until you got hold of him, that is." A shrewd glint came into his eye. "First you tell Jones that Kristin has been to see you twice; then you ask Goodwin that question about the back seat of his car. Wonder what the two of them talked about last night?"

"Or what each of them is thinking about this morning," I added.

Draining off the little coffee that was left, I set my cup on the front corner of the desk.

"What do you think she'll do?" I asked. Then, before he could answer, I changed my mind. "What do you think she *should* do?"

"You mean, should she lie to save her husband?" He looked away, slowly shaking his head. "If she really loved him, it wouldn't even be a question for her, would it?"

Gathering up the two neatly bound briefs, Horace fastened his robe at the collar.

"I have to get into court," he said, glancing at the clock.

Then he was gone. Horace was never late.

Neither was Irma Holloway. With a brief glance at the jurors, she perched on the edge of the high-backed black leather chair, stretched her thin arms forward, and clasped her hands.

"You may call your next witness," she advised the defense.

All morning and halfway through the afternoon, the defense summoned one witness after another to testify that Marshall Goodwin could not possibly have had anything to do with the murder of his wife. Then, an hour and a half after we returned from lunch, Richard Lee Jones rose from his chair and announced that he had called his final witness. Sitting just below him, Goodwin fidgeted restlessly and his eyes shifted from one place to the next.

Holloway asked if the state had any witnesses it wished to call for rebuttal.

"Yes, your honor," I replied, as Goodwin's head jerked up. "The state recalls Kristin Maxfield."

She had the look of a woman who had gone to bed crying. I did not even pretend to be kind.

"The testimony you gave here before was not in all respects entirely truthful, was it, Ms. Maxfield."

Sternly, I stood at the counsel table and waited.

Her eyes drifted toward the other end of the table, where her husband was also waiting to hear what she would say.

"Ms. Maxfield?"

Her eyes came back, for an instant met mine, and then looked down at the floor. Gradually, as if she were coming to terms with a decision she knew she could not avoid, she raised her head.

"No. I was not entirely truthful."

"You get one more chance, Ms. Maxfield. Now, did you or did you not deliver a sealed envelope to Travis Quentin the day he was released from the county jail?"

She took a deep breath. "Yes, I did."

"And did that envelope come from the defendant, Marshall Goodwin?"

She glanced at her husband and said, as if to let the world know how wretchedly unhappy she was that she could no longer lie for him, "I'm sorry."

"Ms. Maxfield?"

Digging her nails into the arm of the witness chair, she nodded. "Yes," she whispered, her eyes downcast.

"I didn't quite hear you," I said sharply.

"Yes," she replied, raising her head.

"The night Nancy Goodwin was murdered, the night you were working with Marshall Goodwin, did you have sex with him?"

Biting her lip, she nodded.

"I'm sorry. You'll have to give your answer out loud."

"Yes."

"Describe to the jury, please, where that took place."

Nothing, not a word, not even a blink of her eye.

"Did it take place in Marshall Goodwin's car, in the back seat of his car?"

Still nothing.

"Ms. Maxfield?"

She watched me without expression.

"Yes," she said finally.

"And when was the next time you had sex with Marshall Goodwin?"

For a moment, she hesitated, her lips parted, as if she hoped I would change my mind and ask her something else.

"He said he didn't want to be alone."

"It was the same day Nancy Goodwin was buried, wasn't it?" I asked. "The night of her funeral?"

"Yes," she admitted.

I stared hard at her and then, crossing my arms, lowered my eyes and walked toward the jury box.

"You were asked these same questions in the grand jury, weren't you?" I asked, as I spun around.

"Yes."

"And you lied to the grand jury, didn't you?"

"I was trying to protect my husband."

"You lied," I insisted.

"Yes."

"And when you testified before in this courtroom, in front of this jury," I said, waving my hand toward the twelve men and women who were sitting on my right, watching her closely, "you lied then too, didn't you?"

"I was trying to protect my husband," she repeated.

"Are you telling the truth now?"

"Yes," she replied in a subdued voice, contrition in her eyes.

I eyed her sternly. "You're not holding anything back? Everything you say here is the truth?"

"Yes," she promised.

"Good," I said, with a quick nod of approval.

I walked back to the counsel table as if I were finished. When I reached my chair, I hesitated—and then stood straight up.

"But you haven't told us the whole truth, have you, Ms. Maxfield?"

She blinked. "Yes, I have."

"You haven't told us that when you delivered an envelope to Travis Quentin you knew what was inside it. You knew you were giving him instructions on how to murder Marshall Goodwin's wife, because you were part of it from the very beginning, weren't you?"

"No!" she insisted. "I wasn't. I didn't have anything to do with it. I didn't even know he had anything to do with it, until . . ."

"Until what?" I demanded, as I put both hands down on top of the table and bent forward, glaring at her. "Until what?"

"Objection!" Jones shouted, as he sprang out of his chair.

"Until what?" I demanded. "Until he told you he had her killed?"

Ready to clutch at anything that might yet give her a way out, she cried, "Yes! He told me."

"Objection, your honor!" Jones shouted again, beating the table with his open hand.

Judge Holloway hammered her gavel with such force that the silence when she stopped was a kind of physical shock.

Bending forward, the wooden gavel dangling from her hand, she darted a glance first at Jones, then at me. "Mr. Antonelli—"

Before she could say another word, I held up my hand. "No further questions, your honor."

Jones was still on his feet, his mouth trembling. "Your honor, I ask the court to strike the testimony of this witness. The prosecution was badgering her with questions even after I had made an objection."

"Denied," Judge Holloway ruled, without hesitation. "Do you want to examine this witness?" she asked, with studied indifference.

Jones muttered something under his breath.

"What's that, counselor?" Holloway asked sharply.

"Yes, I would."

He looked at Kristin Maxfield, huddled in the witness chair, and in a calm, steady voice, appeared to take her side.

"This has been a difficult time for you, Kristin—"

Judge Holloway interrupted. "A witness is never addressed by his or her first name."

"Hasn't it, Ms. Maxfield?" he asked, his eyes still on her.

"Yes, it's been difficult," she agreed.

"Must be a little frightening to know that your husband has been accused of something as awful as this, and that you yourself are under some kind of suspicion?"

She lowered her shoulders. "Yes." She sighed. " 'Frightening' would be a good word for it."

"You've been under a lot of pressure, not only because of what your husband has been going through but because the prosecution has made it clear to you that if you didn't change your testimony they were going to try to indict you for this crime as well. Isn't that true?"

"Yes," she acknowledged, her eyes locked on his.

"As a matter of fact, you've had two meetings with Mr. Antonelli in which all this was discussed, isn't that true?"

"Yes, but—"

Jones held up his hand, the smile still on his face. "No, that's enough. No further questions," he added, without so much as a glance toward the bench.

On redirect, I simply asked, "Was the testimony you gave here today truthful?"

"Yes," she said, staring down at the floor, "it was."

"No further questions," I announced wearily, with a brief, dismissive wave of my hand.

Jones just shook his head when he was asked if he had anything more.

As she rose from the witness stand, Kristin tried to catch her husband's eye, but he refused to look at her. She let her gaze linger a moment longer, as if she were giving him one last kiss good-bye, and then, turning away, walked out of the courtroom as quickly as she could.

It was time for closing arguments. The prosecution always goes first and, because it has the burden of proof, is given a second chance, after the defense has finished, to convince the jury that it has proven the guilt of the defendant beyond a reasonable doubt. In less than thirty minutes, I outlined the evidence that had been presented and then sat down, waiting to see how Richard Lee Jones would try to argue that his client had been wrongly accused.

Among the unexamined propositions that pass thoughtlessly from one generation of lawyers to the next is the advice to argue the *law* if the *facts* are against you and to argue the *facts* if the *law* is against you. For the better part of three hours, Richard Lee Jones made his closing argument to the jury and seldom mentioned either one. Instead, he talked about trust and insisted upon suspicion. He described every graphic detail of the rape and murder of Nancy Goodwin and then reminded the jurors of what they had seen on the face of the man who had done it.

"Was there any remorse? Was there any regret? Did Travis Quentin leave you with anything except the certainty that, given half a chance, he'd do it all over again?"

Then he reminded them of what they had seen on the face of the man who was accused of hiring the killer.

"The prosecution claims that Marshall Goodwin had Travis Quentin brought to his office, that he spent an hour with him, that he knew everything about him, his record of violence, his record of murder, a record that would leave no doubt at all that he was completely indifferent to human life, and that then, knowing all this, he paid him to kill his wife."

Gripping the railing of the jury box with both hands, he dared them to believe it.

"You've seen them both: Travis Quentin and Marshall Goodwin. Do you really think a husband could have done that? You've seen them both," he repeated, "Travis Quentin and Marshall Goodwin. Which one of them would you believe on anything that was of serious importance to yourself?"

Moving away from the jury, he tossed his head back.

"But the prosecution claims corroboration. The prosecution wants us to believe that we can take the word of a murderer and a rapist because Marshall Goodwin withdrew ten thousand dollars from his bank account."

Pausing just long enough to cast an accusatory glance in my direction, he turned back to the jury.

"Now, how do we know Travis Quentin was paid ten thousand dollars to murder the defendant's wife? Why, because Travis Quentin told us so. And it must be true, because it matches perfectly, including the hundred-dollar denominations, the money that everybody agrees the defendant had in cash. Travis Quentin couldn't have just made that up, could he?" he asked. "After all, he couldn't possibly have known that the defendant had removed exactly that amount in exactly that denomination unless someone told him, could he? And we certainly wouldn't want to suggest that the police or the prosecution might just have happened to mention that little piece of information to him during one of their lengthy conversations, would we?"

I considered objecting, but instead I scribbled a note to myself and then sat back and watched the rest of his performance.

His words laced with condescension, Jones ridiculed the evidence and insisted that the only reason a case was brought against the defendant was the malice and incompetence of the prosecution. The most savage criticism was reserved for the very end, when he tried to explain away the testimony of the defendant's own wife.

Even more than the defendant, Kristin Maxfield was the victim of an "overzealous prosecution begun by the police, who were embarrassed because they had failed to catch a killer, and continued by the powerful political enemies of a decent man they knew they could never otherwise defeat."

Perspiring, a curling shank of black hair plastered to his forehead, Jones waved his hand in the air.

"She came into this courtroom and she told the truth and the prosecution did not like it and so they threatened her with prison until she came back in here and told a lie. And the only question left is whether we're going to let them get away with it!"

There was a dead silence when he stopped, as if, all emotion spent, everyone was too exhausted to breathe.

Facing away from the jury, I began to beat the second knuckle of my finger against the hard edge of the table, a tangible reminder that there was something yet to come.

Peering down from the bench, Judge Holloway invited me to give the second closing argument.

"Mr. Antonelli?"

Ignoring her, I continued to tap my finger against the hard wood surface, as if I were mesmerized by the sound.

"Mr. Antonelli?" she repeated, more loudly.

My head snapped up and I looked at her, a startled expression on my face. "Yes?" I asked.

Everyone was watching, concentrating now on what was playing out in front of their eyes, Richard Lee

Jones's incendiary words already receding from the forefront of their conscious minds.

"The prosecution gets to make two closing arguments, Mr. Antonelli. Or did you decide to call it quits with one?"

I was on my feet, walking toward the jury box, before she had finished.

Standing in front of the jurors, I started to say something, then closed my mouth, shook my head, and stared at the floor.

"I was about to summarize again the evidence that has been given in this case," I said, glancing up. "But I've already done that. You heard the evidence, you watched the witnesses, and you can tell for yourselves who told the truth and who did not. No, I'm not going to summarize the evidence again," I went on, looking across at the counsel table. "The truth of it is, I'm almost embarrassed to stand up again after what we've just heard from Mr. Jones. It seems somehow unfair. I shouldn't be able to address the jury twice," I said earnestly. "He should. I'm not the prosecutor in this case, he is. He's not defending a client charged with the murder of his wife, he's accusing everyone else involved in this case with a conspiracy to 'murder' his client."

My eye stayed a moment longer on Richard Lee Jones, and then, turning away, I paced back and forth in front of the jury.

Repeating each allegation he had made, I offered the same rebutal, tedious and infallible: There was not a scintilla of evidence to support anything he had said.

"But of course," I reminded them, with a sidelong glance at Jones, "that only proves his point, doesn't it? What better demonstration that a conspiracy—those powerful political enemies—is behind everything that's happened than the very fact that there's no evidence that it ever existed?

"Well, that isn't quite right, is it?" I asked, searching the eyes of the jury. "Mr. Jones did not just accuse unnamed political enemies, he also accused the prosecution. And he did more than just name me, he told you what I had done to further the ends of this conspiracy. He told you I had threatened a witness with prison if she didn't change her testimony, change it in a way that would be helpful to the prosecution and damaging to the defense."

Pausing, I pivoted a half step back and faced Richard Lee Jones.

"Let me say this just once. Kristin Maxfield was not threatened with anything, and the only thing I ever asked her to do was to tell the truth."

I turned back to the jury.

"What does it all come down to? The defense insists she was lying when she told you that she delivered the sealed envelope to Travis Quentin; lying when she told you that she first had sex with Marshall Goodwin the night his wife was being murdered and then again the day his wife was buried; lying when she said he confessed to the hired murder of Nancy Goodwin. And what is the best reason they can give you to explain why she decided to lie? Because I threatened her with prison. For what? If none of it happened, what could she have been sent to prison for?"

I began to walk away and then stopped and turned around.

"Mr. Jones told you in his closing argument that all you really have to decide in this case is whether you should believe someone like Travis Quentin or someone like Marshall Goodwin."

One at a time I looked at them, twelve ordinary people summoned to decide if someone else should live or die.

"There really isn't that much difference between them, is there? They were both willing to kill to get what they wanted. Travis Quentin got his freedom and ten thousand dollars. Marshall Goodwin got Kristin Maxfield and a million dollars. I'll bet not even Richard Lee Jones would try to tell you it was worth it."

| xvii

LATE THE NEXT MORNING, THE CASE WENT TO THE JURY. With nothing left to do but wait, I took the elevator two floors down and, as quietly as I could, slipped into the back row of Horace Woolner's courtroom, the only observer of what appeared to be a routine request for attorney's fees.

"The contract plainly states that, should a dispute arise between the parties, the losing side must pay the reasonable attorney's fees of the other side, your honor," a young sallow-faced lawyer explained.

Horace rolled his head toward the other lawyer and waited.

A paunchy, round-shouldered man, the shiny elbows on the sleeves of his tight-fitting dark-blue suit coat betrayed the dismal career of a sole practitioner forced to take whatever case he could get.

"That's just the point, your honor," he replied. "It says *reasonable* attorney's fees."

Horace moved his eyes from one side to the other.

"These *are* reasonable attorney's fees," the younger, expensively dressed lawyer insisted. "A complete account of the time records kept in this case has been supplied to the court."

His eyes still hooded, Horace rested his elbows on

the bench and scowled. "This case was settled out of court, wasn't it?"

"Yes, your honor," he answered proudly.

Horace ran his left thumb up along the rough-edged side of the voluminous court file. "There's enough in here to write a textbook on civil procedure."

"I tried to be thorough, your honor," he said.

Lifting up the file cover, Horace withdrew a two-page document that was on top. "Yet the whole thing started with this, a simple page-and-a-half complaint in which Mr. Barkley there"—he gave a quick nod toward the older attorney—"filed an action for breach of contract on behalf of his client."

Folding the first page over the second, Horace went on, "Now, I'd like to point out that right at the very end the plaintiff asks for damages in the amount of seven thousand two hundred and fifty dollars."

"Yes, but—"

"And the first thing you do," Horace continued, extracting another document from the folder, "is file a counterclaim in which *your* client alleges damages in the amount of one hundred thousand dollars. And then you proceed to file motion after motion, until finally the plaintiff can't afford to pursue it. Instead of his day in court, what he gets is a chance to buy himself out of any more expenses. And *now* you come in here and submit a bill for attorney's fees for thirty-six thousand four hundred and fifty dollars!"

Horace was as angry as I had ever seen him.

"Well, you'll get your attorney's fees. One hundred dollars. That's the amount I consider reasonable. And let me tell you one other thing. You want to practice law like some game where the side with the most money wins? Try it again, and I'll see you're brought up on charges. Now, get out of my courtroom!" And Horace lurched to his feet and stalked out of court.

I went around the other way and entered his chambers unannounced. He was standing next to the coat rack, tugging at the clasp that held his robe together. It would not come undone, and he clamped his thick fingers around it and pulled down as hard as he could, ripping it off. Grabbing the first book on the shelf nearest him, he sent it sailing across the room. Glancing off the top of his desk, the book hit the wall and fell, face down, pages bent, on the floor.

"What are you doing here?" he demanded.

"Horace, what the hell is wrong with you?" I asked, alarmed.

"Goddamn lawyers."

The stacks of files and documents, usually organized in the rigorous arrangement required by his insistence on perfect order, had been scattered all over the desk and onto the floor. He did not seem to notice, or, if he did, he did not care.

He started to sit down, changed his mind, and laid his right hand heavily on the near corner of the chair.

"You think you can just walk in here whenever you feel like it?" he snapped.

"My mistake. It won't happen again." I turned on my heel and headed for the door.

"Don't go. I didn't mean it," he called after me.

I let go of the handle and swung around. Horace had sunk into the chair.

"It hasn't been a good day," he said, by way of apology.

Warily, I sat down, holding my briefcase in my lap.

"I'm sorry, Joe," he said softly.

"I saw what you did in there," I said. "What's going on, Horace?"

"He deserved what he got. Guys like him have never done anything in their lives. They go to college, they go to law school, they join some downtown firm so they can lease their new cars and buy their new houses. They live their little lives and never think twice about anything except how they can make more money this year than they did last. The hell with them," he whispered. "The hell with them all."

Abruptly, he pushed himself up and walked in purposeful strides across the room to the coat rack. He bent down, picked up the crumpled black robe, shook it out with one hand, and draped it over one of the brass hooks. From another hook, he retrieved his suit coat and struggled into it.

"You want to walk out with me?" he asked. "I've got a meeting."

We walked in silence through the corridor and rode the crowded elevator down to the ground floor without exchanging a word. Outside the courthouse we said a brief good-bye.

Horace had followed every detail of the murder trial of Marshall Goodwin. He knew the case was going to the jury this morning, and he had not asked a single question about it.

WHAT HORACE HAD NOT ASKED, HELEN COULD NOT wait to answer.

"Jury will be back before three," she said, as soon as I shut the office door behind me. She said it the way she said most things, with absolute assurance, as if she had inside knowledge.

She fluttered all around me while I got a cola from the small refrigerator and walked through the open doorway to my desk. As I pulled one arm out of my suit coat, I felt her take it by the shoulder and then help me out of the other sleeve. I fell into the chair and looked up at her.

Carefully folding the jacket down the middle, she laid it over the arm of one of the two wingback chairs in front of the desk and sat down in the other.

"I haven't said this before," she began, looking at me from under long pointed lashes, each one of them coated black. "But this was a lot of trouble to go to if you're going to be a one-case lawyer." With a wave of her hand she encompassed the things she had done to transform a vacant suite into a functioning office.

"What's the matter? Don't you think they'll give you your old job back at the firm?" I asked.

She cocked her head. "Thanks, but if I want to be dead, I'll do it myself."

"Did you really think I'd ask you to leave your job if I wasn't sure I was going to do this for good?"

She lowered her eyes, slightly embarrassed. "I knew you wouldn't do that," she replied, fidgeting. "I just wanted to be sure." She looked up. "So where are all the clients?"

"What kind do you think we should have? I've been thinking maybe we should do something more exciting than criminal law. What do you think about divorce cases?" I tried to look serious.

"Why don't you do both? Defend the people who shoot divorce lawyers." She made it sound like a form of justifiable homicide.

A few minutes before three, the telephone rang. "I told you so," Helen said, without looking up, as I passed her desk on my way out the door.

There was a verdict. Before the hour was out I would know whether the jury had decided that Marshall Goodwin was guilty or whether I had failed to make a strong enough case and he would walk out, a free man.

The stifling heat had passed. Everyone outside on the sidewalks walked easily now, under the clean light of the sun, breathing in the first nostalgic hint of autumn.

I took my chair at the counsel table and waited. There was not a single place left to sit anywhere in the courtroom. The door behind the bench swung open, and Judge Holloway appeared.

Lowering herself into the tall leather chair, she rested her arms on the bench and folded her hands together.

"Bring in the jury," she said firmly, looking straight ahead.

As if he could have an effect on them even now, Richard Lee Jones sat straight up and stared at each juror as they filed into the box.

The motorcycle mechanic had been chosen foreman. He held the verdict in his hand.

Following the time-honored practice, Judge Holloway inquired, "Has the jury reached a verdict?"

"Yes, we have, your honor."

The clerk moved across the front of the courtroom.

"Would you hand the verdict to the clerk, please?"

The paper was brought back to the judge, who read it with as little expression as she might have perused an article in the newspaper. She handed it back to the clerk.

"The clerk will please read the verdict."

Out of the corner of my eye, I studied the reaction of Marshall Goodwin as he waited a last few agonizing seconds while the clerk cleared her throat and began to read. He had a lost look in his eyes, the look someone gets when they abandon hope. It was close to what I imagined

Nancy Goodwin must have felt when she waited for the knife. I turned away and watched the mouth of the clerk pronounce the last few words of the verdict.

Evenly and without emotion, her eyes moving left to right and back again, she read the word *guilty* and then took a half step back.

Beating her gavel, Irma Holloway quieted the crowd. "Sentencing will be in thirty days," she announced.

It was over. There was nothing more to do except gather up my belongings and run the gauntlet of reporters waiting outside. When I turned to go, there were only a few stragglers left in the courtroom.

"Mr. Antonelli," said a distinguished-looking man in his early sixties. He was standing next to the gate at the railing, waiting for me.

"Yes?"

He extended his hand. "I just wanted to thank you. I'm Thomas Redfield, Nancy's father."

"It's a pleasure to meet you, Mr. Redfield. I wish it could have been under different circumstances."

His handshake was strong and firm. He placed his other hand on my shoulder.

"If it hadn't been for you, he would have gotten away with it. If there is ever anything I can do for you . . ." His hand slipped off my shoulder and he let go of my grasp. Without another word he turned away.

Somewhere in one of the Platonic dialogues Leopold Rifkin first told me about is the argument that it is better to suffer injustice than to commit it. Watching Nancy Goodwin's father walk out of the courtroom, I had a hard time believing it was a choice anyone should ever have to make.

In the corridor I stood under the television lights, surrounded by a mob of reporters.

"How does it feel to beat Richard Lee Jones?" some-one shouted from the back.

"No one who has the good fortune of having Mr. Jones as his attorney can ever complain they did not receive a fair trial. He's one of the best defense attorneys I've ever seen."

Harper Bryce was waiting for me on the courthouse steps. "That was pretty damn shrewd, Antonelli," he remarked.

I kept on walking. "The case is over, Harper. There isn't anything more I can tell you, on or off the record."

On cool days, he had no trouble keeping up. "Two sentences, and you put Jones in the position of having to explain how his client didn't get a fair trial when he had him as his lawyer and then you give him that back-handed compliment about being 'one of the best.' That'll just kill him when he hears it."

"You don't think he's one of the best?"

"That's not the point."

"What is the point, Harper?" I asked, walking briskly.

"You know damn well what the point is. Jones doesn't think he's *one* of the best. He thinks he *is* the best."

"Maybe he is, Harper. He's damn good."

"He lost."

I stopped still and looked at him. "That's the mistake everybody makes. The verdict doesn't decide how well you've done your job. If we had changed sides—if I'd defended and he'd prosecuted—do you think the verdict would have been different?"

For a moment, he said nothing, the loose folds around his eyes wrinkling up as he studied me. Nodding slowly, he said quietly, "Yes, actually, I do."

I started walking again, Bryce right alongside.

"There is something I wanted to ask you about. Could we talk for a few minutes?"

Helen leaped up as soon as she saw the columnist behind me. "Hello, Mr. Bryce," she said, flashing an almost girlish smile.

"Aren't you going to ask what the verdict was?" I inquired when, of her own volition, she brought two cups of coffee into my office.

"Guilty," she said nonchalantly as she left, shutting the door behind her.

Cradling the cup in his soft, pudgy hands, Bryce asked, "How did she know that?"

"Who knows?" I shrugged. "She can always tell as soon as she sees me. . . . There was a question you wanted to ask?" I reminded him.

"Kristin Maxfield. What is going to be done about her?"

I smiled back. "Do you think something needs to be done?"

"You may have forgotten, but the first time we talked—our first off-the-record conversation—I distinctly remember you said that Marshall Goodwin had not acted alone. In fact, I remember putting something like that in the paper." He bent closer. "I hope you weren't just using me."

"How could you possibly think a thing like that?"

"What are you going to do?"

"Nothing."

He put down his cup. "Nothing? You don't think she was in on it from the beginning? That she knew what was inside when she took that envelope to Quentin?"

"I'm going to tell you something—off the record," I said seriously. "I don't know if she knew what was inside that envelope or not, and I certainly don't know if she played any part in planning the murder. Maybe she was telling the truth. Maybe she didn't know anything about it. All I know is that without her testimony Goodwin could never have been convicted, and I'm going to give him the chance to get even. I'm going to give him the same offer they gave Quentin. He tells us everything he knows about Kristin, and he gets life instead of the death penalty."

Slowly, Bryce got to his feet. "Whatever happens, it's another great day for journalism. One murder solved, and someone else is murdered."

He seemed surprised I had not heard.

"Not your usual murder, either. One of the most prominent people in town. You must have heard of him. It was the headline in this morning's paper. Russell Gray."

A VAGUE PREMONITION HAD COME OVER ME, WHICH lingered long after Harper Bryce had left. It was still nagging at me that evening when I sat at the desk in the library and opened the volume of Aristotle to the place where I had quit the night before. Only after the third attempt to get through the first paragraph was I able to clear my mind.

I went into the kitchen and turned on the small television on the counter while I made a cup of tea. The weather report was for intermittent showers the rest of the week. The kettle had just started to whistle when the telephone rang. Harper Bryce apologized for calling so late.

"I just wanted to be sure about this story. I'm assuming you'll be representing her, right?"

Cradling the phone, I turned off the burner and poured water over the teabag in the cup.

"I don't know what you're talking about, Harper. I'm not representing anybody."

There was an awkward silence at the other end.

"Who am I supposed to be representing?"

Harper cleared his throat. "Alma Woolner. She's been charged with the murder of Russell Gray."

|xviii

THE BLINDS WERE CLOSED, THE WINDOW A SILHOUETTE of thin striped light.

"Why didn't you call me?"

Horace stared at me and said nothing.

"I tried to reach you for more than an hour last night, until sometime after midnight, but you never answered."

Still nothing.

"I came here first thing this morning. I waited outside for more than an hour, until you got here." I bent closer, until my hand was touching the edge of the desk. "I know how awful this must be for you, but you have to talk to me."

"There's nothing you can do," he said finally.

"Of course there is," I said impatiently. "Alma needs a lawyer."

He nodded his head. "I'll find her a lawyer."

"You don't want me to help?"

"I can take care of Alma," he said, resolute.

"You can't defend her," I retorted, glaring back at him. "And unless you want to find someone who can do it better, I can."

He looked down at the wrinkled black skin on his oversize knuckles. "I have to take care of this myself," he muttered. "I can't ask you to get involved. You're too close."

"I can treat Alma the same way as someone who just walked in the door."

It was a serviceable lie, and we both knew it. His shoulders hunched forward, Horace drew his eyebrows together and studied me.

"I've always thought one of the reasons we became friends is that you never ask me about myself unless it's something I bring up myself," he said. "How much do you really know about Alma and me? You may find out things aren't all what you thought they were."

Horace was right. Neither one of us talked much about the things we had done or the things we had felt. That was another generation, a younger one, which wanted to share everything and did not yet have any secrets they needed to hide. But nothing in any of the contingent details of Horace's past history or his everyday life could change the two most important things worth knowing about anyone: I knew I could trust him, and I knew that neither he nor Alma could do anything wrong. In that respect, I was more certain of him than I was of myself.

"Unless you can look me in the eye and tell me you believe Alma would be better off with another attorney," I said, as I stood, "I'm taking the case."

I looked at Horace, sitting on the other side of the shaft of light given off by the reading lamp, and the longer I looked at him, the farther away he seemed to be. I wondered what was waiting for us, Horace and Alma and me, on the other side of the nightmare that was already changing the way we thought about one another.

From Horace Woolner's chambers, I went directly to

the DA's office. Advising the receptionist that I was representing Alma Woolner, I asked to see whoever was in charge of the case. A few minutes later, Gilliland-O'Rourke appeared.

"I thought I'd be hearing from you today," she said. Dressed in a black pinstripe suit and a white blouse, every inch the professional woman, she held open the door to her office and waited for me to go in.

"You're going to prosecute this yourself?"

"Don't look so surprised."

"I'm not surprised," I replied. "Just disappointed."

She swept past me and settled into the cushioned high-backed chair behind her writing desk.

"Who are you to be disappointed in me?" she demanded.

"It's the second time, Gwendolyn. First Leopold, now Horace."

"Horace isn't charged with anything. It's his wife." She fixed me with a steady gaze. "You're out of line saying something like that to me. I know you're friends, so I'm going to let it go, but I'm warning you, I've just about had it."

I forced myself to be civil. "You know Alma. You've met her. If there's anybody who isn't capable of murder, it's Alma."

"I didn't think Marshall was capable of murder," she interjected.

"No, you didn't think he'd run the risk," I reminded her. "Alma *couldn't* hurt anyone."

"Would you like to know why she was arrested?" she asked, with aggravating indifference. "Or would you rather just assume that I made the whole thing up?"

She dragged a polished nail back and forth across the hard shiny surface of the table.

"You should never have agreed to prosecute the case against Marshall."

"You don't think he was guilty?" I shot back.

"That's not the point. The point is, you didn't know. I watched part of that trial. You haven't lost a thing. You're still the best lawyer I've ever seen, the best at winning. But that's also your weakness. You wouldn't last a day in politics. You can only see one side of things."

"That's what I'm supposed to do."

"All you could see was the way the evidence proved what you wanted it to," she went on, ignoring me. "Marshall was supposed to be guilty, and everything followed from that, didn't it?"

My hand on the arm of the chair, I sat straight up.

" '*Supposed* to be guilty'?"

Raising her chin, she studied me a moment, her hands resting in her lap.

"Did you ever consider the possibility that Kristin knew what was inside that envelope she delivered to Quentin?"

"Of course."

Her chin came up just a little higher.

"Did you ever consider the possibility that she knew what was inside it because she put it there herself?"

It hit me like the news of my own imminent death. I could think of nothing to say. All the wretched soul-searching I had done at the beginning had counted for nothing once I walked into court and started the trial. I had to win, and that meant Marshall Goodwin had to be guilty. Even now, after it was over, I did not want to admit that I might have been wrong.

"Are you suggesting that Goodwin didn't know anything about it? That she acted alone?" I asked. "He was the one who had the conversation with Quentin. He was the one who dropped the charges," I said, trying to sound more confident than I felt.

She laughed at me. "Maybe the search was bad. Maybe Marshall decided to have a little fun with him before he dismissed the charges. Marshall does things like that. Or maybe he really did talk to him to see if he could use him as a witness in that drug case. He talked to a lot of people about that."

She went on, waving her hand in front of her. "Marshall loves to talk about himself, and Kristin, who was practically his deputy, was always willing to listen." Her eyes sparkled with malice. "He would have told her the whole thing, especially the part about Quentin asking who he had to kill."

I felt like someone on trial listening to a witness destroy the only alibi he had.

"What about the money?" I asked, forcing myself not to look away.

"Maybe it was just the way he said it was. Maybe he took it out to invest it. Kristin wouldn't have had any trouble coming up with the same amount."

The only thing I could do was turn it back on her. "Do you think that's what happened?"

She shook her head. "I don't know. The point is, it could have."

For the first time in my life I was face-to-face with the question that everyone liked to ask and no one really wanted to answer: What was it like to convict an innocent man?

Arching her eyebrows, Gwendolyn fixed me with a dismissive stare. "You won. Isn't that all you've ever wanted?"

She bent forward at the waist, her back still straight.

"Now, about Alma Woolner. Russell Gray was murdered, and her fingerprints are all over the gun. With that kind of evidence, we have to prosecute, and you know it."

I tried to appear indifferent. "So her fingerprints are on the gun. It might help if she had a motive."

"She was having an affair with him," Gwendolyn replied.

"That's a lie," I said automatically.

"Why?" she asked, her eyes flashing. "Because Alma Woolner couldn't do a thing like that?"

The question faded away, unanswered, a silent reminder of the long afternoons Gwendolyn and I had once spent, when we were both much younger, in lonely out-of-the-way motels.

"Even if they were having an affair," I said finally, "that's not a motive."

"It is if he wanted to break it off and she didn't."

"She didn't do it," I insisted, as I rose from the chair.

Instead of a reply, Gwendolyn picked up the telephone. "What time is the arraignment?" She held her hand over the receiver. "Can you be in court at one o'clock?"

"Of course."

"That will work," she said into the phone, and hung up. "As a favor to Horace, I'll do what I can to keep this out of the hands of the media."

For Gwendolyn, a favor did not count unless you got credit for it.

"I'll see you in court at one," I said.

The district attorney was as good as her word. Every reporter and news organization that called to find out when Horace Woolner's wife was going to be arraigned for the murder of Russell Gray was told the same thing:

Arraignments were scheduled by the court. No one bothered to ask whether, given that unremarkable fact of criminal procedure, the arraignment had already been scheduled. Instead, the caller would hang up and call the court, but there were lots of courtrooms and lots of clerks, and, even if they were sitting at their desks eating lunch, no one answered telephones between the hours of twelve and one.

Harper Bryce did not bother to call anyone. Wearing a different suit, but the same tie he had on the day before, he waited outside the entrance to the courthouse and, when he saw me coming, held open the door.

"What do you know about Russell Gray?" I asked, as we walked together toward the elevator. I moved slowly, keeping to his normal pace.

"You mean off the record?"

We stood waiting for the elevator to arrive. At a quarter to one, the hallways were still largely deserted.

"Actually, I know quite a good deal about the unfortunate Russell Gray," he said, once we were alone inside the elevator. "How much do you know about Alma Woolner?"

I threw him a warning look. "Not even off the record."

"Lawyer–client privilege. I understand. Fair enough." He looked straight ahead, staring at the elevator door. "Russell Gray liked women. A lot." Without moving his shoulders, he turned his head until he was looking at me. "Don't be surprised if one of the women he liked was your client."

"Do you know that?"

"Let's just say that Russell Gray wasn't the kind of man I'd trust my wife with, if I had a wife," he added.

"Or my husband, either, if I was the sort of fellow who had one of those."

"He was interested in men too?" I asked, not entirely surprised.

The elevator stopped and the door slid open.

Bryce shrugged. "Russell Gray was a man who believed in pleasure. From what I've heard, he took his pleasure where he found it. Sometimes he found it with women; sometimes he found it with young men." Casting an ominous glance, he added, "Very young."

"How young?" I asked, as we walked toward the courtroom of Judge William West.

Bryce rolled his eyes. "As I say, wherever he could find it."

We stopped outside the courtroom door. Bryce inspected the empty corridor. "I wonder why I'm the only one here."

"All the others must still be at lunch."

There was no one inside, and I sat alone at the small blond table just inside the bar, thinking about what Harper had told me and what it eventually might mean for the case. I sat back, crossed my ankle over my knee, and pulled up my sock. I checked my watch. Three minutes before the hour. If you listened hard you could hear the only sound in the room, a dim distant whirring of the air filtration system coming from somewhere in the ceiling. My stomach made a slight noise, and I remembered I had had nothing to eat since the night before. Nothing to eat and hardly any sleep, staring out the bedroom window, worried whether I would go mad trying to keep thoughts of what I might have done to Marshall Goodwin separate from thoughts of what I had to do for Alma Woolner. The words of Gwendolyn

Gilliland-O'Rourke had played in my head until I feared I might never be able to think about anything else again.

At one o'clock the court clerk burst in from the side of what was one of the largest courtrooms in the building. Following a few feet behind her, William West, trim and fit, with a quick athletic step, took his place on the bench. Gwendolyn Gilliland-O'Rourke materialized at the counsel table a short distance from where I had scrambled to my feet.

With his dark expressive eyes and angular face, West had the brooding aspect of a poet. He looked directly at Gilliland-O'Rourke.

"Are we ready?"

"Should be any minute," she said, and glanced down at a thin file folder she had placed on the table in front of her.

"Nice to see you, Mr. Antonelli," he said, in a calm, relaxed voice.

"Your honor," I acknowledged.

Looking around, I saw Harper sitting quietly in the last row, a reporter's notebook, the cover thrown open, balanced on his knee.

Dressed in the dark-blue cotton jail uniform, Alma looked like a little girl in her mother's clothes. The V-neck top slipped sideways over one shoulder. Pulled as tight as they would go, the bunched drawstring trousers dragged along the floor. The jailer carried the handcuffs that should have been on her wrists.

Brought to the counsel table, she waited until the guard moved away. Then she took my arm in her hand and rose up on her tiptoes until her mouth was next to my ear. "Where's Horace?"

"I'm going to represent you," I said.

"He said he'd be here," she said, tightening her grip on my arm.

Before I could say anything, Gilliland-O'Rourke began the formal arraignment. She was willing to mislead the press, but that was the only concession she would make. Alma Woolner was a defendant in a murder case, no different from anyone else charged with a serious crime. The state opposed a conditional release.

I argued what seemed obvious, that Alma had long-standing ties to the community, was not a flight risk, and was certainly not a threat to anyone.

Standing next to me, her shoulder rubbing against my arm, Alma stared down at the table, a startled expression on her face, as if it had just occurred to her that she was in the middle of something serious. Nodding to himself, West had reached his decision.

"Bail will be set in the amount of one hundred thousand dollars."

Neither Gilliland-O'Rourke nor I had anything else for the court. West rose from the bench, hesitated, looked at Alma as if he wanted to say something, and then, deciding against it, gave her a brief smile of encouragement and walked quickly out of the courtroom.

I caught a glimpse of Horace standing next to the double doors that led to the corridor outside. His arms were folded in front of him and his chin was on his chest. He was looking right at me, but his eyes were full of some private meditation.

"There's Horace," I said.

Alma looked up. "Where?"

He was gone, the only sign a slight shudder of the door as the handle clicked back into place.

Outside in the corridor, a half dozen reporters and a television cameraman were moving at a quick trot toward the door. I left Gilliland-O'Rourke to deal with them while I went in the opposite direction, hoping to catch up with Horace.

I found him in his chambers, next to the coat rack, slipping out of his suit coat and putting on his robe.

"Bail is set at a hundred thousand," I said, catching my breath. "You can get her out in a couple of hours."

"I can't," he said, his eyes tense, expectant.

"What do you mean, you can't?"

"I don't have a hundred thousand dollars," he explained.

"Well, if you don't have it, Horace, go get it," I told him. "Go to the goddamn bank, get a loan, take out a second mortgage, do whatever the hell you have to do. Just get it!"

He shook his head. "I can't do that, either."

"You can't—or you won't?"

"I can't. I'm already mortgaged up to my neck. I couldn't borrow ten cents if my life depended on it."

"I'm sorry, Horace," I said. "I didn't know. It's all right, I'll take care of it. She'll be home tonight."

"I'll handle it," he insisted. "It'll take a few days, that's all."

"You can pay me back when you have it."

Something ominous entered his eyes. "I appreciate what you're trying to do," he said slowly, as if he had to force himself to speak the words. "I'll have her out in a couple of days." He put his hand on the door, ready to go into court.

"Don't worry about it, Horace," I said, trying to give him some assurance that things would work out. "I'll have her out this evening."

"Listen to me," he hissed. "She got herself into this. Let her sit in jail for a few days and think about it."

The door slammed shut behind him, and I was left alone in the dimly lit room, wondering if he believed his wife capable of murder.

ALMA WOOLNER WAS OUT OF CUSTODY BY THE END OF
the day. Horace had found a way to cover bail.

"She didn't do it, Joe. She didn't do anything," he
said, as if it were the first time we had talked about it.

"I need to talk to her, Horace. As soon as possible."

"Tomorrow soon enough? I gave her a sleeping pill
and put her to bed."

"Can you bring her down to the office?"

He hesitated. "I thought it might be good to get out
of here for a while. I thought we'd take a drive up the
gorge. Why don't you come along? There'll be plenty of
time to talk."

The next morning, with Alma at the wheel, the three
of us left the city behind and drove east along the river,
following it as it broadened out, gradually covering
everything between the dark wooded high-walled
plateaus on each side of the Columbia Gorge. On the
other side of the Cascades, where the river moved
through the high desert, you were in one of those places
where you begin to think that God must have became
bored creating the world and repeated himself to get it
over with.

We drove deep into the gorge, following the straight
line of the road, parallel to the narrow railroad tracks.

Above us, a shallow stream plummeted over a cliff and fell like a silver thread to a pool more than three hundred feet below.

Horace sat in the back, one long leg stretched stiffly out across the seat, and Alma kept her attention focused on the road. Conversation was brief, an awkward self-conscious intrusion into the silence.

Alma pulled into the parking lot at the waterfall. Passing a long line of tourist buses, we walked across to the visitors center and down the rough stone steps to the railing that ran around the pool at the bottom of the waterfall. Spray filled the air around us and a fine mist settled on our faces.

We bought coffee from the concession stand and found a place to sit at the far end of an empty table on a rock-walled landing with a view of the falls. In the branches of a fir tree just above us, a hummingbird, buoyed on whirring wings, waited motionless in midair and then darted away.

"We haven't been here in a long time," said Horace, as he lifted the paper cup to his mouth.

"It's funny how that happens," I replied, though the remark had not been addressed to me. "You live somewhere and you never really spend that much time looking around. I haven't been up to the lodge at Mount Hood since I was a kid."

Alma looked at me, curious. "Why not?"

Whenever she asked me a question, I felt struck by the urge to say something interesting, something she had not heard before.

"Maybe it's because some things should only be seen from a distance. Maybe it's just a matter of perspective."

Her eyes, always sympathetic, watched me a moment

longer. "Is that the reason you haven't married? Because the absence of distance might spoil the effect?"

I glanced at Horace, but his eyes were on the waterfall.

"No," I said, turning back to Alma. "I just never met the right woman."

Her eyes never left me. "Yes you did," she insisted.

"The Alexandra I knew never existed. She pretended to be someone she wasn't."

"We all do that, don't we? Pretend to be something. Isn't that really who we are? Who we pretend to be?"

A shadow slanted across the table between us before I realized Horace was getting up.

"You two need to talk," he announced.

As he moved behind his wife, he laid his hand on her shoulder and then let it go. I watched him descend the stone steps, holding on to a steel banister, placing one foot carefully before he lifted the other. Shoving his hands into his trouser pockets, he joined the crowd that stood at the guardrail, caught in the clean enchantment of the water that had been falling for thousands of years.

"We used to come out here a lot," Alma remarked, watching my eyes follow Horace. "When we first came here, Horace loved this place. It was like therapy for him. It helped him forget."

Down below, Horace rested his arm on the railing, spread his feet wide apart, and stared into the shallow rock-bottomed pool.

"Forget?" I asked, my eyes coming back to her.

"Not forget, really," she said, trying to explain. "Helped him realize it was good to be alive. He was still very bitter, back then, about the war and what had happened to him."

She looked at me in a way that made me feel as if she were older than I.

"He was drafted a week after he graduated from law school. How many twenty-five-year-olds do you think got drafted?" she asked, an edge to her voice. "And do you think they put him in the adjutant's office? No, they put him in the infantry."

She glanced away, searching until she found Horace, as if she had to be sure he was safe.

"When his legs were blown off," she went on, looking at me again, "they called him a hero and gave him a medal, and they all felt proud—not so much of Horace, they didn't even know him—but of themselves. It made them proud of what a great country this was. Horace proved everything they wanted to believe about themselves. He proved this wasn't a racist country, because if it was, why would he have saved those white boys when he knew he might die doing it?"

"Then why did he do it?" I asked.

"Horace never talks about it," she said, looking away. "There was an attack, late at night, out in the middle of the jungle, and they were surrounded. Horace's unit fought its way out, but a lot of them didn't make it. Horace wanted to go back for the wounded, but no one else dared. So Horace went back by himself and brought them out, one at a time. He was shot in the shoulder when he brought the first one back, and shot in the arm when he brought in the second. They were still too scared to help him, so he went back the third time and got another one out. He was going back for a fourth when the grenade came. Even after that no one came to help. They let him lie there, not more than a hundred feet away, convincing themselves he was already dead."

She took a deep breath. "You want to know why he did it? Because he was black, and he had to prove he was better than they were."

"I don't believe that, Alma," I said quietly. "I think Horace did it because he *was* better than they were."

There was something in her eyes, but whether it was a reflection of the anger buried deep inside her over what had happened to her husband or the first sign of the terror she must have felt about her own impending ordeal, I could not tell. Reaching across the table, I grasped her arm.

"We don't have to talk about this today," I said, trying to ease her into the conversation we had to have. "But if you feel you're up to it, why don't you just tell me what you know about this. We have to figure out how your fingerprints got on that gun."

She pressed her lips together, as if she were thinking about something, and then, a moment later, pulled them back into a wistful, almost rueful expression.

"Horace told me I should tell you the truth."

Until she said it, it had not occurred to me that she was capable of telling me anything else.

"I was there the night Russell was murdered."

"You were at the house?" I asked, wondering whether I had heard her right. "But Horace told me you were home with him that night."

"It was the first thing he could think of. He wanted to protect me."

It was getting warm. Taking off my windbreaker, I draped it over the bench. Down below, Horace stood against the guardrail, his back to the falls, taking the late-morning sun full in the face.

"Start from the beginning," I told Alma. "What were you doing at Russell Gray's house that night?"

"We had a board meeting there for the ballet company. Not the whole board, the executive committee. There were seven of us, counting Russell and myself."

"What time did it start?"

"Eight o'clock. By the time everyone got there, it was probably eight-fifteen."

"Why did you meet at his place?"

"Russell was the chairman of the board and he always offered," she explained. "His house is beautiful, up in the west hills with a wonderful view of the city and Mount Hood. You used to live up there; you know what it's like."

"What time did the meeting end?" I asked.

I was not sure she was listening. Her gaze drifted away, out toward the trees that covered the hillside and above them, to the soft white clouds that were scattered across the sky.

Quietly, I asked her again. She looked at me and blinked, as if trying to remember what we had been talking about.

"Ten-thirty or eleven," she said. "I stayed a while longer. There were some things we had to discuss."

"What happened after everyone else left?"

"I was there for about an hour. I was just getting ready to leave. It must have been close to midnight. I was in the bathroom when I heard it."

"The shot?" I watched her as she stared straight ahead, living it over again in her mind.

"I don't know *how* I could have heard it," she said, strangely detached. "The bathroom is enormous. The door must be two inches thick."

"Are you sure you heard it?" I asked, trying to keep her attention on what we had to talk about.

"I wonder if I did? Maybe I just felt it, but somehow

I knew it. Anyway, I found him in the living room, where I'd left him. He was on his stomach, in the middle of a Persian rug, his face turned to the side. His eyes were wide open. I saw the blood underneath him. Then I saw the gun, lying a few feet away. Everything was so still. I could hear my own breath when I knelt down next to him. I kept expecting him to move, say something."

She did not have to tell me what she did next. "Why did you pick up the damn gun?" I asked, suddenly angry that she should have done something so stupid.

Her eyes were filled with a puzzling intensity. "I don't know. I hate guns. Maybe that was the reason. I'd never been close enough to touch one before. And there it was lying there, something that had just brought death to someone I knew, someone I cared about. Whatever the reason," she said, lowering her gaze, "I picked it up and looked at it."

As she clutched the near-empty paper cup, a shudder ran through her. She raised her eyes and looked directly at me.

"When I became aware of what I was doing, I dropped the gun on the floor and ran out as fast as I could. I panicked. I should have called the police, but all I could think about was getting as far away as I could."

She seemed haunted by what she had done. Her eyes stayed fixed on mine, but she was looking right through me.

"Where did you go?" I asked.

"When?" she asked blankly.

"When you dropped the gun and ran out of the house."

"I went home."

"Straight home? You didn't stop anywhere?"

"No," she insisted, with a trace of annoyance. "I didn't stop anywhere."

"When you got home, was Horace still awake?"

"Horace wasn't there. He has dinner with some of the other judges once a month."

I was more interested in something else. "Go back to the gunshot. Try to think. Did you hear it, or didn't you?"

She cocked her head. "I must have."

"Did you wait in the bathroom until you thought it was safe, or did you run out immediately to see what had happened?"

She hesitated. "I'm not sure. I think I opened the door a crack and listened and then went out to the living room."

"And what did you hear?"

"Nothing. So I left the bathroom and went to the living room."

"Nothing?" I asked, watching her intently. "You heard nothing at all? You hear a gunshot, you open the door, and you hear nothing at all?"

"No."

"You didn't hear the sound of footsteps running away, of a door slamming shut, the kind of noise someone trying to get away in a hurry would have made? You heard nothing?" I asked.

She reached across with her hand and took hold of my wrist.

"Joe, it's me, Alma. Everything that happened is all mixed up. I don't remember hearing anything. I'm not absolutely sure I even heard the shot. But I must have. I think I did."

Her hand tightened around my wrist.

"Joe, I didn't do it," she said. "I'm telling you the truth. You do believe me, don't you?"

I slid my wrist away from her hand and straddled the hard bench, my side to the table, staring out at the steep hillside, watching the light climb toward the summit as the sun kept moving west.

"Tell me about Russell Gray. What was he like?"

"He was fascinating."

With my knuckles, I beat out a hollow rhythm on the bench between my legs. The surface was rough, irregular, and badly in need of paint. I remembered Russell Gray—charming, urbane, and, I suspected, literate and superficial.

"He loved the arts," I heard her saying, in the low, somber tones of a eulogist. "He went to London every year for the theater and to New York for the ballet." The sun hit the side of her face, adding a luminous glow to her skin.

"Tell me about his personal life. I understand his involvements were not limited to women."

"You really are a moralist, aren't you, Joe? His 'involvements.' " She laughed quietly. "You want to know whether Russell went both ways, don't you? Well, the answer is, one, I don't really know, and, two, I would not be the least bit surprised." With a mocking glance, she added, "It's not all that uncommon, you know."

There was something in her voice, something in the way she looked at me that I did not like. It was condescending, too much the attitude of someone asked to explain the ways of the world to someone else who is never going to be any part of it.

Over her shoulder, I caught a glimpse of Horace. He had taken a seat on a bench on the other side of the walkway. He was sitting erect, both feet on the ground, his eyes open, waiting for whatever was going to happen next.

"And what about you, Alma? Were you part of Russell Gray's sophisticated world?"

"Are you asking me whether I slept with him? Whether I had an affair with him?"

"I have to know everything. If there was anything—anything at all—between you and Russell Gray, I have to know," I said.

"No," she said, "there was nothing going on between us. We were just good friends."

She saw the doubt in my eyes.

"There was no affair. I never slept with Russell Gray."

"Gilliland-O'Rourke says you did," I replied, watching her closely.

She tossed her head back. "People tell stories. There wasn't any truth to them." She glanced over her shoulder to where Horace was still waiting.

"I have to know, Alma. I can't help you unless I know the truth."

Her eyes lit up. "I know," she said brightly, as she sprang to her feet, "let's get Horace and go somewhere else. We have all afternoon."

I watched her move gracefully down the steps and take her husband by the arm. She was lying to me. I wondered if it was because she was hoping Horace would never have to find out.

AUTUMN CAME AND THE NIGHTS GREW LONGER. SIDE-walks were slick with faded yellow leaves. At the northern edge of the city, dark smoke curled up from the black-funneled freighters riding on the murky waters of the Columbia. Winter was more than a month away, and I was already dreaming of spring.

Harper Bryce was not dreaming of anything. He was too busy gathering whatever information he could for his next story. He had just drifted in, unannounced and uninvited, a dripping black umbrella in his hand, obviously in a reflective mood.

"It occurs to me we have something in common, you and I," he said, as he dropped into a chair. "Other than your one-time fling as a prosecutor, you represent people accused of crimes and I report on what happens in those proceedings. We both tell stories about what happened to other people. And that makes us both outsiders, doesn't it? Do you ever wonder what it's like, to sit at that counsel table and listen to you and the lawyer on the other side describe what happened, and you're the only person who really knows? You ever imagine, when you're up there telling a jury that the evidence doesn't even come close to proving the defendant did what he's accused of, that your client is sitting there laughing his head off because he knows he did it? It's kind of a strange business all the way round, isn't it? Clients lie to their lawyers, and lawyers hardly ever tell the whole truth to reporters." His nostrils flared as he drew in a breath, and his chest seemed to sink as he let it out. "Do they?"

"I wouldn't go that far," I replied. "Some clients tell their lawyers the truth."

He laughed appreciatively. "Those must be the ones who plead guilty."

"Not everybody is guilty, Harper. And even when they are, they're not always guilty of the crimes they're charged with."

Making a wry face, he conceded that perhaps only a large majority of people accused of breaking the law were guilty. "There are a few who aren't." He lifted an eyebrow. "I'm even willing to concede that Judge Woolner's wife might be one of them."

"You can count on it," I said firmly.

"I'm just a reporter," he said cagily. "I try not to count too much on anything, especially when it involves murder, and particularly where it might be what they used to call a crime of passion."

I gave him a blank look. "Crime of passion?"

"There are rumors out there, my friend," he said, trying to gauge my reaction.

"There are always rumors when you have a murder trial, Harper. You know that."

"And I know that sometimes rumors are true, and even when they're not they sometimes point to something that is."

Leaning back, I held up my hands in surrender. "All right. What rumors are you talking about?"

"The rumor that the late Russell Gray was having an affair with the accused. Care to comment?"

"I never comment on rumor, and I never comment on a case."

"Off the record."

"Off the record, on the record, doesn't matter. Alma Woolner is innocent, absolutely innocent." But I did not stop there. "It's bad enough she's charged with murder. Now she has to defend herself against charges of infidelity? How the hell do you think this is going to make her husband feel?" I exclaimed angrily.

Harper sat up. "I didn't start it. I just told you about it."

In silent apology, I held up a hand again. "You're right," I said, looking at him.

Hastily, Harper tried to change the subject. "You have two weeks before that case goes to trial. Tomorrow morning you have the sentencing of Marshall Goodwin. What's going to happen?"

"What do the rumors say?" I replied.

"There aren't any rumors." Pausing, he cast a shrewd glance at me. "And there isn't any comment from the other side, either."

"Richard Lee Jones refuses to talk to the press? That's a first."

Harper was amused. "I didn't say he wouldn't talk, I said he wouldn't comment. Actually, he talked a lot. He said Goodwin was innocent, said he was sure he'd eventually win on appeal. What he wouldn't comment on was whether his client was going to turn state's evidence in return for a lesser sentence."

He tugged on his sleeve and wiggled the fingers of his free hand, apparently trying to increase the circulation in his arm. It was a miracle that his heart held out against the burden of that corpulent, undisciplined body.

"I'm afraid I can't comment, either, Harper."

He had been around the courthouse too many years not to know what was going on.

"You made him that offer, and he hasn't made up his mind?"

"What do you think happened, Harper? You were there through the whole trial. You take almost verbatim notes."

He took a deep breath and slowly let it out. "Remember the testimony of her former fiancé? What was his name?"

"Atkinson," I reminded him. "Conrad Atkinson."

"Remember what he said? He was in love with Kristin Maxfield, but she wasn't in love with him. I think that was the reason he was in love with her, and I think that's the reason Goodwin was in love with her," he said.

"All right," I said. "And?"

"They both knew—with a woman like that you'd have to know—that they could never really have her, which made them want her even more, and that made them willing to do whatever they had to do to get her. You could see it on Atkinson's face when he testified, a sense of relief that he'd been saved from his own madness." He paused. "What I'm trying to say is, whether she knew what was inside that envelope or not, she's the reason Goodwin killed his wife."

I tried to make it sound like a casual observation, a chance remark. "What if it was the other way round? What if she knew what was inside the envelope because she put it there herself? What if Goodwin didn't know anything about it?"

Sitting immobile, he stared down at the floor, frowning.

"Are you afraid you convicted the wrong one?" he asked, glancing up.

Looking out the rain-streaked windows, I watched the traffic crawl over the steel bridges. The door in the outer office opened. Helen was back from lunch.

"Tell me something, Harper," I said, locking my fingers together behind my head as I leaned back in the chair. "You must have thought about becoming a lawyer at some point in your life. Why didn't you?"

He snorted. "Legal technicalities would have made me suicidal. Besides, they don't let you in law school if you haven't graduated from college."

"You didn't graduate?"

"I didn't go." His eyes rolled around his head. "And I didn't go because they won't let you in unless you graduate from high school first." He gave a shrug of nostalgia. "I was sixteen years old, a little on the precocious side, certain I knew everything worth knowing. I got a job on a small-town weekly and worked my way up from there. Couldn't do it today. Nobody would take a chance on a kid."

Helen stuck her head inside the door. "Good afternoon, Mr. Bryce," she said, flashing a smile at Harper. "Can I get you anything?"

Harper shook his head. "No, thank you. I need to get going."

"It's no trouble," she assured him.

Reluctantly, he declined again. She turned to go, and then, almost as an afterthought, glanced back and said to me, "Don't forget, you have someone at one-thirty."

With an effort, Harper got up from the chair.

"Thank you for your time, counselor," he remarked. "It's always a pleasure."

As soon as he was gone, I said to Helen, "I didn't know I had a one-thirty appointment."

Holding the door with one hand, she put her other hand on her hip. "You don't. You have a two o'clock at the other end of town. I wasn't sure you'd want Mr. Bryce to know about it."

"Mr. Bryce. You never called any of my clients *mister*."

"Why would I? They were all crooks." She thought of something. "I always called Judge Rifkin *Judge Rifkin*. And," she added soberly, "I always say *Mrs. Woolner*."

THE INVESTMENT BANKING OFFICES OF CONRAD ATKINson occupied the top floor of a high-rise building on the other side of the river. Several pairs of serious men in dark pinstripe suits moved in different directions across the high-ceilinged lobby, engaged in the intense whispered conversations of high finance. A slender brunette rose from behind the reception desk and with an abbreviated smile led me down a windowless corridor to a glass-walled office.

It was Atkinson's firm, and he dressed the way he wanted. I could imagine that he always wore a suit to a business meeting and never to the office. He was dressed instead in a double-breasted blue blazer, with a white button-down oxford shirt and a muted yellow silk tie. He had on a pair of oxblood loafers, not the tasseled ones that lawyers often wore to court but the old-fashioned kind, the penny loafers high school kids used to wear, the kind worn by middle-aged men who had gone to prep school, men who played tennis at places with ivy-covered fences and then cooled off with a gin and tonic in dark paneled rooms where everyone knew each other by their first names and no one had to explain the rules.

Atkinson looked as tanned and well rested as someone on a summer vacation. When I commented on it, he explained that he had just returned from a week in Barbados.

"By the way, congratulations," he said, looking at me from behind his glass-topped desk. He sat with one leg crossed casually across the other, swinging his foot back and forth. "It was good you put away that bastard, Goodwin. Even better that you did it with that baboon, Richard Lee Jones, defending him."

"Jones is good."

"I'm sure he is," Atkinson replied, glancing away.

"You handled yourself well with him," I said, remembering the way Jones had tried to bully him.

With an appreciative nod, he swung around and faced me directly. "What can I do for you, Mr. Antonelli?"

"Russell Gray once told me the two of you were good friends. What can you tell me about him?"

His brownish-blond eyebrows shot up. "We knew each other, that's true, but I couldn't honestly tell you we were good friends. In the first place, when you were dealing with Russell, it wasn't always easy to know what was true and what wasn't. He had a remarkable facility for creating rumors about himself."

Pulling himself away from the desk, Atkinson settled back against the upholstered chair and rested his hands in his lap.

"Russell was a collector."

"A collector?"

"Yes. Art, among other things," he added vaguely. "He probably had the largest private collection in the city. He certainly made that claim. You couldn't have a conversation with him without hearing about his latest acquisition."

He looked down at his hands.

"But there were always rumors," he remarked, raising his eyes. "Rumors that some of the things he had were really nothing more than very good forgeries, and that he knew it. That some of the things he had were unquestionably authentic and enormously valuable, but almost certainly stolen. Russell knew what the rumors were and would never deny any of them."

"Perhaps he couldn't," I suggested.

"I don't believe that," Atkinson said. "I don't think any of the rumors were true at all. I think most of them were started by Russell himself. You see, Mr. Antonelli, I believe he wanted there to be a sense of mystery around him."

"What else did he collect besides art?"

"He liked women," he replied.

"What about men?"

He frowned, not because he regarded the suggestion as unseemly but because, as he explained, he simply did not know.

"That might have been another rumor Russell started about himself. On the other hand," he observed, with studied indifference, "it might have been true."

"What about the women? Was there anyone in particular?"

"No, I don't think so. With Russell, everything was always temporary."

"Did he ever talk about Alma Woolner?" I asked.

His easy affability faded away, and he became serious.

"He thought she was one of the most gifted and talented people he had ever met. And he felt sorry for her."

"He felt sorry for her? Why?"

"Why do you think?" he asked. "She's gorgeous and gifted and so light-skinned that people who meet her think she must be Indian or Egyptian or something else exotic, and look who she married," he explained, his voice trailing off as he refused to put into words the thought he was sure I would understand.

"Yes?" I prompted.

"Let's just say someone who doesn't quite fit in with the kind of people who can really appreciate someone like her."

"And is that because he's a judge who makes less money in a year than most of your friends make in a week, or is it because he walks funny—having your legs blown off will do that to you—or is it just because Horace Woolner is so damn black?"

"That isn't the way I feel," he hastened to assure me. "But there are people, and Russell Gray was one of them, who still have those prejudices."

"Was he having an affair with her?" I asked him point-blank.

It caught him off guard. "I don't know," he said tentatively. "They were together quite a lot. But she ran the ballet company and he was chairman of the board, so there wouldn't have been anything unusual in that."

"There's something else, though, isn't there?"

His arms rested on top of the glass desk and he stared at his two thumbs, pressed tight together. The lines in his forehead deepened.

"It's nothing more than an impression. It just seemed to me that whenever she was around him, she seemed completely consumed by him."

"Do you think Gray was in love with her?"

He threw me a glance that told me I understood nothing at all. "I told you. He was a collector. If he was ever in love with her, it would not have been for very long. But again," he added, "I don't know whether anything ever happened between them or not. And even if it did, I don't see what it could have to do with his murder."

"It could supply a motive," I suggested.

He dismissed it out of hand. "It's easier for me to believe that Kristin was planning a murder with Goodwin while she was living with me than that Alma Woolner had anything to do with the death of Russell Gray."

That reminded me. "Marshall Goodwin is going to be sentenced tomorrow morning," I told him.

"Yes, I know," he replied, treating it as a matter of no importance. "Let me tell you about Kristin. I answered the questions you asked me at trial, but there were other questions you could have asked. I told you I didn't think she was in love with me. I didn't tell you that my lawyer insisted she sign a prenuptial agreement—and she refused."

He stroked his chin, lost for a moment in his thoughts.

"She didn't do too badly as it was," he observed, a wry expression on his face. "I'd given her a lot of jewelry. She took that, of course. She also took the Mercedes. I hadn't given her that. She even had the temerity to ask me for money."

As I got up to leave, I thought of something.

"If you don't think Alma could have done it, is there anybody you can think of who might have?"

With a lithe step, Atkinson moved around the desk and walked me to the door. "No, not really." Grasping the door handle, he gazed down at the carpet as if he was trying to decide how far to go. "Despite what he told you," he said, looking up, "we weren't that close. His best friend was Arthur O'Rourke."

I should have thought of it before. Russell Gray, Conrad Atkinson, Arthur O'Rourke: they were all part of the same circle, people with the kind of money that made a difference in whether something important got done. I could still see Arthur O'Rourke, with his gray candid eyes and friendly patrician manner, telling me, as if it was something he would have loved to do himself, how much he admired those who battled things out in courtroom disputes. They all had that—Russell Gray and Arthur O'Rourke and Conrad Atkinson, too, for that matter—the self-deprecating manner by which they let you believe that whatever you did was far more interesting than anything they had done or could ever do. They left you with the feeling that they wanted to know everything about you, and only later did you realize that they never revealed anything about themselves.

Perhaps it was this very insistence on privacy that had drawn Kristin Maxfield away from Conrad Atkinson and toward Marshall Goodwin. Kristin loved money, but she loved something else more, and whether it was excitement or power, it required a kind of publicity that no one in that circle would have allowed.

KRISTIN'S NOW-NOTORIOUS HUSBAND HAD MORE IM-portant things on his mind the next morning, when I sat down across from him at a small table in a windowless conference room. Silent and morose, he sank back against the armless metal chair, glaring at me while his lawyer patted his arm.

"He isn't going to take the deal," Richard Lee Jones said gruffly. "We'll win on appeal."

He tilted his chair back and put one foot against the edge of the table. He was wearing his expensive boots. We were going into court for sentencing and the jury box would be empty.

"But only one of you will be waiting on death row to find out," I snapped.

"I'll take my chances," Goodwin said. "I really don't have any choice," he added, when our eyes met.

"You can agree to testify that Kristin knew what was in that envelope she delivered to Quentin," I reminded him. "You'll get a life sentence and a chance to get parole someday."

He was not wearing any of the tailored suits and hundred-dollar ties he had worn to court as a defendant; he was dressed like every other inmate of the county jail.

"I can't tell you anything about Kristin because there isn't anything to tell," he insisted. "I didn't do it; I didn't hire Quentin; I didn't have anything to do with killing my wife."

I searched his eyes, trying to find something that would tell me if what he said might possibly be true.

"If you didn't give that envelope to Kristin, that means she did it on her own."

He shook his head. Getting to my feet, I put my hands on the back of the folding chair and looked down at him.

"In a few minutes you're going in there," I said, nodding toward the courtroom next door, "and you're going to be sentenced to death. And while you sit there on death row, waiting year after year while your lawyer files one appeal after another until he's exhausted every legal argument to save your life, Kristin is going to be living in your house, driving your car, spending whatever is left of the million dollars you got for the death of your wife and your unborn child." I bent forward and fixed him with a cold stare. "And I'll be very surprised if she spends any more time mourning you than you spent mourning Nancy."

Goodwin shot to his feet, knocking over his chair. "You don't know what you're talking about!"

Grabbing his shoulders, Jones held him back and motioned for me to leave. "We don't have anything more to talk about," he said.

THE CROWD THAT HAD WAITED FOR THE VERDICT WAS not there for the sentencing. Less than a dozen people were scattered along the gleaming wood benches. The ubiquitous Harper Bryce sat alone, jotting something in his ink-stained notebook. Kristin Maxfield sat in the back of the courtroom, the same place she had occupied throughout the trial. When Goodwin, handcuffed and shackled, was brought into court, his eye sought her out. He seemed to draw encouragement from her affectionate glance.

Solemn and aloof, Irma Holloway peered down from the bench.

"Do you have anything to say before I pass sentence?" she asked tersely.

Goodwin's head jolted up. "Your honor, I swear to you, I did not have anything to do with the murder of my wife."

The judge's eyes stayed on his. "If that is true, Mr.

Goodwin, then a serious miscarriage of justice has taken place. However," she went on, "you were found guilty by the unanimous verdict of a jury that considered all the evidence presented during your trial." Pausing for just a moment, she narrowed her eyes. "It is a verdict fully supported by the evidence, a verdict which, had this case been tried to the court alone, I would have reached myself."

Lowering his eyes, Goodwin stared down at the floor and did not look up while Irma Holloway sentenced him to death.

"My only regret," she said sternly, "is that Oregon law does not provide a penalty for the death of an unborn fetus. As far as I'm concerned, you're guilty of two murders, not just one." And rising from the bench, she disappeared through the door behind the bench.

Jones exchanged a few words with his client as the jailer approached.

"I didn't do it," Goodwin insisted, his eyes burning into mine, as the guard helped him to his feet and led him away.

When I turned to leave, I looked for Kristin. She was already gone. In the corridor outside, Harper Bryce, notebook in hand, started to ask me a question.

"Not now, Harper. Not today," I said, as I walked away.

Three steps later, I changed my mind.

"I'm sorry," I said, as I waited for him to catch up. "That was rude of me."

His shoulders hunched forward, Harper looked at me with a sympathetic eye. "Doesn't matter how much someone deserves it, I've never yet seen anybody come out of a death sentencing feeling good about it."

Nodding, I put my hand on his shoulder as we

started to walk toward the elevator. "I never had any-one sentenced to death."

"That's one of the benefits of winning all the time: you don't have to worry that because you made a mistake, an innocent man . . ." His voice trailed off.

The elevator door opened and we stepped inside.

"I don't know," I said, rubbing my eye with the heel of my hand. I was tired to the bone, and all I wanted was to go home and go to bed and try to forget everything that had happened. "I never used to worry about that and now it seems to be all I think about."

The elevator doors opened on the ground floor.

"Did you believe him?" I asked abruptly.

"They all say that," he replied. "They're all innocent. No one ever did anything."

"He could have gotten life," I said, not convinced.

Outside, on the courthouse steps, we stood facing the park.

"Let it go," Harper counseled. "You did your job. That's all anybody can do. That sort of thing can eat you alive if you dwell on it. The system usually works."

I listened to him repeating all the well-worn words of comfort and was grateful for the lie.

"Spend your time worrying about what's going to happen in the Woolner trial."

"That reminds me," I said, as we moved down to the sidewalk. "What do you know about Gilliland-O'Rourke's husband?"

He stopped and looked at me, a quizzical expression on his face. "Arthur O'Rourke?" he asked. "One of the wealthiest men in town. Some say it was a marriage of convenience. More like a merger of money and power, if you ask me."

"Yes, but what do you know about him?" I asked, as we started to walk again.

"Not much. Why? What do you think you've got?"

"Just questions." I sighed.

"Questions have answers," he drawled. "I'll take a look into this."

I left him at the corner, wondering what I was after, and went the rest of the way to my office alone. My client was waiting for me.

ALMA WOOLNER SAT IN THE BLUE WINGBACK CHAIR ON the other side of the desk and told me the same story she had told me at least half a dozen times before. She assured me she had told the truth: there had been nothing between her and Russell Gray.

"The prosecution has your fingerprints on the murder weapon. They have to show motive. If you were having an affair with him and he tried to break it off and that made you angry," I tried to explain. "Or if you tried to break it off"—this seemed to me a more plausible alternative—"and he got angry, tried to force you, and you shot him in self-defense."

"There was nothing between us," she repeated.

After Alma left, I wondered if she had been telling me the truth. I had no reason to doubt her, except for a rumor passed on by people who did not know if it was anything more than that. There was only one person I could think of who might know. I asked Helen to place a call to Arthur O'Rourke. A few minutes later, she opened the door to my office.

"I called Mr. O'Rourke's office," she informed me. "He's on a business trip and won't be back until sometime next week. Shall I make a note to call then?"

"Yes, you better," I replied. "I need to talk to him."

• • •

ON SATURDAY MORNING, TWO DAYS BEFORE THE START of her trial, I had one last session with Alma. I was surprised when she walked in alone. Each time before, Horace had come with her and waited in the outer office while we talked. A certain distance had opened between us, and his manner had become formal and at times almost abrupt. He said hello and good-bye and that was it. I stopped joining him in his chambers, and I was not invited to their home. As nearly as I could tell, they kept to themselves and did not go out at all.

A dove-gray sweater was thrown around her shoulders. She tilted her head to the side and watched me through small round glasses as I sat behind my desk in my shirtsleeves.

"Am I really going to have to testify?"

I bent my head and rubbed the back of my neck. "I've told you every time you've asked. You have to. You're the only one who knows what really happened. You're the only one who can tell the jury."

Alma seemed to shrink into the chair. Tucking her legs beneath her, she pulled the sweater closer around her throat.

"Horace says I don't have to testify."

I sat straight up. "Technically, that's right. You don't have to testify. No one can make a defendant in a criminal case take the stand. You're the only one who can make that decision." I paused, then added, with as much encouragement as I could, "But you have to do it."

"Horace says I don't have to," she persisted.

"Horace is right," I agreed. "You don't have to if you don't want to, but the jury needs to hear you explain why you stayed behind after everyone else left." I hesitated, and then asked, "Why are you worried about testifying? What are you afraid of?"

"I'm afraid I'll make a mistake," she said simply.

I changed the subject. "What can you tell me about Arthur O'Rourke?" I was still not convinced she was telling me the truth.

If the question surprised her, or if she was worried about anything he might know about her, she did not show it.

"He was a friend of Russell's."

"Did you see him very often?"

"Hardly at all. He wasn't involved with the ballet company."

When she got ready to go, she slipped her arms through the sleeves of the sweater and cast a sympathetic glance at me.

"Everything is going to be fine," she said. It was the kind of thing a lawyer says to a client when things are not going well at all.

LATE INTO THE NIGHT AND ALL THE NEXT DAY, I WENT over everything, making certain that I had not missed something that might make a difference in the trial. I was thinking like a defense lawyer again. They would put on their usual line of witnesses; they would make their case. Russell Gray was killed by a bullet fired from a gun covered with the fingerprints of the defendant. But if she shot him, what was her motive? That was the question the prosecution would have to answer. I was left with a question too. If she did not shoot him, who did?

I was in my office before dawn on Monday morning,

going over everything one last time. I made it to the courthouse with barely a minute to spare. The court reporter bent forward, holding his tie in place with one hand, and opened the four-legged metal stand under the stenotype machine with the other. Alma sat in a wooden chair at the counsel table, gazing at the empty jury box.

"Are you all right?" I asked, as I put my briefcase down on the floor between us.

"Fine," she replied softly, turning her gentle eyes on me.

At the far left side, a door opened and the clerk entered the courtroom, followed by the judge. Settling into the narrow black leather chair, William West looked down from the bench and invited the prosecution to open the proceedings.

Gilliland-O'Rourke, her red hair piled on top of her head, stood next to a young man in his early thirties wearing wire-rimmed glasses and a dark blue suit.

"Your honor," she explained in a formal voice, "I wish to advise both the court and defense counsel that Mr. Victor Jenkins of my office will be serving as co-counsel."

The deputy DA had a piercing stare that conveyed an attitude of conscious superiority. His voice was a high-pitched effeminate lisp; I looked again to confirm that the sound came from him.

Within an hour we started voir dire and did nothing else for the rest of the week. Watching Richard Lee Jones talk to jurors about reasonable doubt, I had thought he was a fraud; now, listening to myself, I did not question my own sincerity.

With ruthless affability, I engaged prospective jurors, one after another, in a gentle wide-ranging interrogation designed to test their neutrality and encourage their bias. Gilliland-O'Rourke took less time and went right to the point. She limited her questioning to the obvious issue of whether they were willing to follow the law.

"No matter how much you may like or even admire the defendant," she asked one juror, "would you be able to enter a verdict of guilty if the evidence proves beyond a reasonable doubt that she did it?"

I asked the same juror if he would return a verdict of not guilty even if he thought the defendant did it, if the prosecution had failed to prove guilt beyond a reasonable doubt. His answer was yes to both questions.

Precise and orderly, with little of her old flamboyance, Gilliland-O'Rourke asked her questions and listened without expression to the answers. At times she seemed not exactly bored or even indifferent but preoccupied.

When we were finished, we had a jury evenly divided between men and women. Raising their right hands, they stood in the box and swore to the oath administered by the clerk. An all-white jury would now decide whether a white man had been murdered by a black woman.

At the end of each day of voir dire, Alma would tug on my sleeve and say good-bye, and I would not see her again until the next morning. I never saw Horace at all. He went about his business as if nothing had changed. Alma rode in with him in the morning and left with him in the afternoon, but that was all I knew. He stayed away from the trial, and he stayed away from me.

On the morning both sides were to give opening statements, I sat next to Alma in the courtroom a few minutes before nine as the last juror, a heavyset woman, straggled past the gate in the wooden railing and across to the jury room. At the other end of the counsel table, farthest from the jury box, Victor Jenkins concentrated on a stack of three-by-five cards covered with hand-written notes. Gilliland-O'Rourke had not yet arrived.

The door at the side swung open and the court clerk walked in. I looked back at the door, waiting for Judge West. He never came. Halfway to her place at the side of the bench, the clerk changed direction and headed toward the counsel table.

"Judge would like to see counsel in chambers," she said, bending forward so no one else could hear.

Holding a cup of coffee in his hand, William West was sitting sideways to his desk, listening to jazz on the radio. Turning down the volume, he motioned for us to take chairs.

"I understand that the district attorney won't be here today," he said, looking at Jenkins. "You're prepared to go forward?"

"Yes, your honor," he replied. "I was called last night."

"Illness," West explained, glancing at me.

Pursing his lips, he thought about what to do next.

"I'm not going to give the jury a reason for her absence. I'll just indicate that she won't be with us today and that you will be making the opening statement for the prosecution. Fair enough?"

It was not a question.

"Mr. Antonelli," he called out, as I followed Jenkins out the door. "May I see you for a moment?"

I turned around and let the door close behind me.

"Gwendolyn's husband had a heart attack."

"When did it happen?" I asked. "Is he all right?"

"All I know is that it happened sometime yesterday and that he survived it. He's in intensive care." West frowned. "At his age, I suppose things like this are to be expected. Still, it must be very difficult for Gwendolyn."

I barely listened while West informed the jury that Victor Jenkins would give the opening statement for the prosecution. We had been trying to reach Arthur O'Rourke for the last two weeks. Helen had called again yesterday and had been told he was still out of town and was not expected back before the end of the week. But he had not been out of town at all, or, if he had, he had returned. Why would Arthur O'Rourke go to so much trouble to avoid my call?

Victor Jenkins was standing in front of the jury box, and right from the beginning he had their undivided attention. It was an oddly arresting combination, a look of masculine severity and that effeminate lisp. What was strange about him became the mark of his own authenticity as the opposite extremes canceled each other out. The lisp became less noticeable because of the way he looked, and his features softened because of the way he sounded. The longer he talked, the more likable he seemed.

Pausing frequently, Jenkins outlined the evidence the state would offer. It was all routine, the kind of thing said at the beginning of every case. Resting my arm on the table, I stared down at my hands and rubbed my thumb against first one finger, then another, pulling the skin back from the nail. In the background, Jenkins was saying something about the gun. I listened long enough to hear the words *murder weapon* and then let my mind drift.

Listlessly, my gaze moved from Jenkins to the jury, from the jury to the court reporter, and from the reporter up to the bench, where Judge West had lowered his eyes to study some papers he had brought into court.

We were all the part-time performers of a permanent play, repeating itself over and over again, and as I watched, I felt something, the soft shudder of a wing beating out into the dusk, and had an eerie sense of something indefinable, a kind of knowledge just beyond my grasp, an inexplicable certainty that everything was wrong.

"Mr. Antonelli," I heard a voice say.

Before I knew what I was doing, I found myself standing up, facing the bench. "Yes, your honor?"

"Does the defense wish to make an opening statement at this time?"

I had committed to memory what I wanted to say, but now I changed my mind.

"No, your honor. The defense would like to reserve its opening statement."

The prosecution would now have to put on its case without having heard anything about what the defense intended to do.

THE NEXT MORNING, GILLILAND-O'ROURKE APPEARED in court as if she had never been away. Resuming her place as lead attorney, she called the first witness for the prosecution.

His thin knees pressed together and his manicured hands folded in his lap, Andre Barbizon settled into the witness chair, cast an insolent glance at the crowded rows of spectators, and waited for the first question.

"How long were you employed by Russell Gray?"

Her voice, her manner, the way she moved toward the witness, then toward the jury, none of it had changed. Whatever she felt about what had happened to her husband, the world was never going to know it.

"Three years next month," Barbizon said. He seemed to take a certain satisfaction in the precision of the answer.

"And what did your duties include?" she asked.

"I managed the household, hired staff, took care of the accounts, and made certain everything was done in the proper manner."

Nodding, she faced the jury. "Where were you the evening your employer, Russell Gray, was killed?"

"That was my night off. I had dinner with friends in town."

"Approximately what time did you return?"

Barbizon stroked the side of his nose. "Ten minutes after midnight."

Gilliland-O'Rourke walked toward him. "Exactly?"

"It was twelve minutes past when I went into the living room. At least that was what it said on the mantelpiece clock."

"What did you find when you entered the living room?"

"Russell. I mean Mr. Gray. He was on the floor. Dead. A gun was right next to the body."

"How did you know he was dead?"

A look of disgust spread over his face. "His eyes were wide open. There was a lot of blood. He wasn't breathing. Just to be sure," he added, with a slight shudder, "I checked his pulse."

"What did you do then?"

"I called the police," he said.

She was standing right in front of him, her arms folded in front of her. "What did you do while you waited for the police?"

He thought about it for a moment. "I went into the

kitchen and poured myself a glass of wine. I wanted something to steady my nerves. I was upset."

"Your witness," Gilliland-O'Rourke remarked, as she returned to her chair.

I stood at the side of the counsel table and squinted at him.

"You lived in Russell Gray's home. Is that correct?"

"Yes."

"Where exactly did you stay? Did you have separate quarters outside the main house, an apartment inside the house itself, a room?"

"I have a two-room suite on the second floor."

Nodding, I moved across the hardwood floor to the front of the jury box.

"It's a very large stone house. Three full stories, I believe. Correct?"

"Yes," he said, watching me carefully.

"High ceilings, solid floors, long hallways that run off in a number of different directions?"

"Yes," he replied, a touch of impatience in his voice.

"A house in which it would be extremely difficult to know whether someone else was present or not?"

"If you mean, is it hard to hear people moving about, yes, of course."

"When you're upstairs in your private quarters, for example, people visiting Mr. Gray in the living room would not know you were in the house, would they?"

"No, they wouldn't," he agreed. "Unless, of course, Mr. Gray happened to mention it."

I looked at the jury, and then I looked back at him. "You mentioned that among your other duties, you hired staff. Did any other employee of Mr. Gray live in the house?"

"No. The rest of the staff—the cook, the maid—were only there during the day or as needed."

"When someone came to visit Mr. Gray or called him on the telephone, did you answer the door or answer the telephone when the maid wasn't there?" I moved closer to him, running my hand along the railing of the jury box.

"Yes, of course."

"So during the course of the nearly three years you worked for Mr. Gray, you became fairly well acquainted with most of the people he knew, didn't you?"

"Yes," he said with assurance.

"Thank you, Mr. Barbizon. That's all I have."

I took a step toward my chair and then glanced back. He was looking at the judge, waiting to be told he could go.

"One last thing. In a house that large, how could you be so certain after you found the dead body of Russell Gray that the killer wasn't still somewhere on the premises?"

"I just assumed it," he stuttered. "I saw the gun on the floor."

I held up my hand. "No further questions."

Barbizon was excused, and the judge announced that because of another matter before the court, we would stand in recess until after lunch. As soon as the jury left, I moved over to where Gilliland-O'Rourke stood, closing her briefcase.

"I'm very sorry about your husband," I told her. "Is he going to be all right?"

She finished fastening the clasp on her briefcase before she turned to look at me.

"He'll be fine," she said tersely.

"Which hospital is he in?"

"He's in a private clinic." She swung the briefcase off the table and held it in front of her, waiting for me to finish whatever I had to say.

"I'm glad he's going to be all right," I said, and started to turn away.

"If you wanted to talk to my husband," she said, with an icy stare, "You should have talked to me first."

"I beg your pardon?"

"You've been calling his office for weeks."

"Yes, that's true. I wanted to talk to him."

"What about?" she demanded.

Her husband was in the hospital with a heart attack. I tried to make allowances.

"Look, Gwendolyn," I whispered. "This isn't the time—"

"What did you want to talk to him about? Something about this case?"

"He was Russell Gray's best friend."

"They barely knew each other," she said, with a dismissive glance. "If you had asked me, I could have told you that," she added, as she turned on her heel.

"If it's that simple," I said, sympathy exhausted, "why didn't *he* just take my call and tell me that?"

She hesitated, as if she was going to stop and turn back, but then she walked away.

ANDRE BARBIZON HAD FOUND RUSSELL GRAY'S BODY
on the living room floor. The next witness called by the
prosecution explained how he got there.

Dr. Reuben Santana walked to the witness stand in
long, brisk strides. He had close-cropped hair and a
thin, slightly off-center nose.

"You performed the autopsy on the decedent, Russell
Gray?" Gilliland-O'Rourke asked, standing at the
counsel table, her long painted fingernails resting on the
edge.

"Yes," the coroner replied. His brief nod seemed to
parallel the clean, efficient movement of a surgeon's
hand.

"Based upon your examination of the body, Dr. Santana, what in your professional judgment was the cause
of death?"

Shifting his gaze to the jury, he replied, "Trauma
from a gunshot wound. The victim was shot in the
chest. The bullet essentially exploded the pulmonary ar-
tery. Death was instantaneous."

Gilliland-O'Rourke went to an easel, where she removed a blank sheet of paper that had been covering a
simple line drawing of a front view of the human body.

"When you examined the corpse of Russell Gray, were you able to discover the precise entry wound?"

Santana left the witness stand. With a felt-tipped pen, he carefully drew a small circle in the middle of the chest area. "The bullet entered here."

Standing at the side of the easel, he waited while Gilliland-O'Rourke unveiled a drawing of the back view.

"Were you able to find an exit wound?"

Santana drew a circle halfway across an imaginary line running between the lower edges of the shoulder blades.

"Taking into account the location of both the entry and the exit wounds," he was asked when he returned to the witness stand, "what conclusions can be drawn about the trajectory of the bullet that killed Russell Gray?"

"The line was virtually horizontal."

"Which suggests that the gun did not go off during a struggle, for example?"

This called for speculation, but I decided not to object.

"All I can say with certainty is that he was shot by someone firing at neither an upward nor a downward angle."

Gilliland-O'Rourke wanted to make certain everyone understood. "So he couldn't have been shot, for example, during a struggle to get the gun away from the other person if the barrel was forced either up or down as it went off?"

"No."

On the following day, Gilliland-O'Rourke took up the same line of questioning with her next witness.

Pigeon-toed and round-shouldered, Detective Thaddeus Oliver brushed his mustache with his fingers, waiting for the chance to answer.

"Were there any signs of struggle when you investigated the scene? Furniture thrown around, things broken, anything like that?" she asked briskly.

"Nope. Everything was in the place it was supposed to be."

"What about the victim's clothing? Anything that showed signs of a struggle?"

"His shirt was torn where he got shot," Oliver replied, his eyes darting toward the jury, thinking he had made a joke.

"Nothing else?" Gilliland-O'Rourke asked, with a glance of disapproval.

"No," he said, looking down at his feet.

Moving closer to the witness, she lifted her head. "This is very important, Detective Oliver. Were there any powder burns, any evidence of any sort, that would indicate that the victim had been shot at close range?"

A well-trained witness with years of courtroom experience, he looked directly at the jury. "There was nothing."

"If someone had been shot while struggling for a gun, would you expect to find such evidence?"

"Yes, we would," he replied firmly, his eyes on the jury.

It was a preemptive strike, an attempt to prove premeditation by eliminating the possibility of either sudden impulse or self-defense. Gilliland-O'Rourke was thorough, but it was all beside the point. Our defense was simple. Someone else killed Russell Gray.

• • •

DAY AFTER DAY, THE PROSECUTION CALLED ITS WITnesses and fastened together each link in the chain of evidence against Alma Woolner. Lab technicians and forensic experts testified that the bullet that killed Russell Gray had in fact been fired from the gun found beside the body and that the only fingerprints found on the gun belonged to the defendant. It was almost a relief when they finally called a witness who did not spend most of her waking hours staring down a microscope.

The old woman leaned on the silver knob of her black lacquered walking stick and reluctantly raised her right hand while the clerk recited the oath. When Gilliland-O'Rourke asked her to state her full name and spell her last name for the record, she looked at her as if she could not believe the younger woman was really serious.

"Roberta Hope Caldwell," she said finally, each syllable pronounced like the next note in a building chorus of resentment. Resting her liver-spotted hands on the knob of the walking stick, she spat out the letters of her last name: "C-A-L-D-W-E-L-L."

Mrs. Caldwell served on the ballet company board and, though few people were old enough to remember it, had once been one of the most beautiful women in Portland.

"You were vice-chair, and Russell Gray was chairman, is that correct?" asked Gilliland-O'Rourke, keeping her distance.

"Yes," she replied, sniffing the air as if there were something not quite right about it.

"You attended the meeting of the executive committee the night of his death?"

"I did." She planted herself on the walking stick and waited for the next question.

"How many people attended the meeting?"

Raising her wispy eyebrows, she thought about it for a moment. "Six, I think. No, seven. Counting Mrs. Woolner."

Gilliland-O'Rourke had carried with her from the counsel table a pencil which, consciously or not, she kept tapping against her finger.

"What time did the meeting end?" she asked patiently.

"I suppose about ten or ten-thirty. I didn't check the time."

Pensively, Gilliland-O'Rourke gazed down at the floor. "And did everyone leave at the same time?"

"I stayed behind a few minutes. I had something I wanted to say to Mr. Gray in private."

Her eyes still lowered, Gilliland-O'Rourke nodded and then moved a few steps toward the jury. Pursing her lips, she tapped the pencil on her finger, then stopped abruptly.

"Did any of the others," she asked, looking up, "including Alma Woolner, happen to come back to the house during the few minutes you were still there?"

"No," Mrs. Caldwell replied slowly.

"So when you left, Russell Gray was entirely alone?"

"Yes."

I was certain she was mistaken and as soon as it was my turn to examine the witness I tried to prove it.

"Mr. Gray lived in a very large house, didn't he?" I asked, as I approached her.

She did not seem to think so. "No larger than my own."

"But large enough that someone could be in one part of the house and someone in another part wouldn't know it?" I asked the question as if it were a matter of no great importance.

"Yes, of course."

"So then, as far as you know," I asked, turning up my hands, "Alma Woolner could have been down a hallway somewhere—in a bathroom, perhaps—and you only assumed she left with all the others?"

Gripping the walking stick, she stared down at her sensible oxfords. "That would be possible," she agreed, as she lifted her gaze, "except for the fact that I said good-bye to her myself outside and watched her drive away."

It was the last answer I expected, and I had to force myself to sound as if it was the only answer I wanted.

"You saw Alma Woolner leave. Good. No further questions, your honor." I headed toward my chair.

Gilliland-O'Rourke was on her feet. "Mrs. Caldwell, just one or two more questions. What was the reason you wanted to have a private word with Russell Gray before you left?"

"I wanted to confront him with some rumors I had heard."

"What rumors were those?"

For the first time, she seemed to lose a little of her self-assurance. Her eyes moved away from Gilliland-O'Rourke and settled for a moment on Alma, who was now following every word.

"Rumors that he had started an improper relationship with Mrs. Woolner," she replied finally. "Mr. Gray was rather well known for that sort of thing," she added as she shifted her attention back to Gilliland-O'Rourke. "Surely you knew."

Gilliland-O'Rourke passed it over.

"What did you say to Mr. Gray?" she asked, as she turned away and faced the jury.

"I told him that he was to leave Mrs. Woolner alone, that she was a married woman, and that if he persisted, I would have him removed," she said, raising her withered chin.

Gilliland-O'Rourke looked back. "Removed?"

"Yes. As chairman of the board. Everyone thought he was so charming," she muttered. "Not a bit of it. He was a beastly man, willing to take advantage of anyone."

It made no sense. Alma had told me she had stayed behind, and Mrs. Caldwell had just sworn that she left. And she was not the only one. Everyone who had been at Russell Gray's home that evening came into court and testified to the same thing.

ALMA DENIED IT AND ARGUED SEMANTICS. SHE HAD NOT left with the others, she insisted, not in the sense of going for good.

"I left with everyone else. Then I remembered I needed to talk with Russell, so I went back," she explained.

We had gone to my office, late in the afternoon, after the prosecution had finished with the last witness who saw Alma leave.

"That isn't what you told me," I reminded her. "You told me you stayed. You never said anything about leaving."

Dark clouds closed out the sky, and the rain had begun to fall, the way it would for months, sweeping in from the sea, day after dismal day. Standing at the window, my hands in my pants pockets, I took a deep breath and let it out in a slow, despondent sigh.

I turned my head, just far enough to see her. In the shadows of the fading yellow light of the lamp, her smooth skin glowed like burnished brass.

"What does it matter?" she asked softly. "Whether I stayed, or whether I left and came back a little while later? I was still there."

"They'll say you left, and when you were sure he was alone you came back, and that you came back carrying a gun," I replied, as I crossed the room and sat down next to her.

She looked at me without expression.

"They'll say you were having an affair with Russell Gray, that you were in love with him but he wasn't in love with you, and when you found out he didn't want anything more to do with you, you couldn't stand it and you killed him."

"I didn't kill him," she insisted.

"But you were having an affair with him."

She denied it, as she had done so many times before. I held up my hand and shook my head.

"Don't," I warned her. "It's too late for that now. You didn't suddenly remember there was something you wanted to talk to him about. You left because you didn't want anyone to know you were spending time alone with him. If you weren't having an affair with him, you wouldn't have thought anything about staying behind after everyone else was gone. Only a guilty conscience produces that kind of concern with appearances."

She stared at me and said nothing.

"That's the reason you didn't want to testify, isn't it? You didn't want it to come out, because you don't want Horace to know."

There was no reaction, no visible sign of what she felt, or that she felt anything at all. Nothing, just the look of someone who has slipped away to a place where no one can find her. I had known her for years. Now, I realized, I did not know her at all.

"You're going to be convicted of murder, Alma, and there isn't anything I can do about it, not unless you start telling the truth. You had an affair with Russell Gray, and you have to admit it, no matter how much it hurts. That's the reason you came back to the house, and you're going to have to say so when I put you on the stand. All right?"

She did not answer. Instead, she glanced at her watch.

"I have to go," she said, as she rose from her chair. "Horace is meeting me outside."

She was not going to say anything more. Reluctantly, I got to my feet and, taking her arm, walked her out.

"I've tried to call Horace three times this week. He doesn't take my calls."

"He's been very busy," she explained.

"I want him in court. He has to be there, sitting where the jury can see him. He has to show by his presence that he believes you're innocent. He knows how important that is."

We rode the elevator down to the lobby and I walked her out to the rain-slicked sidewalk. Horace was waiting in the car. Holding an umbrella, I opened the door and helped her in. When I said hello, Horace, looking straight ahead, nodded and said nothing in return. As they drove off, I stood on the curb, watching the taillights disappear into traffic, wondering what I had done.

I had hours of work to do, and as I walked across the lobby, my footsteps echoing off the dark red marble floor, I debated whether to stay in the office or take it home with me.

The door to my office was open, just the way I had left it. Everything else on the floor was locked up for the night. Closing the door behind me, I stopped at Helen's desk and thumbed through the telephone messages that had been accumulating over the last week. Most of them I discarded, but a few looked important and I studied them more closely as I walked back into my office.

"I hoped you were still here."

Startled, I looked up. In the shadows on the other side of the desk, the same place where Alma Woolner had been sitting just a few moments earlier, a woman in a long dress and a black fur coat was staring at me. She laughed at my surprise.

"Have you forgotten me already?"

Settling into my chair, I looked at her, all dressed up, taunting me with her eyes.

"What can I do for you, Kristin? Or did you just happen to be in the neighborhood?"

"I thought maybe you'd like to take me to dinner," she said, her glossy black hair falling back over her shoulder as she tilted her head to the side. "I have a date, but I can get out of it."

"Your husband was just sentenced and you have a date. You didn't waste much time, did you?"

"He was sentenced a month ago." She made it sound like a lifetime. "And it really isn't a date. I'm just having dinner with a friend. You remember him. Conrad Atkinson."

I could not hide my surprise.

"I know what he said at the trial. He was angry with me. He deserved to be. But Conrad knows I could never have had anything to do with what Marshall did."

She read the skepticism on my face. Reaching across, she picked up the telephone and dialed.

"I'm not going to be able to make dinner tonight," she said into the receiver. Her eyes on me, she activated the speaker.

There was no mistake. The voice at the other end was Conrad Atkinson.

"I'll call you later on," she promised, before she hung up.

She was still watching me.

"Take me to dinner. I'll tell you some things about Russell Gray you might find interesting."

We drove in her black Mercedes—the one she had taken when she broke off her engagement to Conrad— to a small French restaurant in the northwest section, five minutes from downtown. At a quiet table in a corner, with her glistening fur coat draped over the back of her chair, Kristin tried to convince me that she was one of the few people I could trust.

"What would you like to know about Russell Gray?" she asked as she sipped on a glass of red wine.

"You met him when you were engaged to Atkinson, right?"

"Yes, but I had heard of him when I was still handling misdemeanor cases in the district attorney's office." She dragged the end of her middle finger across her lower lip. "A teenage boy claimed Gray had given him a ride in his car and tried to molest him. I interviewed the boy. I believed him. Gilliland-O'Rourke told me to dismiss it. Insufficient evidence, she said. I'd prosecuted dozens of cases just like it. But this was different, because it was Russell Gray and Russell Gray was one of them."

I thought I knew what she meant, but I wanted to hear it from her.

"Them?"

Her mouth curled back at the corners and she looked at me, derision in her eyes.

"You don't understand these people—Russell Gray, Gilliland-O'Rourke, even Conrad—do you? They aren't like you or me."

"Because they're rich?" I laughed.

"Because they can do whatever they want so long as they don't embarrass each other. They protect their own—to a point. After that, if they can't cover things up, they abandon them as if they had never known them. Look at what Gwendolyn did to Marshall."

I was not sure what she meant.

"If it hadn't been for you," she explained, tracing her finger around the edge of the half-empty glass, "he would never have been charged in the first place."

The waiter appeared. After we ordered, I reminded her that Travis Quentin had confessed to the state police.

"Gwendolyn would have told them there was no case. Quentin was a murderer trying to save his life, and all the other so-called evidence was circumstantial. She wouldn't have done anything that would embarrass herself. Why do you think she's prosecuting the case against Alma Woolner? Because she thinks she did it?"

She shook her head.

"She couldn't trust anyone else. She's afraid of what might come out. They're all afraid. Russell Gray was involved in things they don't want anyone to know about."

I barely touched my food, while Kristin was finishing nearly everything on her plate.

"What's the connection with Arthur O'Rourke?"

She put down her fork and leaned across the table. "Did you really have an affair with Gwendolyn?"

"No. Where did you hear that?" I replied with as much indifference as I could summon.

"I don't believe you," she said, pulling back. "It doesn't matter. She must have had a lot of affairs. What choice did she have?" Kristin took another mouthful. "They don't have a marriage," she said, as she wiped her mouth with a napkin, "they have an alliance. One of the richest families in the state and one of the most powerful political families. People must have thought it was the start of a dynasty. How was anyone to know Arthur O'Rourke was gay?"

Suddenly serious, and a little withdrawn, she looked down and etched a figure into the tablecloth with her nail.

"It's too bad," she said. "Arthur is a very nice man. It must have been difficult for him, growing up when he did, knowing he could never let anyone know the way he really felt, the way he really was."

She looked up, reached for her glass, and took a drink, her eyes still on me.

"Poor Arthur. Everyone used him. Gwendolyn knew what he was before she married him—she had to have known—but she did it anyway because she wanted the money and everything that went with it. Russell was even worse."

I sat across from her, an attentive audience, and listened to her describe the ways in which Russell Gray had exploited his friend.

"A long time ago, when they were both much younger, they were lovers for a while."

"Arthur O'Rourke and Russell Gray?"

"Yes. Arthur is ten or fifteen years older, and when Russell was a young man he was really quite good-looking: thin, blond, blue-eyed. Arthur fell in love with him."

She paused.

"Was Russell in love with him?" I asked.

"Arthur was always a very generous man, and Russell never did anything to discourage generosity."

"I thought Russell Gray was one of the wealthiest men in town."

"He wanted everyone to think so," she said, a shrewd glint in her eyes. "His family had been wealthy, though nothing like as rich as the O'Rourkes. But Russell had to split the inheritance with a brother and a sister. And then, of course, he spent a good deal of what he had. Without his good friend Arthur O'Rourke, I'm not sure what he would have done, especially in the last year or two."

She took another sip from her glass before she went on.

"He was in serious financial trouble. He was borrowing money anywhere he could get it. He even borrowed some from Conrad. But of course he borrowed more from Arthur, a lot more. They were friends, but even with friends there is a limit. Apparently, Russell started making threats, suggesting that he hoped he could find a way out of his financial difficulties before he started talking about things he shouldn't."

She gave a short, dry laugh. "Even when they blackmail each other, the rich try to be polite."

I was not interested in their manners. "Are you telling me you think Gray was killed by someone he was trying to blackmail? Arthur O'Rourke?"

She laughed again. "Have you ever met Arthur?"

When I told her I had, she looked at me as if I had

just answered my own question. "Arthur O'Rourke isn't capable of hurting anyone, but Gwendolyn may be," she said. "And she isn't the only one. There are a lot of people who would have wanted to prevent the kind of scandal Russell Gray might have caused. Although, when you think about it," she said, settling back against her chair, "Gwendolyn had the most to lose. What do you think it would have done to her political career if people knew her husband was involved with someone like Andre Barbizon?"

"Barbizon? The one in charge of the household?"

Her eyes opened wide. "I suppose that's one way of describing what he did." The look of derision passed. "Arthur O'Rourke was a decent, lonely man, and his friend Russell introduced him to people who were willing to provide him comfort." She paused and considered what she had just said. "Yes, that's perhaps the most charitable way of describing what Russell did for his friends."

We ordered coffee, and while she stirred her cup I asked her about Russell Gray and Alma.

"They were having an affair," she reported matter-of-factly. "Everyone knew."

"Conrad Atkinson told me he didn't know if they were or not," I retorted, interested in what her reaction would be.

"They take care of their own," she said, casting an indulgent look at me. "Conrad didn't lie to you. He just didn't tell you the truth."

"So everyone knew?"

"It wasn't a secret."

I had to ask. "Do you think her husband knew?"

She held her cup with both hands, elbows on the table. "He wouldn't have been difficult to fool. Horace

Woolner is a straight arrow if there ever was one." She put the cup down, folded her hands together, and rested her chin on top of them. "And who would have told him? He doesn't exactly move in the same circles, does he?"

I placed a credit card on top of the bill and waited until the waiter took it away.

"And what about you, Kristin? Why did you decide that wasn't the circle you wanted to be in?"

"Marshall was exciting," she said, her eyes perfectly still. "Conrad and his friends are all a little too predictable." A slow smile started across her mouth. "You wouldn't fit in there either. You'd be bored out of your mind. Under the surface—" she said, and broke off. Tossing her head back, she laughed. "There is no under the surface."

She took my arm when we left the restaurant and kept holding it while we walked to the car. As we drove across town, I asked her why she had told me.

"I wanted you to know that I trust you," she replied, her eyes on the road. "And because I want you to trust me." She glanced over. "I didn't have anything to do with what Marshall did. You have to believe that."

She pulled up in front of my building and turned off the engine.

"Tell me something. Did Marshall really admit to you that he had his wife killed?"

A brief, enigmatic smile floated across her mouth. "It's what you wanted me to say, wasn't it?"

"I wanted you to tell the truth."

"And I just thought you wanted to win. That's what I always liked about you. The way you do whatever you have to do."

"I wanted you to tell the truth," I insisted.

"The truth is that Marshall did it, and I had nothing to do with it. That's the only truth worth talking about."

I opened the door and started to get out.

"You've never seen my house, have you?" Her voice was a soft whisper. "We could go out there for a while and talk. It might be good for both of us."

I looked back at her. "I'll be up half the night, getting ready for tomorrow. You remember what it's like, preparing for trial."

I stayed in the office just long enough to gather up everything I needed and then drove home, trying hard to convince myself that liars sometimes told the truth and that Marshall Goodwin might be guilty after all.

| xxiii

I REACHED ANDRE BARBIZON JUST IN TIME. WHEN HE answered the door, he thought his cab had arrived and began pointing toward the bags on the floor of the entryway before he realized his mistake.

"Taking a trip?" I asked, as I stepped inside.

He remembered my face, but he could not quite remember my name.

"Antonelli," I reminded him.

"Yes," he replied, a look of impatience flickering across his mouth. "What can I do for you, Mr. Antonelli?"

"You can tell me all about your relationship with Arthur O'Rourke, and then you can tell me about everything else you did for Russell Gray."

His eyes darted toward a dark mahogany grandfather clock.

"I'm afraid you'll have to change your travel plans. You're coming back to court."

He refused to believe it. "I've already testified. I finished with that. The judge excused me."

I handed him a subpoena.

"You're coming back to testify for the defense."

He still did not want to believe it. He tore the subpoena out of my hand and began to read it.

"You're making a mistake," he said after he examined it. "Arthur didn't have anything to do with this. He was with me when it happened. We had dinner together that night. Remember I said I was having dinner in town with friends?"

A car pulled up in front, and a moment later the doorbell rang. It was the cab Barbizon had been expecting. He gave the driver a few dollars and explained he did not need a ride after all.

I spent an hour with Andre Barbizon, and at the end of it I was convinced that Kristin had been right. There were a lot of people who would have wanted Russell Gray dead, but Arthur O'Rourke would have been the last person to kill him.

"Russell may have taken advantage of Arthur," Barbizon told me, as we said good-bye at the door. "I don't know anything about that. But I care about Arthur, and I'm worried about him."

"A heart attack is serious," I replied. "But at least he's in stable condition."

"You don't understand, Mr. Antonelli. I don't think he had a heart attack. That was just an excuse so you couldn't talk to him. They didn't want you to find out about him and Russell."

I did not know whether to believe him. Barbizon was afraid, and fear feeds on itself. Everyone involved with Russell Gray had found they had something to fear. Most of all, they feared that people would learn they were living a lie.

WE CAN SPEND A LIFETIME MISLEADING OTHERS AND DE-ceiving ourselves, but most of us still believe there is nothing more important than the truth. I could see it on the faces of the clerk and the judge as they walked single file toward the bench, the twelve men and women who entered the jury box, the spectators who waited on benches for the proceedings to begin. A courtroom is the only place in which no one is allowed to answer a question who has not first sworn an oath not to lie.

Serious and precise, Judge West explained to the jury the next stage in the trial.

"You will remember that last Friday the prosecution finished with its case. It is now the turn of the defense, if it wishes, to call witnesses of its own. Let me remind you all," he said gravely, "that because the burden of proof is on the prosecution to prove the defendant guilty beyond a reasonable doubt, the defense is under no obligation to do anything."

As he turned toward me, I rose from my chair.

"Is the defense ready to proceed?"

"Yes, your honor."

"You reserved your opening. Do you wish to make it now?"

When I said I did, he looked back at the jury.

"At the beginning of the trial, Mr. Jenkins made an opening statement in which he gave you an outline, a preview, of the evidence the prosecution was going to offer. Mr. Antonelli is now going to do the same thing for the defense. I will tell you again what I told you then. The statements of the attorneys are not evidence; they are simply a description of what they believe the evidence will be."

Unbuttoning the jacket of my dark pinstripe suit, I stood at the end of the jury box and stared down at the floor.

"The state has methodically put on one witness after another to prove that the defendant, Alma Woolner, was in Russell Gray's home the night he was killed and that her fingerprints were on the gun that killed him." I moved my feet closer together. "She was there," I said, raising my head. "Her fingerprints are on the gun. But what does it mean? Does it mean that the prosecution is right, that she left with everyone else, came back later with a gun, shot him point-blank, and then, having gone to all this trouble, left the gun with her fingerprints on it for the police to find and just ran away?"

Gilliland-O'Rourke jumped to her feet. "Objection! He's supposed to be making an opening statement, not a closing argument."

Judge West raised his moody eyes from what he was reading. "She has a point, Mr. Antonelli."

"Yes, your honor," I replied. We exchanged a brief glance.

"The state has proven that the defendant's fingerprints were on the murder weapon," I said, as if I were starting over. "The defense will explain how they got there. The defendant, Alma Woolner, will tell us. She will tell us that she was in another part of the house, she heard something, she came into the living room, she found Russell Gray lying dead on the floor, she saw the gun, and in a state of shock she picked it up, looked at it, and then, terrified, let go of it, and, too frightened to know what to do next, ran away."

Pausing, I looked around the courtroom until my eyes settled on Gilliland-O'Rourke.

"But if Alma Woolner did not kill Russell Gray, who did? The defense will call a witness who may be able to help us answer that question."

Her face a rigid mask, Gilliland-O'Rourke stared back at me, waiting for what I was going to say next.

"The prosecution knows all about this witness. They

called him first. Andre Barbizon will now testify for the defense."

There was no reaction, nothing in her green eyes to tell me what she felt or what she thought.

"Andre Barbizon will testify that he did rather more for Russell Gray than run his household. He will testify that he was once the lover of Russell Gray and, over the course of time, the lover of several of Mr. Gray's prominent friends as well."

She shot out of her chair. Judge West hit his gavel once and then, with a baleful stare, waited until the last sound died away.

"Ms. Gilliland-O'Rourke, did you wish to make an objection?" he asked laconically.

"Mr. Antonelli's remarks are deliberately inflammatory, your honor."

He looked at me, waiting for my reply.

"It's what I expect the witness to testify," I insisted, my eyes locked on Gilliland-O'Rourke.

"Go on, Mr. Antonelli," the judge instructed, as he sank back in his chair.

I turned to the jury. "Andre Barbizon has had a number of lovers, and Russell Gray knew about all of them. He used that knowledge for his own advantage. When he needed money—and in the last year or so of his life he needed a great deal of it—he borrowed it from people who wanted to keep their private lives private. He borrowed money, but everyone understood it would never be repaid. Finally, someone decided this had to stop. But there was only one way to stop it, only one way to make sure he would never be able to reveal the secrets he knew, secrets that would have ruined the lives and destroyed the careers of more than one well-known person in this city."

I had everything I needed. Barbizon's testimony would convince the jury that there were powerful people who had every reason to want Russell Gray dead. Alma Woolner's testimony would convince them that she was incapable of murder. We were going to win. I knew it. All Alma had to do was walk to the witness stand and swear she did not kill Russell Gray.

Wearing a white high-collar dress with large black buttons down the front, Alma sat on the witness chair and looked at me with large, frightened eyes. I began with the only question that really mattered.

"Mrs. Woolner, did you kill Russell Gray?"

She took a long time before she answered. "Yes," she said finally, "I did."

Had she misunderstood the question? "No," I said quickly, "I asked you if you killed Russell Gray."

"I didn't want to, but I did."

In ten words Alma had destroyed my defense. Everything I had just said to the jury would be seen as the lie of a lawyer who did not even know what his own client was going to say. I was trapped. All I could do was keep asking her questions, hoping she would say something that would give me a way out. If I stopped now, Alma Woolner would be convicted of murder by her own confession.

"Why don't you just tell the jury what happened?" I suggested, trying to pretend that none of this was a surprise.

She became remarkably calm. Looking away from me, her eyes came to rest on the jury.

"I had been having an affair with Russell Gray," she explained. "It had been going on for some months. That night I wanted to see him alone, to tell him that it was over. That's the reason I left and then came back. He got very upset. He told me I'd change my mind after we'd gone to bed again. He tried to force me, and that's when it happened. I told him to leave me alone and I pointed the gun at him. He laughed at me. I didn't mean to shoot him. It just seemed to go off. I was scared. I didn't know what to do."

My mind was racing. She was telling the truth about her affair, that much I was certain about. But if she had shot Russell Gray in self-defense, why would she not have told me that right away? It did not make sense. She was lying, and I did not know why.

"Russell Gray was trying to force you to have sex with him?" I asked.

"Yes," she replied, her eyes downcast.

"But somehow you got away?"

"I managed to pull away. That's when I got the gun," she explained, looking again at the jury.

"Yes, the gun. Let's talk about that." I walked up to the jury box. "It was your gun?" I asked, looking straight at her.

She looked down. "Yes."

My hands behind me, I leaned against the jury box and crossed one foot in front of the other.

"Where did you get the gun?"

"I bought it."

"Where did you buy it?"

"At a gun store."

"The gun that killed Russell Gray was not registered to anyone. How do you explain that?"

For the first time, she looked at me, a puzzled expression on her face.

"I remember. I bought the gun when I was on a trip to New York. A friend of mine helped me."

"I see. You happened to be in New York, and you just happened to decide you wanted a gun?" I asked.

"It was my gun," she insisted, looking away. "I shot Russell. I didn't mean to, but I did."

Three times I took her through her story, from the moment she first arrived early in the evening until the moment she supposedly shot Russell Gray late that night, and each time it was always the same, the artificial account of someone who had memorized the words because there was nothing real to remember. She insisted she was the one who killed Russell Gray and she had not meant to do it.

Meticulous and remorseless, Gilliland-O'Rourke made her repeat it.

"Is it your testimony that after you left Russell Gray's house with the other board members, you came back alone?"

"Yes."

"With a gun?"

"Yes."

"And is it your testimony that your hand was on the gun when it was fired and Russell Gray was killed?"

"Yes, but I didn't mean—"

"Thank you," Gilliland-O'Rourke interjected. "That's all I have, your honor."

Alma sat down next to me. She started to say something but changed her mind and stared down at her hands, lost in thoughts of her own.

"You may call your next witness, Mr. Antonelli."

Gilliand-O'Rourke did not give me the chance.

"Your honor," she said, "I'd like to request that we recess until tomorrow morning. There are matters that need to be discussed between counsel."

"Mr. Antonelli?"

For a different reason, I had been about to make the same request.

"No objection, your honor."

The jury was sent home for the day, and I took Alma into a small conference room down the hallway. Angrily, I demanded to know why she had done it.

"You didn't kill Russell Gray, not by accident, not in self-defense. Why did you say you did?" We were standing just inside the doorway. She had to bite her lip to stop it from trembling. "You would have told me if it had happened that way. You wouldn't have waited until now. You made up the whole thing, didn't you? Why?"

I grabbed her arm, ready to shake the truth out of her if I had to. She pulled away, her eyes flashing. She stared at me, biting even harder on her lip. Then I knew. There was only one way it could have happened.

"Horace told you to do this, didn't he?"

Her eyes grew wider and she still would not speak.

"Horace told you it was the only way to explain how your fingerprints were on the gun, didn't he?"

She looked away and would not look back.

"You weren't even there when Russell Gray was killed, were you? You left with everyone else, and you never came back."

She would not answer. She did not have to.

THIRTY MINUTES LATER, I SAT IN FRONT OF GILLILAND-O'Rourke's ornate writing table and listened to her make an offer only a fool would turn down.

"Plead her to manslaughter. She'll do two years."

"You were charging her with murder."

Brushing a strand of hair away from her eye, she reminded me of Alma Woolner's testimony.

"She admitted it. No one can prove it didn't happen the way she said it did. There was no premeditation."

She was talking like an overworked prosecutor, anxious to deal out one case so she could get on with the next one.

"It doesn't matter what she said in there," I said, before she could remind me again. "She didn't do it. I have another witness to call."

She assumed I meant Barbizon. "That would be a very serious mistake," she warned.

"Are you trying to threaten me?" I asked as I stood up. "You really think you're in a position to do that?"

Her hands folded on the table, she fixed me with a murderous stare.

"I've made you a plea offer," she said in a hard, thin voice. "You have an obligation to take it to your client. Let me know what she decides."

Turning away, she picked up the telephone as if she were late making a call.

Outside, on the courthouse steps, breathing in the misty air, I heard the voice of Richard Lee Jones echoing in my mind, describing the secret pleasure we feel when the powerful are brought down. I had been so eager to believe that Russell Gray had been killed to conceal a scandal that I had missed what had been right in front of my eyes. I was certain now who had done it, and the only thing I felt was pain and a growing sense of anger.

All that evening I sat in the book-lined library at home, plotting the destruction of one of the few people I had ever really admired. In the middle of the night, unable to sleep, I wandered aimlessly down the creaking hallway and through the empty rooms, listening to the hollow beat of the endless rain, and in the first somber light of dawn, I stared out the window at winter's ruined landscape. When it was time, I dressed and drove down to the city.

I had been lied to from the beginning, lied to by people I thought I could trust, but even the worst news has a certain cathartic effect. The feelings of anger and betrayal gradually subsided until, when I entered the courthouse, all that was left was the strange sense of relief that comes with the knowledge that something has come to an end and nothing will ever be quite the same again.

Two hundred people crammed the courtroom benches and rose as a single body when Judge West appeared at the side door and began his short journey to the bench.

"Please be seated," he said, as he settled into place.

For a moment, the room was filled with a muffled rumble and then, once again, total silence.

"Are there any matters to take up before we begin?" he asked, glancing at me with an expectant look.

"No, your honor," I replied.

He seemed surprised. Pursing his lips, he studied me through eyes half hidden by dark lashes. "In that case," he said finally, motioning toward the clerk, "bring in the jury, and we'll get started."

She disappeared inside the jury room and emerged a few moments later, all twelve jurors in tow. As they filed into the box, one of them, a slight bespectacled man in his twenties, stumbled on the step and sprawled against a first-row chair. Embarrassed, he pulled himself to his feet and grinned sheepishly at the judge.

"Are you all right?" Judge West asked, looking down from the bench.

"I'm fine, thank you," the juror replied, as he turned and found his assigned seat in the back.

The judge nodded affably, leaned forward, put his elbows on the bench, and clasped his hands together.

"Mr. Antonelli, please call your next witness."

"Your honor," I announced, clearing my throat, "the defense calls Horace Woolner."

The prosecutor was on her feet. This was not the witness she had expected.

"Ms. Gilliland-O'Rourke?" Judge West asked, waiting to hear her objection.

She changed her mind. "Nothing, your honor," she said, sinking back down.

There was a noticeable stir among the crowd when Horace entered the courtroom and made his way up the aisle. His eyes stayed focused on a point ten feet ahead of him as he made his way toward the wooden gate. Other than Alma, he was the only black person in the room. I wondered how often before he had found himself running a gauntlet of white resentment or sympathy.

Like insubstantial shades, some witnesses make little impression while they testify and are impossible to remember after they have been excused. From the moment he walked in, however, Horace dominated the room. Every eye was on him. He sat completely still and fixed me with a steady gaze.

"You are the husband of the defendant, Alma Woolner?"

She was sitting right next to me, staring at him, too frightened to move, but his eyes never strayed from mine.

"Yes," he replied. His deep, sonorous voice seemed to come from everywhere at once.

Still in my chair, I asked, "How did you first meet?"

"We met in New York. A mutual friend introduced us."

Slowly, I pushed back from the table and got to my feet.

"When you met," I asked, as I moved toward the jury box, "she was a dancer with the New York City Ballet, wasn't she?"

He sat there, immobile, his eyes following me wherever I went.

"Yes," he answered.

"She had a very promising career ahead of her, didn't she?"

"Everyone said so."

"When you first met, was that before or after you were in the war?"

"After."

Folding my arms, I looked down at the floor. I would have given anything to have been somewhere else.

"You suffered a serious injury in Vietnam, didn't you?"

There was no response, and when I looked up I found myself under that same implacable gaze he used to use on a witness who tried to lie. In that moment, I had the vague sensation of having done something wrong and not being able to remember what it was. I lowered my eyes and began to pace slowly back and forth in front of the jury box.

"You lost both your legs in the war, didn't you?"

Again there was no response. Stopping, I looked up. "Didn't you?" I insisted.

"Yes," he said, and somehow made that one word sound like an accusation.

"And you went through a long period of adjustment, didn't you?" I did not wait for his answer. "And your wife did everything she could to help you through that period of adjustment, didn't she?"

"Yes," he said. For the first time, he looked away.

"She gave up her career for you, didn't she?"

"Yes."

"She gave up her friends, her family, everything she knew, and left New York, so you could come out here to Portland, didn't she?"

In a long, slow arc, his eyes moved back to mine.

"Yes, she did."

"You were in love with her, weren't you?"

"Yes."

The tight self-control, the formal, concise answers, the way he seemed aloof from the proceedings as if he were presiding from the bench instead of testifying from the witness stand, brought it all back again—the resentment, the anger, the sense of betrayal. I turned on him with a vengeance that surprised even myself.

"It just about killed you when you found out she was having an affair with Russell Gray, didn't it?"

Clutching the arm of the witness chair, Horace glared at me.

"She was all you had—she was everything to you—and you found out she was sleeping with another man. How did that make you feel?" I demanded. "Knowing she was going to bed with someone else: a man so wealthy he could fly off to New York for the ballet, to London for the theater, to all the places you knew your wife dreamed about; a man who was not just wealthy but white; the kind of man who stayed home while you went to war and didn't lose a moment's sleep about it, while you lost your legs because of it!" I was beside myself with anger. "A man who felt sorry for your wife because she was married to you. How did that make you feel, Judge Woolner?"

The sound of the gavel beating on the solid wood surface of the bench brought me partway back to myself.

"You couldn't stand it, could you? They had to pay, didn't they? Russell Gray had to die, and your wife, Alma—the woman who had given you a reason to live—had to take the blame, didn't she?"

The gavel struck again. Dropping my head, I turned away from the witness stand and went back to the counsel table. To stop my hands from shaking, I bent forward, spread my fingers, and put all my weight on them.

"How long had you known that your wife was having an affair with Russell Gray?" I asked, forcing myself under control.

"Long enough," he replied, strangely detached.

"Did you confront Russell Gray?"

Horace was breathing evenly, watching me the way he had before, anticipating not just the next question but the one after that.

"No, I did not."

"Did you confront your wife?"

He clenched his jaw. "I'm not going to talk about anything I may have said to my wife."

I walked behind the counsel table, my hands no longer trembling, and took a position at the corner, next to Gilliland-O'Rourke. She was leaning forward, elbow on the table, her face set in an attitude of rigid attention. On her right, Victor Jenkins was busily making notes on a legal pad.

"Weapons used in the commission of a crime are kept in the police property room, aren't they?" I asked, looking across to the witness stand.

"Yes."

"As a circuit court judge, as a former district attorney, it wouldn't be difficult for you to get access to it, would it?"

"Objection!" Jenkins called out. "The defense is assuming facts not in evidence."

Out of the corner of my eye, I noticed Gilliland-O'Rourke touch Jenkins on the sleeve.

"Withdraw the question, your honor," I said, waving my hand.

"It's not difficult to find a gun if you really want one, is it?" I asked, as I began to move across the front of the courtroom.

"No," he agreed.

"The prosecution has based most of its case on the fact that the defendant's fingerprints were found on the gun used to kill Russell Gray. But isn't it true that if your wife had held that gun in her hand just once—if, for example, you were showing her how to use it—her fingerprints would stay on it until someone wiped them off?"

Jenkins started to get to his feet, but Gilliland-O'Rourke held him back.

"Yes," Horace replied.

"So if someone took that gun—with her fingerprints on it—and was careful to hold it with a handkerchief, or to wear a glove, her fingerprints would continue to be the only ones on it, wouldn't they?"

"Yes, I suppose. If someone did that."

So close to him I could have touched him with my hand, I threw the words back in his face.

"*If someone did that?* It's exactly what *you* did, isn't it? You murdered Russell Gray because he was having an affair with your wife. You murdered him with a gun that had her fingerprints on it so she'd be blamed for what you did."

"You forget," he said, defiance blazing in his eyes, "your client admitted she was there. She admitted she shot him."

"My *client* your wife?" I asked. "Yes, she did say that." I conceded it with a nod. "And we both know she was lying, don't we? She lied because you convinced her it was the only way to explain how her fingerprints got on the gun. She trusted you with her life, and you betrayed her, didn't you? You killed Russell Gray, didn't you?"

He looked away and stared straight ahead.

"Why don't you deny it?" I demanded. "If you didn't kill Russell Gray, deny it!"

Everyone was watching. The judge was peering down at him. But still, nothing, not a sign he had even heard me.

"If you didn't do it, deny it!"

The obstinacy of his silence drove me over the brink.

"She saved your life, she gave you a reason to live, and you want her to spend the rest of her life in prison for something she didn't do? Don't you have any decency left?" I turned on my heel and walked away.

"Russell Gray was sleeping with my wife!"

I stopped and looked back. Horace was bent forward, shaking with rage, pointing at Alma.

"What right did they have to do that to me?"

The words reverberated around the high walls of the courtroom and then, like a complaint thrown at the gods, echoed back.

Exhausted, I sank into my chair. Alma was hunched

over, rocking back and forth on the hard wooden chair, tears streaming down her face.

For a moment, no one said anything. In a voice subdued and distant, Judge West asked if the prosecution wished to cross-examine the witness.

Gilliland-O'Rourke's chair made a harsh, rasping sound as it slid back over the varnished hardwood floor.

"No, your honor."

Horace Woolner left the stand and, his eyes once again on a point ten feet in front of him, walked out of the courtroom.

"Mr. Antonelli, you may call your next witness."

I glanced over my shoulder, searching along the rows of spectators until I found him. Andre Barbizon was sitting on the aisle in the back row. His knees were pressed tight together and his hands were folded in his lap. The corner of his mouth twitched nervously. I had hoped to use him to show that someone other than the defendant had a motive to murder Russell Gray; now the only reason to call him was to have him confirm the affair that had given Horace Woolner a reason to kill.

"The defense calls Andre Barbizon," I announced.

Gilliland-O'Rourke was on her feet. "Your honor," she said firmly, "I have a matter for the court."

We waited while the clerk led the jury out of the room. Tapping his fingers together, the judge looked at Gilliland-O'Rourke.

"Your honor," she began, standing straight, her red hair swept back over a blue jacket, "the prosecution has a duty to pursue justice. That sometimes means admitting a mistake."

I looked over, wondering what she was doing.

"In light of the testimony we have just heard, there can be no doubt that a mistake has been made. The defendant is clearly innocent of the murder of Russell Gray, and it would be a serious injustice to subject her to the hazards of a jury verdict. For that reason, your honor, the state at this time moves to dismiss all charges against the defendant."

The judge did not seem pleased. "Perhaps a more thorough investigation should have been made before the charges were brought in the first place," he said. "That might have been a better exercise of prosecutorial discretion."

Shaking his head, he turned to me. "Mr. Antonelli, I assume the defense has no objection?"

"No, your honor."

"Very well. The case is dismissed."

It was over, just like that. Alma was a free woman, and she looked more shattered than anyone I had ever seen convicted. I started to say something to her, but I could not find the words. She touched my arm, turned away, and disappeared into the crowd.

No one paid any attention to me as I made my way out of the courtroom. Everyone wanted to hear what the district attorney had to say. In the hallway outside, Gilliland-O'Rourke stood in front of a battery of television cameras while a dozen reporters shouted the same question.

"I moved to dismiss the case because it became obvious the defendant is not the person who murdered Russell Gray," she explained patiently.

"How soon is Judge Woolner going to be charged?" someone asked.

I did not want to hear any more. Feeling friendless and alone, I shook my head and started to walk away.

"But there isn't any evidence that Horace Woolner killed Russell Gray, is there?"

I stopped and looked back. On the other side of the crowd, standing next to the last television camera, Harper Bryce was waiting for an answer.

Gilliland-O'Rourke raised her chin and smiled. "He confessed in open court. That's fairly conclusive, don't you think?"

"He didn't confess to anything," Harper replied. One hand shoved into his pocket, he turned the pages of his notebook with his thumb. "Antonelli kept accusing him, kept challenging him to deny it, but," he said, raising his eyes, "I didn't hear any confession."

The smile vanished. "You've obviously forgotten that outburst at the end."

His thumb flashed forward until he found the page he wanted.

" 'Russell Gray was sleeping with my wife. What right did they have to do that to me?' " Harper closed the notebook and looked up. "Did you think that was a confession?"

"The way you read it isn't the way he said it," she replied irritably. She turned her head, looking for the next reporter who had something to ask.

"Before you have him arrested," Harper drawled in a voice she could not ignore, "you might want to have someone check out his alibi."

Her eyes flashed. "Alibi?"

"The night Russell Gray was murdered, Horace Woolner was playing poker with three other judges."

As soon as we were outside the courthouse and free of the crowd, I asked, "How do you know what Horace Woolner was doing the night of the murder?"

Harper started to smile, but when he saw the look in my eyes he became serious. "Because I was there. We've had that same poker game going for years. Just the five of us. Four judges and me." He paused for a moment, a twinkle in his eye. "They needed me. I was the only one who didn't cheat." He paused again and stared down at the sidewalk. "The one thing you can be sure of, whoever killed Russell Gray, it wasn't Horace Woolner."

WHY DID I COME BACK? WHAT DID I ACHIEVE? I CON-
victed a man who may have been innocent and convinced
a courtroom that my best friend was guilty of a murder he
did not commit. The woman who may have hired Travis
Quentin on her own was living on the money intended for
Nancy Goodwin's child, and it was almost certain that no
one would ever know who really killed Russell Gray. The
innocent had been condemned and the guilty had gone
free. I should have stayed where I was, in the solitude of
my library, reading all the books I could, minding my own
business, staying out of other people's lives.

For the second night in a row, I could not sleep. The
two trials played over and over again in my mind,
words, phrases, whole paragraphs of testimony, more
vivid in the way I now remembered them than when I
heard them spoken. I kept listening to Horace Woolner's voice, answering each of the questions I asked, listening this time without any of the anger and outrage I
had felt when I asked them. I kept hearing Kristin Maxfield, swearing her husband had confessed to murder, no
longer certain she was telling the truth.

A few minutes after four, wide awake and restless, I
went downstairs, searching for something I had first
read just weeks before I started the trial of Alma Wool-

ner. In the ninth chapter of the first book of Aristotle's *Rhetoric*, I found what I was looking for.

> And those things are noble which it is possible for a man to possess after death rather than during his lifetime, for the latter involve mere selfishness; all acts done for the sake of others, for they are more disinterested; the successes gained, not for oneself, but for others; and for one's benefactors; for that is justice; in a word, all acts of kindness, for they are disinterested.

It was the perfect abbreviated biography of Horace Woolner, who had been willing to give his life to save three wounded strangers. I stared at those lines, thinking about their meaning, listening again in the solitude of the early morning silence to what he had said. I looked around at the towering book-lined shelves and then down at the writing desk in front of me. I felt like a character in a story written by someone else.

I found him at the courthouse a little before eight, hunched over his desk, his glasses pinched to his nose, lost in concentration as he wrote out a letter in longhand on a sheet of court stationery. I stood at the door, waiting until he finished.

"Come in," he said, without looking up. "Sit down."

I sat on the other side of the desk, watching his large hand move across the page in smooth, unhurried strokes. He signed his name at the bottom, put the pen down at the side, and then, for the first time, looked up.

"My letter of resignation," he told me, as he sat up and placed his hands on the arms of the chair. Pushing himself up, he caught his balance and then, in a halting, jerky motion, made his way to a small table next to a file cabinet on the other side of the room.

"Would you like a cup?" he asked as he poured coffee from the dented metal pot into a chipped white mug.

The clear morning light streamed through the window and ran across the floor, framing his silhouette as he bent his eyes on the simple everyday task that had been part of his routine for more years than either one of us could remember. When he came back, he put the cup on the desk, braced himself with both hands, and lowered himself into the chair. His eyes on mine, he lifted the cup to his mouth and took a drink.

"Why did you do it, Horace?" I asked.

A pensive expression covered his face, as if he was not completely sure himself. Turning away, he sat sideways to the desk, his arms folded over his barrel-like chest, and sipped the coffee, meditating.

"I knew what was going on between Alma and Gray," he said finally, his eyes fixed on the dark-colored surface of the half-empty cup. "I knew it from the beginning. I could tell she was falling in love with him."

"Didn't it bother you?" I blurted out.

His head came up, an ominous look in his eyes warning me I was on dangerous ground.

"It wasn't her fault," he insisted. "It was never her fault."

"And it didn't bother you?" I asked, intent on knowing everything.

Cocking his head, he looked right through me. "Maybe it's time you understood," he said, standing up.

He walked toward the small private bathroom at the far end of the room. A few moments later, I heard behind the closed door the clatter of something hitting the floor. Then he was standing in the doorway, and I had to force myself not to look away. Half of Horace had disappeared. He stood there, like someone who had fallen through the floor. He had removed his suit coat, and his pants, and the legs that held him up. All that was left of him were two black stumps, not even long enough to keep his shirttails from dragging on the ground. He was the grotesque remnant of a human being. Standing up, he was at least six foot two; without his artificial legs, he was less than four feet tall.

"This is what Alma Woolner married," he said, looking at me with the bleakest, most desolate eyes I had ever seen. "This is what she goes to bed with every night. You want to know if it bothered me that she was sleeping with another man? You want to know if I cared?"

His head was shaking hard, his mouth trembling, as he fought to keep at least the semblance of control.

"What difference does it make? Don't you understand? She deserved more than me."

I started toward him, but before I had taken a step, he reached up, grabbed the handle on the door, and threw it shut.

When it opened again, it was Horace the way I had always known him, moving stiffly across to his desk, lowering himself slowly into his chair. Only now, instead of the grinning exuberance and quiet confidence which I had for so many years taken for granted, there was on his face no expression at all.

"Why did you do it, Horace?" I asked again, swallowing hard.

The light from the window struck the side of his face and shadowed his large graying head in a yellowish haze.

"I knew that if you believed I killed Russell Gray out of jealousy, and tried to blame it on Alma out of revenge, that you'd hate me for that, and that you'd put

me on the stand and try to convince everyone that I was
the one who did it, that I was the black man who murdered his wife's white lover. Who wasn't going to believe that?"

I had believed it, and I was his best friend. Caught up
in my own delusion, swept away by the certainty that he
had killed Russell Gray, I had taken his belligerent defiance for an admission that I was right and never once
entertained the suspicion that I might be wrong. I had
done exactly what he had wanted me to do. I was the
last chess piece on the board, and Horace had seen it before the first move had ever been made.

"You're the best I've ever seen," he was saying, while
I thought about how quick I had been to turn on him.
"You did just what I thought you'd do."

I looked at him, almost as angry now as I had been
in court. "And did Gilliland-O'Rourke do just what you
thought she'd do?"

He stared down at his hands, a pensive expression on
his face. "I gave Gilliland-O'Rourke a way out, a way
to protect herself, and I gave her a way to get even."

I still did not understand. "But why? All Alma had to
do was keep telling the truth: that she left and came
back; that she heard the shot; that she picked up the
gun. We would have won."

He raised his head and stared at me, his face an im-
penetrable mask. Then he looked away, and suddenly I
knew.

"She did it, didn't she? Alma killed Russell Gray."

He did not answer, not at first. "Alma is safe," he
said finally. "That's all that matters."

There was nothing more to say. Wearily, I slid back
my chair and got to my feet.

"You don't have to do this," I said, nodding toward his signed letter of resignation. "You didn't commit any crime."

He pushed himself up in the chair and looked right at me. "I was under oath."

"But you didn't lie. You didn't commit perjury," I insisted.

It was a lawyer's argument, and he treated it with contempt. "I didn't tell the truth, either, did I?" He raised his chin and narrowed his eyes. "I knew exactly what I was doing. I knew what everyone would think when I wouldn't answer the questions you were throwing at me. I lied, Joseph, I lied by my silence. I made everyone believe something that wasn't true. So what if I'm not guilty of perjury? It was still a lie, and just because the law won't punish me for it doesn't mean that there isn't a price to be paid." His eyes still on me, he slowly shook his head. "I did enough damage to the law. I'm not going to hide behind it now."

"What are you going to do?" I asked, wondering if he had even thought about it.

"I don't know," he replied without a trace of self-pity. "Whatever I have to do to take care of Alma," he said, looking away. "She needs me."

I could almost hear him, talking to himself, years before, out in that jungle half a world away, each time he carried a wounded soldier to safety and then made himself go back for another.

I NEVER TOLD ANYONE WHAT HORACE SAID THAT MORNING, no one except Kristin Maxfield, and not all of it even to her. When I invited her to dinner a week later, she seemed surprised it had taken me this long to call. She had plans that evening, but, she added after a pause, she could get out of them.

She picked me up in front of my office in a silver Mercedes.

"It was time to get a new one," she explained, as she drove along the busy, rain-spattered street.

We went to an Italian restaurant in the heart of the city and sat at the bar while we waited for a table. It was only a few minutes after six, but on Friday night a lot of people had dinner in town before they headed home.

"Here's to our next governor," Kristin said, raising her glass. "She owes it all to you," she added, after she had taken a drink. "I was there. I watched you crucify Horace Woolner."

She stirred the ice with the tip of her finger, then looked at me, an unmistakable sense of vindication in her gaze.

"Remember what I told you? Those people play by different rules."

"You think it's a better set of rules?" I asked. I took a sip of my scotch and soda.

Her mouth formed the kind of knowing smile that made you believe she knew everyone's secrets, including your own.

"They get what they want," she replied.

Our table was ready. As we left the bar, I remarked "What if I told you that of all the people involved in this, the only one who got what he wanted was Horace Woolner?"

She thought I was making a joke and then decided was only making a mistake.

"Gwendolyn is the one who got what she wanted,

she insisted over dinner. "No one is ever going to find out about her husband, and because of the way the trial ended, everybody believes she was only trying to do the right thing. What did Horace Woolner get? He resigned from the bench, and a lot of people still think he must have had something to do with the murder."

"He saved the woman he loved."

A look of disdain crept along her lower lip. "She was sleeping with Russell Gray, for God's sake."

"You don't think someone can love someone enough to live with infidelity?"

"Would you?" she retorted.

A picture of Horace standing in the doorway, his shirt hanging down to the floor, flashed through my mind.

"I suppose if you loved someone more than you loved yourself," I said.

She was not listening. "What I can't believe is that Gwendolyn got away with murder."

I looked at her and said nothing.

"Her husband isn't capable of it, and she's the only one left with a motive," she explained.

Because the case had been dismissed, she assumed like everyone else that someone other than Alma must have done it. Horace was right. Alma was safe. Not only could she never be tried again, she was now beyond suspicion.

"The night Russell Gray was murdered," I informed her as I paid the bill, "Gilliland-O'Rourke was speaking at a benefit dinner in front of five hundred people."

The waiter took the money and left.

"Of course, that doesn't meant she's innocent, does ?" I asked, as I put my wallet away. "I suppose she uld have hired someone to do it."

There was a question in her eyes, just for an instant, and then it was gone.

It was only when we left the restaurant that she noticed my briefcase. "Why are you carrying that?" she asked with a laugh, as we waited for the car.

"I have to go by the jail. I have some papers I have to drop off with a client," I explained. "Would you mind? It shouldn't take more than a few minutes."

The parking structure across from the courthouse was nearly deserted. Her high heels echoed on the concrete floor as we walked out the front entrance, then faded into silence as we waited on the corner for the light to change.

We cut through the park that separated the courthouse from the correction facility. Inside, under the watchful eye of a uniformed guard, I signed the visitor's log.

"Why don't you come along," I suggested. "You must have come in here a lot when you were in the DA's office." We passed through the metal detector and followed the guard down a long hallway.

"Tell me, what do Conrad Atkinson and his friends think about what happened? They never much liked Horace, did they?"

"I don't see Conrad very often," she replied. "I told you before. We're just good friends."

The guard stopped in front of a door and inserted a key.

"I forgot," I said, peering into her eyes. "This is where the police interviewed you, isn't it?"

She looked at me, wondering what was going on. The guard turned the key, unlocking the door, and then with his hand on it, waited for me.

"Would you take Ms. Maxfield around the corner?" I asked. "She might like to see what it's like to observe someone inside when they don't know they're being watched."

Shutting the door behind me, I sat down at the rectangular table and waited. A few minutes later, another door opened. His wrists handcuffed behind his back and his ankles shackled together with a chain, the inmate was shoved inside by two armed guards.

"Sit down," I said, as I reached inside my briefcase. Placing a hand-held tape recorder on top of the table, I glanced at the two-way mirror on the wall and then looked back at Marshall Goodwin.

"I had them bring you over from the prison because I have something I think you might want to hear."

I pushed the button that activated the tape, a copy of a court-ordered recording of a late-night telephone call between Kristin and her former fiancé. He listened in silence.

Whether it was the often-repeated complaint that she had been seduced by a murderer and a liar, or the sensuous insistence that she could barely wait for the next time she could show Conrad Atkinson all the things she wished she had been doing with him instead of her husband, Marshall Goodwin was no longer convinced that saving Kristin's life had been worth risking his own.

"I'll tell you everything you want to know," he said.

I looked straight at the mirror, trying to imagine the look on Kristin's face as I asked him whether she had known what had been in the envelope she had delivered to Travis Quentin.

"The whole thing was her idea," he replied.

I almost felt sorry for him. Then, remembering what they had done, I felt a sense of relief that I had not convicted the wrong person after all and that, at least this time, no one had gotten away with murder.

I opened the door and motioned the guard to bring Kristin into the room. Her wrists were handcuffed behind her back. They looked at each other like two strangers who for just a moment thought they might have met somewhere once before.

It had almost worked. If Travis Quentin had never killed again, if he had never been arrested, if he had been caught in a state without the death penalty, if the state police had taken what they knew to the district attorney's office instead of giving it to Horace Woolner— if any of those things had happened, the only thing that could ever have found them out was their own guilty conscience, and the odds against that were higher than most people could count.

NEARLY A MONTH WENT BY BEFORE I TRIED TO SEE Horace Woolner again. Early one afternoon I drove to his building and called from the intercom phone. There was no answer, and when I asked the doorman when Horace might be back, I was told that the Woolners had put their condominium up for sale and left for New York. At first I did not believe it, and then I realized it was the only thing that made sense. There was nothing left for them here. Outside, I looked up at the windows of the twelfth floor, remembering the night I was there and the proud, lonely expression on Horace Woolner's face when everyone was applauding his wife. I turned and headed for the street, wishing I could somehow turn back time and change the way everything had happened.

I kept walking. A half hour later, I found myself in front of the courthouse. There was someone I wanted to see.

Scribbling a message from one caller while she answered another line, the receptionist looked up just long enough to get my name. As I took a seat, the door to Gilliland-O'Rourke's office swung open and two young men, engaged in an intense, excited conversation, walked out. A short, energetic young woman bounced right past them on her way in. A few minutes later, the receptionist caught my eye and signaled that it was my turn.

Gwendolyn was standing at a round table on the far side of the room, examining a set of black-and-white photographs of herself.

"Yes, I think you're right," she said, putting her finger on one of them. "We'll go with this one."

Beaming, the young woman gathered up the pictures and, without a glance, left the room as quickly as she had entered.

"I don't have much time," Gilliland-O'Rourke informed me as she sat down behind the glowing antique desk. "The announcement is tomorrow, and there are a thousand things left to do."

There were a lot of things I had thought I wanted to talk to her about, things I could never talk about with anyone else. But now, face-to-face with her, there was nothing to say.

"I just dropped by to wish you luck," I said as I got to my feet. "Give my best to your husband," I added before I turned to go. "I'm glad he's all right."

Except for the years I had been at school, I had lived my life in the city. But now, wandering the streets, I felt out of place, like someone who dreams of coming home only to find when he gets there that nothing is the way it used to be. All around me, people were going about their business, to all appearances certain of what they were doing and why they were doing it. I was adrift, cut off from the world, without anything to which I could look forward. I was desperate for a familiar face, a friendly voice, someone with whom I could talk. I found my way to the newspaper office and asked for Harper Bryce. I was told that he was over on the coast, in Astoria, covering another murder trial. There was no one left for me to go see.

THAT NIGHT, FOR THE FIRST TIME IN WEEKS, I SLEPT straight through and did not wake up until late morning. Sunlight slanted through the bedroom window, and the sky outside was a brilliant blue.

When I was dressed, I started down the long spiral driveway toward the iron gate at the bottom. The paving glistened black, still wet from rain that had fallen sometime before dawn. Water dripped from the branch of a sycamore tree where a bird sat, cocking its head from side to side, searching for a place in its nest to add the twig it held in its beak. After the dead days of winter, spring was about to begin again.

Outside the gate, I picked up the morning paper, tucked it under my arm, and trudged back up the drive. After a few steps, I stopped and, squinting my eyes, turned my face to feel the sun. A noise from down below broke the stillness. Two boys were pedaling their bicycles on the sidewalk that ran along the other side of the spite fence. One called the other a liar, a charge repeated each time it was denied, as they took turns riding their bikes off the curb.

Perhaps we're born with it, this sense of the difference between the truth and the lie, this belief that it is always better to tell the truth and always easier to lie. I had spent a year in a self-imposed exile because I had convinced someone to perjure himself, and everyone I had dealt with since had told lies of their own. Some of them had lied to conceal something they had done, and some of them had lied to protect other people. Maybe that was the difference that mattered, not whether you always told the truth but what you thought was worth lying for.

I sat down on a stone bench below the wooden porch and for a while did nothing but gaze out at the blank sky. The voices of the children had faded away, and the only sound was a slight breeze whispering through the fir trees. The same bird I had seen before flew back to the sycamore, clutching another twig in its mouth. Finally, I opened up the paper and saw the front page picture of Gwendolyn Gilliland-O'Rourke announcing her candidacy for governor. Her husband, Arthur O'Rourke, stood next to her, a slightly distracted look on his face, as if he was not quite certain why he was there.

Down below, outside the gate, the two boys had come back, and I could hear their laughter as they took turns jumping the curb. I put down the paper and leaned back against the side of the house, and wondered what might have happened if someone without lies and secrets of her own to protect had prosecuted the case against Alma Woolner.

I will never know what really happened that night between Alma and Russell Gray. I will never know for sure why she killed him, whether it was because he was ending their affair or whether she acted in self-defense. I cannot even guess how much she told Horace, and how much he knew without her saying a word. I am a stranger to what passes between husbands and wives.

All I know for certain is that while Horace loved the law, he loved her more. It did not matter what she had done. He could not have lived a day without her, and by saving her, he saved himself. It was the least he deserved.

"An excellent legal thriller."
—*USA Today*

THE DEFENSE

by D.W. Buffa

Dynamite defense attorney Joseph Antonelli has never lost a case—or felt the sting of conscience for letting the guilty go free. "I can deceive anyone," he says, "and no one more quickly or more completely than myself." Now the man he most admires, the honorable Judge Rifkin, has asked him for a favor: Defend a drug dealer cused of raping his twelve-year-old stepdaughter. Yet Antonelli's acceptance of the case sets in otion an explosive chain of corruption, betrayal, nd murder that will leave no one unscathed. . . .

Published by Ballantine Books.
Available at bookstores everywhere.